Praise for Erin Nicholas's
Just Like That

"You'll laugh, you'll cry and you'll definitely pant while reading Just Like That, it is a keeper, and if you haven't bought this series yet (why? what are you waiting for?!) Now is the time!!"
~ *Book Lovers, Inc.*

"Just Like That is a fun, sexy, light-hearted read that I definitely recommend."
~ *Smexy Books*

"Just Like That by Erin Nicolas is a fantastic read. I found myself sympathizing with Dankia and how her loss of childhood affected her once she became an adult. Sam tickled my fancy. It's always great to see a man working hard to impress a sexy woman and trying to be "the man." Just Like That by Erin Nicolas is a touching story that I'd recommend to anyone."
~ *Two Lips Reviews*

"Danika is a kick ass heroine! I mean kick ass. She can do what needs to be done and watching her learn to accept Sam's help is wonderful. And watching Sam trying to do things for Danika, try to be the man is just damn sweet. And the sexual tension of the almost but not quite sex. Sizzle! And when the actual sex happens. Worth the wait! Totally worth the wait."
~ *www.scrapsofme.me*

Look for these titles by
Erin Nicholas

Now Available:

No Matter What
Anything You Want

The Bradfords Series
Just Right
Just Like That
Just My Type

Just Like That

Erin Nicholas

SAMHAIN
PUBLISHING

Samhain Publishing, Ltd.
577 Mulberry Street, Suite 1520
Macon, GA 31201
www.samhainpublishing.com

Just Like That
Copyright © 2011 by Erin Nicholas
Print ISBN: 978-1-60928-092-5
Digital ISBN: 978-1-60928-057-4

Editing by Lindsey Faber
Cover by Scott Carpenter

First Samhain Publishing, Ltd. electronic publication: June 2010
First Samhain Publishing, Ltd. print publication: May 2011

Dedication

For Nikoel. No man will ever fully deserve you, but I pray for one that will never give up trying to.

Chapter One

"Not even one?"

"No."

"*Ever?*"

"Ever."

"Are you *sure?*"

Danika sighed. "You don't think I would know if I'd had an orgasm? Even one? Ever?"

The two men sitting at the next table glanced in her direction and she realized she'd let the volume of her voice rise. She quickly lifted her glass, refusing to make eye contact.

Only her sisters would consider this conversation acceptable in a public place.

Abi had been back in town for three days. Which meant Abi and Carmen had been talking about Danika, what was wrong with her life and how to fix it for forty-eight hours—give or take.

They were both blissfully, head over heels in love with their husbands and felt it was inexcusable that Danika didn't have a wedding anniversary to celebrate too. Every boyfriend that came and went increased her sisters' dissatisfaction with her lackluster love life. And their concern. Which then increased their determination to find her a happily ever after.

Having Abi in Denver for the past year had been a bit of a relief. Not that their three-way conference calls didn't often center around the current man in Danika's life and his inevitable shortcomings. Abi's resolve and enthusiasm—and outrageousness—were forces to be reckoned with even long-distance. Her sisters together, in any format—text messages, e-mail, phone calls, even faxes—were impossible to ignore.

Together in person... Danika didn't have a chance.

"You're not a virgin are you?" Abi demanded.

Danika rolled her eyes. "No. Not that it's any of your business." Or the business of the two men sitting close enough to be unable to miss the conversation.

She wasn't a virgin, though she doubted Abi or Carmen would be impressed with her description of her two—count 'em, two—sexual encounters.

"Then how is it possible she hasn't had an orgasm?" Abi asked Carmen, as if it was all Carmen's fault.

"Look at the guys she dates," Carmen said.

"True." Abi glanced at Danika.

Danika drank and pretended to not know what they were talking about.

They were supposed to be celebrating her new job and Abi's return to Omaha after being transferred with her husband's company four times in five years. Now Ryan owned his own business, so no more moving. Abi would be here. Right here. With Carmen. In person. All the time.

It was going to be...great.

"Maybe you're doing something wrong," Abi said.

"Well, we put everything where it's supposed to go," Danika said dryly. "What exactly could I be doing wrong?"

Abi looked to Carmen for help. "Maybe you didn't..."

"Give it enough time," Carmen offered.

Danika looked from one to the other. "Enough time?"

"Or maybe you should have...lit some candles." Abi didn't even look convinced herself.

"Candles. Right." Why hadn't she thought of buying those magic orgasm-inducing candles?

"Do you want to know what I think?" Carmen asked.

No. But she was going to soon enough, she was sure.

"She needs all the help she can get," Abi said.

Wow, nothing like being a sexual charity case.

"I think if she's going to keep picking the guys she picks, then it's up to her to make sure she's having orgasms."

Danika didn't know what to do with that statement—or how to fake that she wasn't interested—so she took another drink of strawberry and tequila.

"Go on," Abi said, leaning her chin on her hand and giving Carmen her full attention.

"I was incredibly attracted to Ryan when I met him," Carmen said. "But in the beginning I had to let him know what I liked and we played around a little."

"Really?" Abi seemed fascinated. "He wasn't offended?"

Carmen laughed. "No. He *wanted* me to have orgasms, so he was all for learning how to do it."

"Luke and I never had any trouble," Abi said thoughtfully. "I don't think I want to know how he got so good at it."

"You've never even had to hint?" Carmen asked, clearly impressed.

Abi shook her head, grinning and looking smug. "Nope."

Danika drank again. She supposed that women who were having regular orgasms could be smug. And grin a lot. And just generally like life a lot.

But grinning was overrated.

"Good for you," Carmen said, sincerely. "Of course, I knew that Ryan would be amazing with practice."

Danika watched her sisters grin at one another and rolled her eyes.

"How did you know?" Danika asked.

"The heat. You know, the chemistry. The fact that from the first moment I met him I wanted to get him naked."

"I thought you met him at The Olive Garden," Danika grumbled. No one fell in love—or lust—at The Olive Garden. Except maybe with the chicken parmesan.

"I did. I was waiting on him and his parents and all I could think about was his mouth and how much I wanted to kiss him. Even with his mom sitting right there."

Abi nodded her head emphatically. "I wanted to rip Luke's clothes off the minute I met him too. In fact, I slept with him on the first date."

The look on Carmen's face was surely an exact replica of Danika's. "I didn't know that!"

"It's not like I was proud of it," Abi said. Then she grinned. "Well, I was. I thought he was out of my league, but I went for it anyway and it paid off. Big time."

She and Carmen snickered at that. Danika took another drink.

Carmen turned to Dani. "Honey, the orgasm thing can work out. Where there is chemistry, there is potential."

Danika pushed an ice cube around her glass with a finger wishing they could talk about *anything* else.

"Maybe she needs some official help," Abi said, looking at Danika again.

Danika raised an eyebrow. *This* did not sound good.

"Like a sex therapist?" Carmen asked.

"That's not an overreaction at all," Danika muttered.

It wasn't like she didn't know why she wasn't having orgasms.

She didn't want to.

Well, that wasn't entirely accurate. Part of her wanted to, of course. But she just couldn't let herself go. She held back. On purpose. And intended to keep doing so.

"Like a vibrator," Abi said.

Danika choked on the sip of margarita she'd unfortunately just taken.

"You don't already have one?" Carmen asked her with wide eyes.

Before she could answer, Abi said, "If she does, she needs a new one since that one is apparently not working."

"Are you using it *with* the guy?" Carmen asked. "Because only one-third of women have orgasms with vaginal stimulation. Most need clitoral stimulation."

Danika couldn't help it. She looked over at the two men at the table next to them. One was facing her and making absolutely no effort to pretend he wasn't listening—or grinning about the crazy conversation. The other's back was to her, but he was closer and could hear everything clearly. The one she could see was very good-looking and very amused. In fact, it seemed they had completely given up talking to one another. Probably easier to hear Carmen and Abi. Not that her sisters were trying to keep their voices down.

"Carmen," she said through gritted teeth. "If you ever say the word clitoral to me in public again, you'll never get another Christmas present as long as I live."

She tried to drink again, but somehow her glass was empty. She waved to the waitress. Judging by the conversation to this point, she was definitely going to need a refill.

She should just pay her bill and leave, but nothing was that easy with her sisters.

"She needs a man who she can experiment with so she can figure out what she likes," Carmen said resolutely. "Clearly the ones she's been with have been duds."

Danika frowned at that. "They have not been duds." They'd all been nice, sweet guys. Unassuming, undemanding...un-lots of things. Just the way she liked them.

"Maybe not duds," Abi said, gently. "But they're...vanilla cupcakes."

"*What?*" Maybe it was the tequila. The conversation just kept getting crazier.

"You love fudge brownies," Abi said. "But you're dating vanilla cupcakes. They're not *bad*, but you don't *crave* cupcakes."

Carmen's grin was huge and Danika groaned.

"That's a perfect analogy, Dani," she said. "You've got to find a fudge brownie."

The thing was, it *was* a good analogy. It was scary how close her sisters had just come to the truth. It wasn't like she was picking cupcakes on accident. She knew her weakness was fudge brownies. And therefore trouble. A great brownie could make her throw all her discipline away, forget her goals and plans. Even a not-so-great brownie—because, after all, even a bad brownie was still a brownie—could make her lose control, decide the pleasure was worth the consequences.

"So I'm supposed to only date men who make me think of food?"

Abi grinned. "Men who make you think about indulgence and devouring and...licking all over."

"Exactly," Carmen said, her eyes twinkling. "It's like your life is a bakery and you have everything to choose from. But you go for the vanilla cupcakes, even though you could have a brownie and that's what you'd really like and what would completely satisfy you."

Her life was a bakery. Terrific.

"I like cupcakes." Danika knew she sounded grumpy, but she was feeling grumpy. And judged. And criticized.

She hated when her sisters were right. Her boyfriends were no more exciting than cupcakes. They were good, just not…worth not fitting into her favorite jeans for.

"Cupcakes are fine," Carmen agreed. "And for some people that's *it*. Their favorite thing. The thing they go crazy for. But not for you."

"You have to find a fudge brownie," Abi agreed. "A big one."

"No pun intended," Carmen giggled.

"Luke's a fudge brownie?" Danika asked Carmen, attempting to show her how stupid that sounded.

"Oh, no. He's a great big slice of cheesecake." Carmen winked at her. "Brownies to me are like cupcakes to you. But cheesecake? That's what I *want*."

Danika thought about Travis and Rob and Paul. Vanilla cupcakes, for sure. Travis had been a vanilla cupcake with sprinkles at least, but he hadn't even come close to brownie status.

He was a good guy, a sweet guy, undemanding. Which had made it easy to break up with him. The conversation had gone something like, *"Travis, you're a sweet guy, but I just don't feel like this relationship is going anywhere." "Oh, that's too bad. But we'll still be friends, right?" "Sure." "Okay, take care."*

He hadn't even argued with her. Ever. About anything. Which was why she'd dated him. And ultimately why she'd broken up with him. There was no emotion, no spark, not a smear of fudge frosting in sight. It made Travis, and every other guy she'd dated, safe. But expendable.

She knew it was dysfunctional. But she didn't care. "I'm fine," she told her sisters. "I'll get a new vibrator and a *real* brownie—maybe two—and I'll be fine."

"And you're going to keep dating cupcakes?" Carmen asked.

It was very likely.

"I'm not dating anyone right now."

"That's not good either," Abi said. "I mean, I'm a fan of vibrators, but all the toys are more fun if you have someone to play with."

"Maybe I should just have a one-night stand," Danika said, hoping to show her sisters how nuts all of this sounded.

"Maybe you should," Abi said, obviously considering it.

"You've got to be kidding."

"You wouldn't have to worry about finding a reason to

break up with him," Carmen said.

"What do you mean?" But she was afraid she knew.

"You broke up with Rob because he rearranged your living room."

"Right." He hadn't even asked.

"He did it because he bought you a new couch. One that you'd definitely liked and wanted."

"It was *my* living room." She didn't like surprises. Never had, even as a kid. Their mom's illness had been enough of a surprise and the unpredictable course of the disease had made Danika conscious of the importance of planning and making decisions and having expectations.

"You broke up with Travis because of his work shifts."

"He worked every night." Travis was a detective on the police force and was often gone all night, sometimes without a break for days if he was on a case.

"You knew that the minute you met him," Carmen pointed out.

"So?"

"So," Carmen repeated in the same tone. "I think you make up reasons to break up with the guys you date."

She shrugged without answering. Carmen wasn't entirely right. Or wrong. Danika didn't make the reasons up. The reasons were there and real. What her sisters didn't know was that she was aware of those reasons, and that she was going to use them to end the relationship, nearly from the beginning.

The thing Abi and Carmen would never understand was that she honestly didn't want heat and chemistry. It was so much easier without...all of that. Her relationships weren't exciting, or spontaneous, or wild...or a multitude of other words. Like messy or painful. Or...desperate. She'd never felt desperate about a guy—to kiss him, or be with him, or see him. She'd never *needed* a guy. Very intentionally in fact. It kept things from being, well, messy and painful.

She rather suspected none of the guys she'd dated needed her either, though.

They'd had some laughs, enjoyed a few good conversations, seen some terrific movies. There had even been a few nice kisses and two sexual encounters that had been good, if not spectacular. Then they'd parted ways without any heartbreak, major emotional upheaval or...desperation.

"You were attracted to him, though?" Carmen clarified.

Danika shrugged again. "I guess." She'd found him handsome. He was a good dresser.

"Were you hot for him?" Abi asked. "Did you want to tear his clothes off? Could you not wait until you were alone? Did you sit across the table from him at dinner and think about taking the sugar packets and shaking them out all over his body and then licking it off?"

Carmen and Danika stared at her. Abi looked from one to the other.

"What?" she asked.

"Luke is a lucky guy," Carmen finally said.

Danika had to chuckle. "No, I never thought about covering him in anything. Or licking him."

She heard one of the men choking at the next table. She resisted looking in that direction.

"I think you're doing it backward," Abi told her.

"I'm doing what backward?" Danika felt the need to clarify, especially with Abi. It was never safe to assume that Abi was talking about anything conventional.

"Finding a relationship."

"Backward how?" Danika wasn't sure why she kept asking questions. Not that her sisters needed her participation to keep the conversation going, but they might mistake the questions as encouragement.

"Most people have a physical attraction first, then they get to know each other and put the two together to find out if they're compatible. You're doing it backward."

"Because I'm choosing to date men that I want to talk to versus men I want to lick?" Danika clarified.

"Yes." Abi looked very pleased that Danika was understanding.

"Are you kidding?"

"No."

"So I should just go to bed with the first fudge brownie I see and then hope that he can actually string words together into a sentence?"

"Right."

"Isn't that the opposite of the advice a normal, sane person would give to someone?" Danika asked.

"You need an orgasm, not political opinions or the history of the mining of tanzanite."

"What if the guy can't even spell tanzanite?"

"If he can help you find your G-spot, who the hell cares?" Abi asked. "Once you figure out what does it for you, then you can teach the guy who stimulates your mind how to stimulate your—"

"Abi!" Danika interrupted.

There was a snort of laughter from the next table. Ignoring it—kind-of—Danika asked, "You want me to pick up a random stranger?"

"You might have to get some new clothes first," Carmen said.

"What's wrong with my clothes?"

"You dress like a kindergarten teacher," Abi inserted.

"I do?"

"And no guy thinks of kindergarten teachers as sexy," Carmen said.

"Unless you turn it into a fantasy, role-playing, sexy-teacher-naughty-student thing," Abi piped up. "Sometimes Luke and I—"

"Stop!" Danika held up a hand. "The last thing I need in my head is the idea of you and Luke in costume having sex."

The men at the next table laughed out loud at that.

"Learning to have orgasms with you would be like learning to play chopsticks with Beethoven. She couldn't find a man with more expertise." Ben Torres was grinning widely at his best friend and brother-in-law.

"Thank you very much." Sam Bradford raised his beer bottle in salute. He drank, then set the bottle on the table. He should have turned the conversation to his sister's upcoming surprise birthday party, or sports, or weather, or anything else, but he couldn't take his attention away from the woman behind him.

"You think I should offer to coach her?" he asked, trying to act cavalier.

"Definitely. A chance to put your gift to good use."

"The women I date feel like I put my gift to very good use all the time."

Ben took a swig of beer. "Please don't take my suggestion as an indication that I doubt how satisfied your ladies are."

Sam was sure all of this would be recounted to the rest of their buddies for Ben's amusement. Probably more than once. Messing with Sam was one of his friends' favorite pastimes.

And vice versa.

"Why don't *you* help her out? You know about women and orgasms. Supposedly. Why don't you give her some pointers?"

Ben nodded, unfazed. "Yes, but I happen to be giving out enough orgasms to keep me nice and busy...and tired."

"You're talking about my sister," Sam pointed out.

Ben grinned. "Yep."

"That should probably bug me."

"Probably."

"But she does smile a lot more since you got together."

"For good reason."

Sam chuckled. "And since you made her an honest woman by marrying her, I guess I can't get too upset."

"Thanks," Ben said dryly. "I was worried about you defending her honor."

Sam sat back in his chair, crossing an ankle over his opposite knee. The position put him closer to the women's table. The bar wasn't too crowded yet. It was early, so it wasn't hard to hear two of the three. But the one with the orgasm problem was the softer spoken—or the more aware of the strangers surrounding them in this public place.

Right across the street from the St. Anthony's Emergency Room entrance, the bar was a popular hangout for the hospital staff and Sam knew that it was not a coincidence that Carmen, second-in-command over the ER nursing staff, had chosen this location to have drinks with her sisters. If she wanted to set her sister up with a fling—which seemed more than obvious—what better place to find young, single, willing men that wouldn't be complete strangers? Carmen knew everyone who came to this bar, and could get references, bank account info and probably birth certificates if she wanted to.

Carmen was a beautiful woman. She was also bright, funny and sexy. She was married so he'd—obviously—never tried to take her home. But that didn't stop him from flirting.

Very little stopped Sam from flirting.

So he couldn't help but be interested in meeting her sister. Her apparently single, sexually frustrated sister.

Sam's back was to the women's table and he *really* wanted to take a look. Then again, there was something very intriguing about just overhearing the conversation. He wasn't particular. Breast size, hair color and shape were all secondary concerns. But she did need to be three things—confident, into him, at least for the time-being, and comfortable with her sexuality.

This woman didn't sound like she was, or would be, any of those things.

Still, he couldn't help thinking *Give me an hour, honey, and I'll take care of your problem.*

He was certainly willing to take his time and vary his techniques to give a woman full pleasure, but he wasn't into virgins or prudes.

This one was obviously not the first, but he had suspicions about the second. Her own sisters said she dressed like a kindergarten teacher.

His kindergarten teacher had been older than dirt, and hadn't liked him.

Of course, it had taken him years to know what *recalcitrant* meant, but even as a five-year-old he'd known she hadn't meant it as a compliment.

But his competitive streak had him thinking that it would be pretty sweet to succeed where others had been failing with this woman. The women he usually spent time with were very sexual, uninhibited and, if he was honest, not much of a challenge when it came to talking them into bed. Yeah, he was good, but it wasn't like he made a habit of picking women he wasn't sure of.

"So you're not going to do it," Sam said to Ben.

"I love your sister."

"My life is more fun."

"My hope for you as my best friend is that someday you'll understand why I say 'no way' to that statement."

"Spoken like a happily married man." Sam knew that Ben and Jessica were one of those rare, meant-to-be couples. He also knew that he'd never even come close, so couldn't argue.

Yet, being able to go to this woman and talk to her about orgasms seemed like a very nice alternative to marital bliss.

"Sounds like all she needs is confidence. A lot of the time women are just too self-conscious to be able to relax enough to get into it and enjoy. She probably just needs some sexy underwear."

Ben looked at him for a long moment. "Sexy underwear. That's the key to all of it?"

"Maybe some toys," Sam said with a wink.

Ben leaned to the left, withdrew his wallet and handed Ben a one hundred dollar bill. "You talk her into going shopping with you and I'm buying."

"Is this a dare?" Sam couldn't help but be interested. He hadn't had anything exciting happen for a long time, and what red-blooded male passed up the chance to show off his sexual expertise and buy sexy lingerie for an appreciative female?

He tucked the bill into his front pocket, tossed back the rest of his beer and pushed back from the table. Ben watched with an eyebrow up and a grin.

"See you later," Ben said.

"Not if I'm even half as good as I think I am."

Sam headed for the bar for two more beers. He used it as an excuse to check out the situation at Carmen's table.

The woman in the middle was the first one his gaze settled on. And he felt like he'd just downed a pot of coffee, two energy drinks and five candy bars. His body literally hummed, and he couldn't relax his chest enough to even take a deep breath.

Lord, have mercy.

Every cell in his body was tense and felt like it was vibrating. His mind was completely blank except for one word...*sex.*

It was the most bizarre thing to ever happen to him. He *never* reacted like that to women. Sure there was lust, there was heat and want and attraction.

But *this* was...inexplicable.

She wasn't even the most beautiful at the table.

Carmen, by far, was the sexiest. She wore a fitted top with sparkling threads woven through that caught the light and drew attention when she moved. Her dark blonde hair was up in a sexy twist and her lips were a bright crimson, just begging to be noticed. The one who had been sitting closest to him, Abi, was very beautiful as well, but had a more sophisticated look. She was also dressed for a night out in a black dress with spaghetti straps and plenty of cleavage, and her straight blonde hair was down, sexy and loose.

But their sister was the one Sam couldn't look away from. Her hair was a soft strawberry blonde, and it fell in waves to touch her shoulders. She didn't wear lipstick. The coral color of her lips didn't need enhancing. She was too far away for him to see the color of her eyes, but just then she rose, presumably to go to the ladies' room, and he realized that seeing this woman in lingerie was going to be one of the great pleasures of his life.

And he was suddenly very sure that he was going to do exactly that.

Prude or not, co-worker's sister or not, he was going to give this woman an orgasm.

Not because of her body—the shape of which he could only describe as "nice" considering nothing she wore was fitted or revealing in any way—but because she was, indeed, dressed like a kindergarten teacher. She wore a simple cotton sleeveless dress that buttoned up the front from hem to the V-neck and ended with a flare right at her knees. The best part was that both top and bottom were completely modest and conservative...and white. Virginal white.

Those things, combined with the conversation he'd overhead, was enough to make him want to see her in a leopard-print thong and bustier. If nothing else, because he doubted that she'd ever been seen in one before. Then he wanted to get her naked. She'd apparently been seen that way before, but she hadn't been *appreciated* that way before. If she had been, she wouldn't have been talking about not having orgasms.

He figured this rush of excitement and anticipation was how the great explorers had felt. Undiscovered territory, the first to stake a claim and all that.

He took Ben's beer back to him, then headed toward the doorway that led to the restrooms. He was going to talk to her, but decided he didn't want an audience.

On his way past their table he kicked a chair out and slid into it. He turned to Carmen. "Are you kidding me?"

"What?" she asked innocently.

"You brought your sister to our bar to set her up with a one-night stand."

"No better place."

She had a point there.

"And she's never had an orgasm."

"Oh, you heard that part?" She blinked at him innocently, but he wasn't fooled.

"And I happen to have a reputation for being pretty good at giving those out."

"That you're quite proud of."

"Seems to me we have a formula here."

Abi was looking back and forth between them. "Him? For Dani?" she finally said.

Carmen smiled at her and nodded. "He's definitely on my short list."

"There's a list?" he asked with a frown.

"You're in the top three," Carmen assured him.

"Top *three?*" Sam repeated.

"I didn't know you'd be here *for sure.*" She glanced over his shoulder at Ben.

Sam raised an eyebrow. "I wondered why Ben wanted to buy me a beer."

"Jessica might have mentioned to him that we'd be here tonight."

"So you *did* intend for me to have a fling with your sister."

Carmen looked alarmed. "Not a fling, Sam," she said seriously. "A one-night stand. That's it. *One* night."

Abi was still nodding. "Definitely only one."

"Excuse me?" Sam wasn't sure why he felt offended, but he did.

"She needs to have an incredible sexual experience. She needs to realize that it can happen and what it takes to make it happen. And that she wants it to keep happening. *Then* we want her to fall madly in love," Abi said. "You can only help with the first part."

"Explain," he said shortly. The words *in love* made him squirm, but he was still intrigued. "You know I don't do madly in love, or happily in love, or any other kind of in love for that matter."

"Exactly. But you do do orgasms," Carmen said.

"And..." He was gritting his teeth for some reason.

"If she thinks it might turn into a relationship then she won't let go and let it happen. Once it does happen, she'll realize it's not fatal." Abi laughed. "We want her to realize that she can have, and want, both. Passion *and* love. Then she'll find someone, let him close and finally fall in love and be happy."

"She's unhappy now?" Sam asked.

"She's...unfulfilled now," Abi said. "She doesn't realize it, of course."

"Of course," Sam said softly. Meddling sisters, always thinking they knew best. He totally understood that.

"And maybe she'll realize there are some things she can't do for herself," Carmen added.

Sam turned to face Carmen squarely. "She can do...that...for herself."

Carmen raised an eyebrow. "It's not the same. Trust me."

He grinned. "I'm glad to hear that. I'd hate to become completely obsolete."

"Because that's all you're good for?" Carmen teased.

He felt a sudden cramp in his stomach. "It's definitely what I'm best at," he said with a wink, and hoped that Carmen didn't think he sounded weird.

"Practice makes perfect and all that," she quipped back.

"Right." He sighed. "So you *are* trying to get your sister laid."

Neither of them even flinched. "Yes."

"Why me?"

"Because you came over here first," Abi said.

Carmen laughed and shook her head. "No, seriously. You're perfect, Sam. You're a nice guy, she'll have fun even before...that...and you're good at it," she said. "When women around here think of orgasms, you definitely come to mind."

Sam knew she meant it as a compliment and tried to take it as such. It was strange how his stomach seemed to knot again, though.

"And I know that *you* won't let her have any misunderstandings about it being more than just a one-time, one-night thing."

Sam felt himself frown. Which was stupid. Carmen was right. There was no chance that he was going to lead her sister, or anyone else, on in that department. One night was more than enough. Always.

"So you'll do it?" Abi asked.

He couldn't help but grin, even as he rolled his eyes at how ridiculous this all seemed.

"Thank you, Sam," Carmen said, sincerely.

Well, he'd been thanked *after* sex, why not before? And why not by the woman's older and younger sisters? Sure. There was nothing weird about this at all.

But he didn't care. Weird or not, complicated later or not, he just couldn't stay away from her now. He was going to show Danika just exactly what she'd been missing with all the cupcakes.

She emerged from the alcove outside of the bathroom and started for the bar. He felt his heart rate pick up the moment he saw her and let himself enjoy the surge of adrenaline. This was not going to be a sacrifice on his part.

He pushed away from the table and started toward her.

"Whoa." Carmen was suddenly standing in front of him. "Where you goin' with that look on your face, big guy?"

"What look?"

"That look of determination and..."

"Heat," Abi supplied.

Carmen nodded. "Heat. Definitely."

"I'm going to introduce myself to your sister."

Carmen's eyes narrowed. "I didn't think that you would be looking at her like that."

"I was under the impression heat was what you wanted her to have."

"Um..."

"Look, I'll use a condom and I won't propose to her, but those are the only details or guarantees I'm giving you, so either pick another guy, or get out of my way." He *hated* the idea of this project falling to another man, but stoically stood, making Carmen decide how she wanted this to go. He didn't want to break Danika's heart and he didn't want to piss Carmen or Abi off. Having everything on the table from the beginning was the only way to go.

There was a long pause from the woman in front of him. Then she nodded and stepped to the side. "Fine."

He barely managed to catch a bit of Danika's dress between his thumb and first finger as she sidestepped the jukebox. The material at her waist pulled tight and she turned to face him, her eyes widening with surprise as she realized a stranger held her.

Her eyes were green. A deep emerald green. He smiled. "I don't think you need a sexy-teacher-naughty-student costume."

She didn't try to pull away, which Sam counted as a positive sign. He continued to hold onto her as she glanced back toward the table where only Ben now sat, then back to him. He knew the moment she realized why he'd referenced the sex costumes.

She tipped her head to one side. "Oh? What do I need?"

"A different guy."

She looked intrigued by his answer. Not surprised, not offended, but definitely interested. Sam felt heat settle low in his gut. She hadn't even blushed. In fact, she swayed closer. His eyes focused on her lips for a moment and he felt the sudden need to kiss her. Not just a desire to kiss her, but a demanding, do-it-or-die *need*.

Kissing was one of his favorite pastimes, and he knew the importance of spending plenty of time on it. But usually where he felt pleasure, even anticipation, he now felt hunger. His fingers tightened on her dress and tugged her closer.

She took a step into his personal space, studying his eyes as she did it. "You might be right." Then she smiled. She was gorgeous. She might not be having wild and crazy sex, but she wasn't a prude. Thank goodness. He could definitely take her to bed. It would even, technically, be a good deed.

"I take pride in the fact that no one leaves without a smile on her face. From what I overheard, that makes me someone you're very interested in talking to."

"You're not even going to pretend to be polite and act like you didn't eavesdrop on all of that?"

He grinned. "Not a chance. That was the most interesting thing I've heard in a long time."

She smiled slightly. "Interesting is not the word I would have chosen."

"Speaking of words, just for the record, *orgasm* is one of my favorite words," he said, to get her back on track.

She looked up at him from several inches below his six-foot-three-inch height. Her expression turned sly, her smile seemed seductive—if he didn't know better. "What are some of your other favorite words?"

He pulled her in even closer, flattening his palm against the curve of her hip. "Sex," he said gruffly. "Hard. Hot. Fast. Deep."

Her lips parted and her breathing quickened. "Anything else?"

He dropped his voice. "Wet. Slow. Clitoris. Cock. More. Yes."

She swallowed hard. "Good words," she said just above a whisper.

He loved the effect he was having. He realized some of her reaction came from her innocence. He doubted any man had ever talked to her like this. But he was feeling every bit of heat from her body, reveling in every shaky breath she took, and he wanted to lick right where her teeth held her bottom lip. He was achingly hard for this woman and he did not miss the fact that his reaction was greater than it had been for the past five women or more that he'd taken home.

"And trust me when I say I am very familiar with the definition of each," he said, freeing her lip from her teeth with the pad of his thumb and then stroking back and forth along the soft pink skin.

"You can use them appropriately in a sentence?" she quipped, though her voice was still hoarse.

"I can even demonstrate them. All at once."

She stared up at him and he saw the desire in her eyes. "You're offering to help me?"

"It would be my pleasure," he said leaning in. "And yours."

She sighed and he felt the warmth of her breath against his lips. He wanted to kiss her. Intended to kiss her. But not yet. The anticipation was a lot of the fun and for the first time in a long time he was pretty sure it was going to be just as fun for him.

He wasn't conceited enough to say that the women had more fun than he did. It was just a fact that the sex had grown...not boring, certainly not bad, or unfulfilling. Just not exciting, or particularly memorable. It wasn't like he needed leather whips or big swings hung from his bedroom ceiling and he'd always been just fine with it being just him and a woman. There was no need for extra bodies. But the scene was pretty much the same every weekend.

Now he was looking down at the potential for a very exciting, and memorable, night.

Why wouldn't he take full advantage of it?

"Where do we start?" she asked.

Oh, the possibilities were endless. He gave her a grin and said, "How about with an introduction?"

She visibly hesitated for a moment. "First names only," she finally said. "And no other personal information."

That didn't change his plans much but he was curious. "Why is that?"

"I don't want to get to know you."

Danika shouldn't have been encouraging this conversation.

But she did have the sudden urge to dump sugar packets out all over him and then lick it off.

Just making eye contact with this guy when he'd stopped her had made her feel like she was free-falling from an airplane. Her stomach flipped, her breath caught in her lungs, her head spun. Now that he was against her, and talking dirty, she felt like one big exposed nerve ending. She wanted to fidget. Or maybe she wanted to rub against him.

Yeah, it was definitely more the latter.

It was probably a good thing that this one had been the one facing away from her during the conversation with her sisters. The guy he'd been sitting with was good-looking and would have been tempting to flirt with...maybe even more. But this guy was I'll-do-whatever-you-say-as-long-as-we're-both-naked magnificent.

He had dark blond hair, long enough on top to have that messed-up look, as if a woman had just run her fingers through it. His eyes were a greenish-blue and were now looking at her as if imagining her covered in chocolate sauce and served as dessert. He was well over six feet, making her tip her head to look him in the eye, and he either went to the gym regularly or did manual labor for a living because he was big, but clearly solid muscle.

As if all of that wasn't enough to make an impression, his confidence and sexual energy were thick enough she felt it wrapping around her and pulling her toward him. Strangely, that was what usually made her avoid men like him. She *hated* feeling overwhelmed or distracted or...seduced. But with this guy, being close—as close as possible, in fact—was practically all she could think of.

This was exactly the fudge-brownie effect she'd been worried about.

Besides that, he knew the effect he was having on her and rather than seem surprised by it, he seemed to be taking it for granted. He was so cocky, so confident.

He thought he'd be the first to give her an orgasm. He was sure of it. She could tell.

Which made her want to prove him wrong.

Guys like this always got their way. Especially with women. It might be entertaining to be the first woman to show him that he could be cute and charming and sweet...and still not get everything he wanted.

The guys she dated weren't losers with women. They didn't do it for her, because she wouldn't *let* them do it for her. This guy seemed to think he wouldn't have any trouble. It was cute. And a little hot. She'd never had tingles like this. Not to say she'd never had tingles at all. She just stayed carefully in control of where they led.

That was why she picked the guys were who less threatening to her hormones. It made resisting falling in love with them easier. She was an intelligent woman and knew that sexual chemistry was only one part of a relationship. But if she could mentally review her daily planner or grocery list during a seduction she was much less likely to fall for the guy. It was easier to stay detached if she wasn't overcome with lust and passion. Being distracted by wanting to lick sugar off of someone could make it difficult to stay aloof.

She'd have to be careful with this guy. But she couldn't quite bring herself to say no to him. A red flag in and of itself.

"I can live with only knowing your first name as long as I get to know what makes you moan and pant," he said.

The husky voice nearly did her in then and there. Red flag or not, she was already addicted to the shot-of-whiskey flare of heat he created in her stomach.

Then it traveled lower. She took a deep breath.

"Danika," she said. "And—" she licked her lips, "—I'm not

sure what all will make me moan and pant." She never really got to that point. But just standing near this guy might be enough.

"Sam. And I intend to find out."

Sounded good to her. Which was shocking. She should be panicking right now. Or at least nervous. Instead, what she felt was pure anticipation. She smiled at him. "What's next, Sam?"

"We're going shopping."

Shopping. Not what she'd expected. Dancing maybe. Having a drink together. Maybe even making out in the back hallway. But leaving... "I already have condoms."

That made him pause. Then grin. "Good. That's not what I meant. But good."

"Oh."

He took her hand and turned to head in the general direction of their tables.

"I thought you didn't think I needed a costume." Though she might be willing to wear a French maid's uniform or something for this guy.

"No costumes," he agreed.

They stopped in the space between the table where her sisters and his friend sat.

"Ladies," he greeted.

Carmen and Abi looked up. Carmen's eyes went from his to Danika's to their joined hands. "Um, hi, Sam."

Danika felt a jolt of surprise. Then her eyes narrowed. Her sisters wouldn't look at her. But they were both grinning. At Sam. About Sam. Terrific. They knew Sam. And they approved of her leaving with him. Just terrific.

"I'm going to be helping your sister with a few things tonight so she's going to be accompanying me on some errands right now. You don't need to call her, text her or go over to her apartment tonight. And you're definitely not welcome at my place."

His place.

"Um..." Danika was momentarily distracted from being irked at her siblings.

Sam turned his stomach-flipping grin on her again. "If this is going to work, you're going to have to trust me, Danika."

Oh, she was pretty sure that Sam could make it work just fine. Which meant that trusting him was the last thing she was going to let herself do.

Chapter Two

He was probably the dumbest man to walk the planet, but somewhere between the tiny hallway by the bathrooms and the table where her sisters sat, Sam had decided that he would not sleep with Danika tonight.

She wanted an orgasm. But Carmen was right about what she needed most—the knowledge of what turned her on, what she wanted from a lover, and the confidence to ask for it.

That was going to take more than one night. And he was very, very okay with that.

Her sisters said that it was supposed to be a one-night stand, that she couldn't fall for him. That simply meant he couldn't sleep with her more than once or romance her. They didn't need to worry. He had no intention of *dating* her.

He was simply going to mentor her. In sex.

But if they slept together right away and she had the long-awaited orgasm it would be because he was just that good. All it would teach her would be how much she'd been missing all this time. Not necessarily how to get it again.

It was Sam's new purpose to be sure she knew exactly how to get her maximum pleasure.

Sam put Danika in the passenger seat of his car, then jogged around to the driver's side.

Neither of them said anything until he'd pulled out onto the main road.

"Shopping?" she finally asked.

"Shopping."

"How do you know that I don't already have what we're going to buy?"

"Show me your bra."

"What?"

He looked to find her staring at him with wide eyes. He laughed. "Come on, Danika. Just unbutton a few buttons. I'm trying to make a point. I intend to see a lot more than that eventually."

She narrowed her eyes but undid the top three buttons of her shirt. She pulled the material to one side, revealing a white strap and the white lacy edge at the top of the left cup. It was the smallest glimpse of women's underwear he'd ever been given and it still resulted in a fast, hard erection.

He shifted to try to get more comfortable in his pants and she covered back up. "Have you felt sexy today?" he asked.

"Sexy? No. That wasn't why I picked this bra out."

"Exactly," he said. "You picked it out because..."

He trailed off and gestured with his hand for her to fill in the blanks.

"It wouldn't show through."

"Then your purpose was practical."

She nodded when he glanced over again.

"Now, let's say you were going to seduce a guy. You knew you were going to see him later at a party. What would you wear?"

She didn't reply right away and Sam knew that his point was going to be made rather easily.

"My black bra and panties, I guess," she finally said.

"Did you buy those because they're sexy?"

"No. I bought them for my aunt's funeral."

Sam coughed and looked over at her again. "Excuse me?"

"I needed a new black bra to go under my dress for her funeral. The panties came as part of the set."

"Danika, here's my first tip for you—do *not* wear that bra and panties any time you want to seduce someone."

"But they're the only ones that aren't white or tan."

"That doesn't matter."

"White and tan aren't sexy."

"They can be."

"Do you think red would be better?"

"Do you have red?"

"No. But we could buy some."

"Maybe, but not just because they're red."

"They need to be skimpy? I have a white thong."

The idea of Danika in a thong made his mouth go dry and he had to swallow before he said, "Skimpy isn't the only consideration, either."

"But I don't..."

He put his hand on her knee and squeezed. "The important part of what you wear is how you *feel*. If you feel sexy and seductive, then it doesn't matter what color or how skimpy anything is. To get full pleasure, you have to want full pleasure, expect it, demand it, even. You're not going to be able to do that if you don't feel like you're ready for it."

"Sexy underwear will make me feel like I'm ready to have an orgasm?"

He glanced at her. "It will help."

"I'll defer to your obvious expertise."

He let her think that over for the few minutes it took to get to the shop he had in mind. He pulled into a parking spot and looked over at her in time to see her eyes widen as she looked at the front of the store Tease.

She swallowed as she took in the barely dressed mannequin in the front window. "This is it, huh?"

"This is it."

Sam got out and came around to her side of the car. He opened the door for her and held out his hand to help her up. Danika didn't take her eyes from the storefront for even a second as she took Sam's hand and got out of the car.

She took a deep breath.

They were two of only eight people in the store besides the salesgirl. She drifted around inconspicuously from person to person. The others all seemed to be in couples. Two couples were looking through the racks of—sure enough—costumes including a school girl, a serving wench and a cheerleader. Another couple was at the back looking at sex toys including vibrators of all sizes and colors while the other two were in front of the displays of erotic videos.

"I think we'll start with what you'll wear," Sam said.

As he put his hand on the small of her back and steered her toward the racks of clothes, he could feel her tension, which he suspected was part shock and part excitement. He'd never bought lingerie for a woman, but he'd enjoyed what he'd seen. The truth was exactly as he'd told Danika—it wasn't the lingerie itself, but how the woman wore it. It could be hot pink, glow in the dark, barely there, or conceal-all but if she wore it with the knowledge that it would drive him wild, it worked.

"Pick something," he urged when the only movement she made was with her eyes.

"No, you pick it. You're the expert."

"That won't work," he argued. "It isn't about what's sexy to look at. It's about what you'll feel sexy wearing."

"I don't even know where to start." She glanced at the other couples.

Sam decided that he needed to get her distracted from the fact that there were other people around. This was about her. He moved in to block her view of everyone else.

"I was right when I said you don't need a costume. You'll be absolutely perfect just as you are."

Her lips fell apart.

"So let's talk about how to highlight your assets." He put his hands on her waist, giving her just a moment to adjust to him touching her, then slipped them around to cup her butt. "For instance, this is very nice," he murmured. "I think you might have been right about the thong idea. Don't want to cover this up."

She put her hand on his chest and her pupils dilated as she looked up at him and Sam knew he was getting her mind where he wanted it to be.

He pulled her forward as he dipped his knees to fit the erection that had been nearly constant since he'd first spoken to her in the bar against her. "But this," he said, pressing forward as she sucked in a sharp breath, "is more like wrapping paper around a present of a very distinct shape. You know what it is, but unwrapping it is half the fun." He rubbed against her and she moaned softly. "And as you take the paper off and see it up close and personal for the first time it's even better than you imagined."

He reached up between them and cupped one of her breasts. It was a perfect fit in his palm. "These you definitely want to show off."

Her eyelids drifted shut and she arched her back slightly as he rubbed his thumb back and forth over the nipple that hardened instantly. He took a huge step forward, moving her back until they were completely behind a tall rack of clothes. He deftly slipped the top two buttons from their buttonholes and slid his hand inside the top of her dress, taking her breast in hand with only soft satin between them. He desperately wanted to swirl his tongue around the stiff point, but settled for tugging on it gently as she gripped the front of his shirt in both fists.

"Sam," she breathed.

"Are you feeling sexy, Danika?" he asked gruffly against her ear. "Are you feeling how hard and hot I am for you?" He pressed the proof against her again.

She opened her eyes and stared up at him. Sam knew that his face showed every bit of his desire for her and he did nothing to hide it. The plain truth was that this little woman, who had been settling for nice guys who couldn't take her all the way, had made him harder than he could remember being, quite possibly ever.

She nodded. "Yes."

"I am about this close to begging, Danika. At this moment, if you told me I could have you, I would give you anything to make that happen." She opened her mouth but he quickly put a finger over her lips. "Do you believe me?"

She nodded.

"How does it feel to know that I want you more than anything?"

She smiled then. A slow, sexy, timeless smile that made Sam groan. "Like seeing just how far I can push you before you do beg."

He wanted to hike up her skirt and make *her* beg against the nearest wall. But, somehow, he let go of her and watched as she re-buttoned her dress.

"Hang onto to that feeling. Go pick something out that will make you feel exactly like you do right this minute."

She smiled again and moved to the racks of bra and panty sets. She flipped through several before pulling two out. She held them up and then turned to him, holding one up against the front of her.

"How about this?"

The bra and thong were outlined in solid black satin, but the center pieces that covered the breasts and the crotch were a filmy gray material that was completely see-through. It reminded Sam of sheer black pantyhose. It would more than hint at what was behind the fabric. In fact, everything would be visible, just shaded. There was a hot pink rose at the center of the bra that would nestle between her breasts and a matching rose on each hip of the thong.

He found himself unable to be flippant or even flirtatious. He simply, honestly said, "Any guy who sees you in that won't be able to think about anything but being inside of you."

"Oh," was her soft, surprised response.

It hit him that while he was having vivid dirty dreams about her, she would be wearing the bra and panties in reality—for someone else. But he shook that off as she asked, "Should I try it on?"

It would kill him to think about her having that on just on the other side of a thin piece of drywall. "No. I can tell it will fit."

"You can?" She raised her eyebrows.

He held his palm up against the cup of the bra. "Yep."

Now she blushed. He almost laughed. She hadn't blushed when he'd touched her, or when he'd pressed a very stiff erection against her, but now, when he referred to knowing the size of her breast, she got pink.

"Are we ready to go then?"

Straight to bed for the next three or four days...absolutely. Instead, he turned her toward the back wall. "I'm thinking that you might need some additional help toward the orgasm thing."

"Oh?" Her trepidation upon stepping into the store had disappeared. "Like what?"

"Have you *ever* had an orgasm?" he asked.

"I thought you heard that part."

"I mean...*ever*. Even by yourself?" He wasn't sure why he was torturing himself this way, but he definitely needed to kill Ben. It had been his stupid-ass idea for Sam to give Danika pointers in the first place.

Danika abruptly stopped walking and Sam bumped into her. She turned. "By myself? You mean—"

"You don't have to say it," Sam cut in. In fact, he knew he would not survive hearing Danika talk about pleasuring herself. "Have you?"

"Um...."

He nudged her forward. "I think you need to. That will help

you know what...works...for you."

Oh man, this was *not* a good thing to talk about.

"What do you mean?"

He sighed. He'd taken on the challenge. He'd been attracted to her as soon as he'd seen her. What had he thought would happen? This was all his stupid fault. And Ben's. And Carmen's.

"You have to figure out what feels best for you. Every woman is different. Some like having their breasts touched." He moved in closer and dropped his voice, for modesty's sake, but also because his voice just got rougher when he was looking into those deep green eyes. "Some like oral sex, some like having their clitoris stroked, some like stroking inside."

She was looking at him with an expression that he couldn't decide how to describe. It was either stunned or fascinated.

"You need to find out for yourself what works best for you."

"How do you suggest I do that?" she asked huskily. "It all sounds pretty good."

It sure did. Trying to not just say, *I'll do it for you,* he simply stood watching her. It was good he did. Otherwise he would have missed the tiny curl at the one side of her mouth. He couldn't believe it. She was teasing him.

He grabbed a huge, bright blue dildo from the shelf and thrust it at her. "With this."

She rubbed her hand up and down the length of the toy. "Oh."

Watching her stroke the fake penis was enough to break his carefully held control. "Dammit, Danika, I thought you wanted my help."

"I do."

"Then stop messing around." He grabbed the blue plastic phallus and shoved it back onto the shelf. He moved down a few feet and pulled a small, clear plastic bottle of gel from a basket. He turned back in time to see her take the dildo back and tuck it under her arm with the bra and panties. He growled in frustration low in his throat and handed her the gel.

"What's this?"

"To help you...get ready. It warms up with friction."

"Where do I put it?"

The tone of voice was innocent, but he was watching her

carefully now. He could tell she was still messing with him by the mischievous glint in her eye.

He moved in close, pressing her back until her shoulder blades hit the shelf. "Do you want me to show you?"

She met his eyes directly. "Yes," she said softly.

Sam swore under his breath. Then he cupped the back of her head and pulled her up onto her tiptoes for a searing kiss. It wasn't gentle or romantic. It was full-on, wet and hot, I-want-you-underneath-me-now.

And Danika returned it stroke for stroke, groan for groan.

He wanted her with a ferocity that shook him. He'd been with a lot of women. Women who weren't shy about anything. He thought he was long past losing control.

It was now painfully clear that he'd been wrong.

"Let's go." He let only a millimeter of space between their lips.

"Okay," she breathed.

He let go of her and took a moment to appreciate the hot desire on her face. Her skin was flushed, her hair mussed, her lips wet and swollen, her chest rising and falling rapidly. And this was just the beginning.

He took her hand and started for the front of the store, but Danika took only two steps before tugging him to a stop. "Wait, there's something else."

"There's *a lot* else but we can't do it in here."

She smiled, but shook her head. "No, I mean there's something else I need."

"What?"

"They have videos." She gestured at the wall to her left.

"Right."

"I'm thinking that might help."

He glanced over and chuckled. "They aren't exactly instructional."

"They *could* be. The things they do in those videos are things I need to learn. Watching someone else do it might help."

He could barely walk as it was, yet he still heard himself ask, "Things like what?"

She stepped closer so she could lower her voice. "Oral sex."

He nearly swallowed his tongue. "Wh-what?" he coughed.

"I don't know how to do...that. What to expect. I thought

surely one of those videos would have a scene or two..."

"I can't believe this was my idea. I can't believe that I'm standing here..." Sam continued muttering as he stomped to the wall of DVDs, quickly scanned the titles, pulled two out, read the back of each, returned one to the shelf and handed Danika the other.

"Thanks, Sam."

She said it with such enthusiasm he looked at her suspiciously, but her eyes were focused on the DVD cover.

He had to nudge her toward the cash register. Once there he started to pull Ben's hundred-dollar bill out of his pocket then stopped. He couldn't stomach having another man buy these things for Danika. Not even Ben.

The only man who was going to provide Danika with sex toys and such was him.

At least while he could control it.

He pulled out his own wallet and watched as the girl put Danika's treats in a black bag with Tease in hot pink letters on the side.

Tease, indeed.

What a stupid idea this had been.

He glanced at Danika, who was clearly over her earlier embarrassment and was now looking around the store like a kid who had stumbled upon Santa's workshop.

A stupid idea that had been more fun than he'd had in far too long.

They were nearly back to the restaurant and Danika couldn't believe how hard her heart was still pounding. She would have never walked into Tease by herself, because she wasn't interested in what the store had to offer. At least, she hadn't thought she was. Before Sam.

She wasn't in the market for hot sex or an orgasm either. It didn't bother her that she didn't have them. In fact, she would never date a guy like Sam, a guy who could make her feel the way he did, and think the things she was thinking so easily. There was way too much potential for big-time emotions there. Already she could tell that she could easily feel desperate for Sam. For the way he looked at her, the way he touched her, the way he talked to her, the way he kissed her. One kiss and she was having a hard time imagining never kissing him again without feeling a pang in her chest.

No matter how totally stupid that was.

She didn't even truly know him. She had been with him for about an hour and already she felt more with him than she had with any of her boyfriends.

She had to stay away from Sam.

Eventually.

She could risk one night. After all, not wanting wild sex and intense climaxes on a regular basis didn't mean she shouldn't know about them. When someone was trying to diet, they were coached to identify their triggers, the things that made them lose control. The more time she spent with Sam, the better prepared she'd be for guys like him. Guys who could make her feel all of the things she was determined to stay away from. She'd recognize them more easily...and could more effectively avoid them. In the future.

That rationalization was working for her. This was good.

She could use Sam like a tutor. And Tease was like the library.

She giggled. Yeah. Exactly like the library.

Sam looked at her with a half-smile. "What's funny?"

"I feel better already."

"Better about what?" He was holding her hand.

"Better about the orgasms."

"Just being with me, huh? That's pretty good for my ego."

She laughed. "You've certainly given me hope." She lifted the Tease bag and shook it. "Not to mention paraphernalia."

"Right." He sounded pained.

"I have to pay you back," she said, tucking her hair behind her ear. "This was fun, but there's no way you should pay for this stuff."

He squeezed her hand. "I can't think of anything I would have rather spent that money on."

Somehow she believed him. Which was ridiculous. They'd known each other for seventy-eight minutes. They didn't even know each other's last names. Yet he'd bought her the most intimate stuff anyone ever had and knew things about her some of her closest friends didn't. This was crazy.

And she loved it. Though Sam turned her on more than any man ever had, she had definitely felt the thrill of turning him on as well. It was certainly playing with fire. But she couldn't help it. She always kept the upper hand in her relationships with men and the look on Sam's face when she'd asked for a video about oral sex had ensured that she had as much effect on him as he did on her. Which was the only reason she'd let it go on. She suspected that Sam had finally caught on to the fact that she was messing with him but he'd continued playing.

"I do appreciate it. I can't believe you left your dinner to do this for a stranger."

"I can have dinner with Ben any time. It isn't every day I get the chance to help a gorgeous woman find her sexual chi."

"Do you think I found it?"

"I can't tell you that for certain unless…"

He grinned at her and Danika felt heat spread…everywhere…as he tugged her closer still.

"Unless?" she asked, knowing full well that this was going to lead to more kissing. At least.

"Unless I give you an exam."

Images of Sam dressed in a lab coat with a stethoscope around his neck, looking her over, touching and testing, maybe even the use of stirrups, all floated through her mind and she was confused as to whether she should be nervous or turned-on. "Exam?" she repeated.

"Isn't that what an instructor does after a lesson to see if the student understands the material?"

Ah. An *exam*. Right. She felt her smile stretch even as anticipation sparkled along her nerve endings. "You are exactly right…Professor. But I think I might need some more lab time…" she held up the bright blue vibrator, "…before the test."

Just then a beeping sound erupted from Sam's waistband. He reached for a pager. "Sorry," he muttered, looking at the message. "Damn."

"Everything okay?"

He lifted his head. "I, um…" He glanced back at the pager, then up at her again. "I have a stop I have to make. I would take you back to the restaurant, but I'm on a deadline with this…thing I have to do. Do you mind?"

Prolonging her time with Sam was probably not smart. But

she still wanted to do it. "No problem."

"You'd better call your sisters and let them know where you are. I don't want them to worry. And in spite of my instructions to the contrary, I have a feeling they're going to call you later."

She smiled. That was nice. He was a good guy.

She frowned. He was a good guy.

Not a good thing to realize. It would be much easier to have a fling with him and let herself go physically—a little—if she didn't like him too.

Sam turned right at the stoplight while she sent a text message to her sisters about the change of plans. Ten minutes later they pulled up in front of a quaint blue two-story house.

"Is this your place?"

He gave her a grin, resting his arm along the back of her seat. "I wouldn't have made up a reason to bring you to my house."

She smiled back. "So where are we?"

"This is Natalia's house."

"Girlfriend?"

He laughed. "Female friend, yes. Come on."

The house was dark and Sam took her up to the garage door. "I don't think she's home," Danika said.

"Exactly." He lifted the cover on the keypad next to the door. He punched in six numbers and the wide door slowly rumbled up. He took her hand and pulled her into the interior then to the door leading into the house.

"Should I have brought my black ski mask?" she whispered.

"You don't just carry that with you?" He opened the door that led from the garage into the kitchen. "And you don't have to whisper. She isn't here."

"Sam, what's going on? You do know this woman, right?"

"I know her very well. I'm here to check her light bulbs." He flipped on the kitchen light. "This one works." He grinned at her and crossed the room to the switches next to the sink. He flipped one up, starting the garbage disposal. "Sounds good to me." Then he turned on the faucet. "No trouble there." He shut the water off and faced Danika.

"What are you doing?" She couldn't help smiling at him.

"You want to help?"

"Do what?"

"I'm checking the place over. Making sure everything works, nothing needs repaired or replaced."

"Why?"

"To help Natalia out. She lives alone. She's eighty-three and can't take care of a lot of this herself."

"Why are you breaking into her house when she's not here?"

"I'm not breaking in. I have the code. And because it's easier when she's not here. If she's home she'd insist on cooking for me and hearing about my job."

"Poor baby," Danika said dryly. "How dare she be interested in having a friendship with you?"

He just chuckled. "You want to help or not?"

"What do I do?"

"Go around and turn on anything that's supposed to turn on, open anything that should open, close anything that should close... Look for anything that's not working the way it should."

"Got it." It was a strange routine, but it was kind of sweet.

"I'll meet you back here. Let me know anything that needs attention."

"Sam, seriously why don't you do this when she's home?"

"Because she would never let me do it. She'd insist on hiring someone else or paying me."

"So instead she just thinks that her light bulbs never burn out?"

He shrugged. "I guess."

Danika headed for another room and spent the next twenty minutes checking light switches, running water, opening and closing windows and drawers and checking the vents.

"Find anything?"

She looked over her shoulder to find Sam leaning against the door jamb. She was standing on the kitchen countertop, scrubbing the high window over the sink. She gave it a final swipe, then climbed down. "I fit all of her jewelry in my pockets, but I'm going to need some help carrying out the silver."

He chuckled. "I'll get the burlap bag." He pushed away from the door and came into the room, not stopping until he nearly stood on top of her. "It was sweet of you to help me."

"This is the most interesting evening I've spent in a long

time," she said, smiling up at him. "Did I hear a vacuum running?"

"Yeah."

"You clean to?"

"I only did the steps. If I did the whole house it would be too obvious."

She shook her head. "And why the steps?"

"We do the stuff she can't, or shouldn't, do. Like hauling the vacuum up and down the steps."

"What about the second floor?"

"She has another vacuum up there. It's the stairs that are tricky."

"So she also believes that her stairs never get dirty?"

He just shrugged again. "I guess." He glanced up at the window she'd just scrubbed. He took the dirty paper towel from her hand and tossed it onto the counter. "You didn't have to do that."

"I know. But it saved you some time doing it."

He glanced up at the window again. "I've never scrubbed those windows."

"Why not?"

"Never thought of it." He looked back at her.

"Hmm." She tipped her head. "Glad I could contribute."

His eyes dropped to her lips and he lifted his index finger and traced it down the length of her throat. "Anything else I've missed?"

The heat of his finger against her neck distracted her to the point of having to swallow twice before saying, "There are high windows above the front door too."

His finger traced along her collar bone. "Uh-huh. What else?"

She searched her mind for something that an older woman couldn't do by herself to keep her home going. But her mind was much more interested in Sam's finger. "I'm guessing that she can't...turn her mattresses."

"Now I have thought about mattresses since you've been around." He bent and placed his lips at the base of her throat.

She half chuckled and half groaned as she tipped her head back. "Then there's the fireplace," she breathed.

"We cleaned her fireplace last fall."

"Great." She let her eyes drift closed. "How about the drains? They should be cleaned out. All kinds of grime—dirt, hair—get in there."

Sam lifted his head and her eyes struggled to open. "You're thinking about clogged drains while I'm kissing you? I'm definitely doing something wrong here."

"No, you're... Oh!" Her protest ended as he cupped her butt in both hands and lifted her up against him, pressing his very evident erection against the soft spot between her legs and capturing her lips with his.

He kissed her hot and hard for several long moments, angling his head so he could stroke his tongue even deeper. When he lifted his head, it was difficult to make her eyes focus.

"What were we talking about?" he asked.

"Mattresses," she replied automatically.

He grinned a cocky, I've-got-you-where-I-want-you grin and set her back on her own two feet. "That's better."

Danika struggled to bring air into her lungs. Sam invaded every molecule of the space around her. She could smell him, feel his heat. And she wanted more. Of all of it.

She needed a distraction. Now. "By the way, the ceiling fan in the dining room doesn't work."

He thought about that for a few seconds. "I guess I'll check the wiring." He didn't sound all that certain about the statement.

"Do you know about electrical wiring?" she asked.

"I'm better with light bulbs and loose screws, but if I can't figure it out, Mac can."

"Mac?"

"One of my buddies. He helps with the houses. He'll come over and check it out."

"Houses? Plural?" she asked.

"There are four ladies we check on." Sam ran his palms up and down her upper arms.

Danika loved the feel of his hands on her. The firm heat gliding over her shoulders made her want his hands everywhere else she had skin.

"The gals play cards every Thursday. They rotate whose house they play at. We check the other three houses while they play. I usually take care of Natalia but Ben wanted to have a

45

drink tonight."

He grinned at her and she realized that his friend, Ben, had been in on them both being at the bar tonight.

"Kevin agreed but then got called into work, so asked if I could come over after all. And we don't have much time before Natalia gets home."

"That's...nice." Dammit. Sam was a nice guy. Who made her tingle just walking into the room with her. She had to stay away from him. "Do you have a screwdriver?"

"Yes."

"I'll check the wiring."

"You're going to check the wiring?" he asked with a smile.

She raised an eyebrow. "Not if you're going to act like that."

"Like what?"

"Like you can't believe that a woman would know how to check the wiring in a ceiling fan."

"I guess while you're up on the table I can check out your butt."

"Good. Be chauvinistic. That will help."

He chuckled. "I was just kidding. What will it help?"

"Me not like you so much."

"You can't help liking me, Dani," he said, huskily, pulling her closer.

He was right. Unfortunately. "Get me a screwdriver already," she said, pushing him back before she got too comfortable up against him. "And don't call me Dani."

He let go of her, turning to rummage in the toolbox on the counter next to the microwave. "No one calls you Dani?"

"Men don't."

"Why not?"

"I don't let them." It was too familiar and she didn't like getting to the point of nicknames and endearments with the men she dated.

Sam said nothing to that and he did, indeed, stand behind her as she crawled up on the dining room table to check the ceiling fan. He shut off the electrical switch on the wall and then held the flashlight for her. Along with the light coming from the kitchen it was plenty to see what she was doing. But she felt his gaze on her backside, and her body heated and she had to force herself to focus on the job at hand.

"How do you know how to do that?" he finally asked.

"I make it a point to know how to do things for myself."

There was a long silence as she removed the cover from the center of the ceiling fan, then stripped the plastic coating back from the end of one wire where it had frayed and come unconnected, then reattached it to the one next to it. She lifted the cover back over the inner workings of the fan and inserted the tiny screw into the hole to hold the cover on.

"You already have a vibrator at home, don't you?"

She wobbled and dropped the screw. "*What?*"

What a way to break the silence.

"You didn't need that blue dildo, did you?"

Unable to come up with anything other than, "Um," Danika looked down at Sam. To find him looking at her butt, which was just about eye level for him.

He handed her the screw from where it had bounced across the table. "You said you haven't had an orgasm." He wrapped a big, warm hand around her calf to steady her and looked up. "But you just said that you make a point of knowing how to do things for yourself."

She quickly turned her attention back to the ceiling fan, which made a lot more sense than the riot of sensations that this virtual stranger was stirring up. "I said that I haven't been with a man who gave me an orgasm." She tried to turn the screw but it wouldn't go in straight, just as she couldn't ignore the way his touch seemed to tingle up her bare leg and a very specific spot higher.

"Have you had an orgasm with a woman?"

She wobbled, the screw hit the table again, and his grip tightened on her leg. "Excuse me?"

Sam stroked his hand up and down her calf. Slowly. Completely ignoring the screw this time. "If you haven't had an orgasm with a man, it was an obvious question to ask if you have with a woman."

She took a deep breath, trying to focus on what he'd said versus the feel of his hand on her. They were talking about orgasms. Right. And women. Wrong.

She frowned. "No, I haven't had an orgasm with a woman."

"Too bad." He gave her a bone-melting grin. "I had some pretty good images going."

"I'll bet." She shook off his hand and bent to pick up the screw where it had bounced.

"But you've had one by yourself, right?"

She tossed her hair over her shoulder. What the heck? He knew plenty about her already. Which ensured that she was going to make a point of never seeing him again. "Yes. Several in fact."

"Good." He nodded, apparently pleased with her answer.

"Good?"

"No woman should go without orgasms completely."

She couldn't say why exactly, but that struck her as funny. She grinned. "If only everyone was so certain about their beliefs."

He winked at her and it hit her that he was good-looking. And she needed to never see him again.

She straightened and fit the screw back into the tiny hole. Just then she felt the heat of Sam's hand on her calf again. She braced herself for the stroking that commenced. What she wasn't prepared for was the fact that his hand kept traveling up. And up.

She narrowed her eyes, concentrating on fitting the tip of the screwdriver into the star-shaped notches on the screw. But when her eyes drifted shut as Sam's hand passed her knee and continued up, taking the hem of her skirt up with it, it was very difficult to see anything at all.

Move forward. Move out of reach.

Her legs had no idea what her brain was talking about. Why would she move away from such exquisite feelings?

You cannot do this on the dining room table—that's probably been in the family for generations—of a sweet little old woman who you don't even know.

Still, her legs pretended not to hear.

When Sam's lips met the skin in the middle of the back of her thigh, she felt the heat shoot straight up between her thighs and her knees wobbled.

Then his tongue touched the crease at the back of her knee and she melted.

Literally.

She vaguely heard Sam gasp, "Danika!" but the next true sensation she was aware of was the sharp pain from where her knees hit the table, stealing her breath, and the hot knife that was seemingly dug into her right wrist.

She thought about gasping, or screaming, or swearing loudly, but her chest wouldn't expand.

Holy crap. That hurt.

Holy crap. She was hurt.

"Danika!"

Shit, damn, fuck.

"Danika," he said earnestly. "Are you okay?"

Somehow, without even thinking, he'd gotten her up sitting on the edge of the table instead of on her hands and knees, not breathing and looking white as a sheet.

Now, a few minutes later, she was still not breathing deeply and was white as a sheet. But she was upright.

Her pulse was strong, she wasn't bleeding, she hadn't hit her head. She was technically okay.

"Hmm?"

"Danika? Honey, are you hurt?"

Of course she was hurt. She'd hit the table hard. She'd gone forward, but her legs hadn't moved with her—since he'd had a hold of them—and she'd gone down onto all fours, her hands hitting just milliseconds before her knees.

It was all his fault.

She blinked long and slow three times before he was sure she was focused on his face.

"What the..." She reached to rub her right knee with her right hand, but instantly sucked in a quick, hard breath. "Damn!"

"Your knee?" Had she cracked her kneecap? That was a hell of an injury. His hands sandwiched her knee and he pressed a thumb against the center of the knee cap.

She winced but it didn't elicit an expletive, which had to be a good sign. She shook her head.

"Did I fall on a knife?"

He stared at her. He was positive she hadn't hit her head. "What do you mean?"

"Did I fall on a knife with my hand? It feels like it."

Oh, terrific. Her hand felt like she'd fallen on a knife when she most certainly had not. Sure, that was normal. And fine. Nothing to worry about at all. *Dammit.*

"Let me see." He took her hand gently. It was swelling. Shit. "Where?"

"All of it."

He started moving her fingers one by one. She winced with all of them, particularly when he moved her two middle fingers. He felt along each of the long bones of her hand, again with only slight wincing. But when he tried to move her wrist, she jerked back.

"No!"

"The wrist?" He took her hand back gently. "I'll be easy. But I have to see what's going on."

"I just fell on it funny," she said. "It's just a strain."

"Let's check it," he said grimly. He pressed on the middle of the back of her wrist and she instantly jerked and tears filled her eyes.

He looked at her and sighed. "We have to go to the hospital, Danika. I think you broke your wrist."

On the drive to the emergency room at St. Anthony's, Sam had no idea what to say. Which was so unusual for him, especially with women, that he felt like *he'd* hit his head.

"Stop it."

He looked at Danika in surprise. "What?"

"Stop beating yourself up."

She was cradling her hand against her stomach, with the makeshift ice bag on it that he'd made from a plastic sandwich bag and cubes from Natalia's freezer.

He frowned. "I'm not."

She rolled her head against the headrest to look at him. She smiled. "Of course you are. Any guy who goes to women's houses to check their light bulbs and vacuum is going to feel bad about me falling."

"You broke your wrist. Because of me."

"You don't know that I broke it, and it wasn't your fault."

"You did break it."

"You don't know—"

"I am an excellent paramedic, if nothing else," he interrupted.

"If nothing else?" she repeated. "What does that mean?"

He suddenly jerked the wheel, pulling sharply to the side of the road. He shoved the car into park and turned to her. "It means that being a paramedic and recognizing obvious things like the fact that you broke your wrist when you fell are the only things that I've done right tonight. As usual." He shoved his hand through his hair. "I broke your wrist while trying to seduce you. Jesus, Danika, do you know how I'm feeling right now?"

She raised an eyebrow. "I'm guessing guilty."

That was it. Her only response, her only reaction. She wasn't scared of him, she wasn't angry with him.

"I feel like hell." He swore. "All I've wanted to do since I first saw you was kiss you and now I'm driving you to the ER."

She said nothing, but she dropped the ice bag on the floor. Then she leaned in and grabbed the front of his shirt with her uninjured hand, pulled him close and kissed him.

At first, Sam only let their lips meet, refusing to move them, refusing to reach for her, to pull her close. He didn't deserve to kiss her. He didn't deserve to touch her. Look what had happened when he had touched her.

But she tasted so good. She felt so good. She smelled *so* good.

He gave in with a groan, pulling her up against his chest, angling his head to taste her more deeply, with long strokes of his tongue, his hands stroking over her shoulders, down her back to her hips, desperate to make her feel good, desperate to assure himself that while her wrist hurt, the rest of her was okay.

She moaned in response and Sam let the sound of her satisfaction seep through him. *This* was something he was always good at. This and taking care of emergency injuries.

Which abruptly brought his passion to a screeching halt.

"Emergency room," he rasped against Danika's lips. "Wrist."

"It feels better," she whispered, trying to pull him closer as he tried to pull back.

"It won't in a little bit."

She frowned. "What do you mean?"

He put his lips against the side of her neck, drawing them up to her ear where he said huskily, "The positions I have in mind will put too much pressure on your wrist."

She chuckled. "I have a feeling I won't mind."

"*I* will be so worried about it, I won't be able to concentrate."

"I'm guessing you've done enough of it, you can do it even when distracted."

He rolled his eyes and laughed as he pulled back, as out of reach as he could get. "We're going to the hospital."

She experimentally tried to wiggle her fingers. They moved and she only frowned. Then she tried the wrist. She sucked in a sharp breath and then held it, then squeezed her eyes shut.

"Yeah, exactly," he said dourly, putting the car into drive. There wasn't anything he could do for her wrist here. The sooner they got to the ER, the better.

Chapter Three

"Did you put the tools away?" Danika asked a minute later. "At Natalia's. Before we left? I don't remember."

He frowned. Hell, he didn't remember either, but he'd been so focused on Danika and getting her into the car, he doubted it. "No, I don't think so."

"Did you put the cover back on the ceiling fan?"

He frowned harder. Of course not. He hadn't given the fan one single thought since the hem of her skirt had lifted high enough to expose the silky skin of the back of her thighs. "No."

"We have to go back."

They were five minutes from the ER. "No."

"Natalia's going to get home and see all of that?" she asked. "Not only will it blow your cover but she'll be scared that someone was in her house until she knows it was you."

He sighed. She was right.

All in one night, three things he did very well—taking care of Natalia, seducing a beautiful woman and taking care of an injury—had gotten complicated. As soon as he'd met Danika.

He pulled his cell phone from his back pocket and punched in Mac's number.

"Can you go over to Natalia's and clean up my stuff before she gets home?" he asked, knowing that Mac would know it was him by the incoming number.

"Why? What's up?"

"I had to leave..." He glanced at Danika. "Quickly. Didn't get a chance to clean up."

"Why?"

Mac didn't exactly believe in things like privacy or people

having secrets.

"There's something I had to take care of."

"Something like what?"

It wasn't that Mac was slow. Quite the opposite. For Sam to be giving him vague answers meant that Sam was up to something that Mac would be interested in.

"A woman," Sam said shortly.

"Who?"

"No one you know."

"Will I get to meet her?"

"How long have we known each other?" Sam asked.

"Nine years."

"And in all that time, how many times have I had a woman meet my friends?"

"On purpose or including the times that we showed up anyway?"

"On purpose."

"Once," Mac said. "No wait. We paid that little boy who lives in your apartment building to call us when you got home."

"Yeah," Sam said, sarcastically. "Conner. Cute kid."

Mac chuckled. "Melissa had fun playing cards with us."

"She did."

"I don't think you dated her again, did you?"

"Nope." Sam found it was too difficult to get his relationships mixed up. He didn't want his friends or sisters to get to know any woman he dated. There was always the chance that they would all get along and like her. That just meant even more people to be disappointed or upset when he didn't see her again.

"So you'll do it?" Sam asked.

"Sure."

"Thanks, man." Sam disconnected before Mac could ask any more questions or hear the wailing siren approaching. The last thing he needed was for his friends to find out he'd put a woman in the hospital on their first date.

They pulled around the corner to the entrance of the ER and Sam parked in his employee spot. But it wasn't until the doors slid open that Sam realized it was a mistake to bring Danika to the ER at St. Anthony's. Mac might not have heard the sounds of the ER over the phone, but he knew the entire staff in the emergency room, and they all knew Mac. And everyone else in Sam's life.

It was too late.

"Sam!" Kaylee, the ER receptionist, came around the corner of the counter. "What's going on?"

His arm was around Danika, who was holding her hand against her stomach, the ice pack back in place.

"We need some x-rays."

"Come on back." Kaylee started for a treatment room.

"We can wait," Danika protested, glancing at the two other people in the waiting room.

"No, we can't." He didn't want Danika sitting and waiting, with her wrist hurting and her hand swelling. At least this was one thing he could do for her—get her into the damned ER without waiting.

"Sam, there are—"

"It's fine," Kaylee said.

"No, they were here first."

"But you're here with Sam," Kaylee said with a wink. "That's like showing up with the President."

"I'm not that hurt," Danika tried again.

"Kaylee." Sam squeezed Danika's shoulder. "What are they here for?" He gestured toward the others in the waiting room.

"One's waiting for his dad who's back on the heart monitor, the other one is complaining of stomach pain."

"Get that guy in," Sam said. He knew he should mean it, but for him no one came before Danika. Still, it would make her happy and she wasn't dying. "Then us."

"Dr. Larson is on his way," Kaylee said. "And the guy won't see anyone else."

Sam looked down at Danika. "No reason to wait."

"Fine." She let him guide her down the hall to the second exam room.

Danika slid up onto the exam table with one hand. "Like being with the President, huh?"

He shrugged. "I bring the front desk staff bagels on Tuesdays."

"Kissing up?"

"At first." He grinned. "But now it's because I like them." He was thinking about finding a reason to sneak out before the on-call physician came in. It didn't matter who it was, he knew them all, and they would all be sure that everyone else knew about this fiasco.

"Hey, Sam." Lisa, another of the ER clerks, poked her head into the room. "Kaylee said you were here. Tommie's here. He wants to talk to you."

It was the perfect excuse to get out of seeing Danika's doctor. "What the heck?"

"Room two," Lisa said.

"Of course." Tommie had a thing for even numbers and had an aversion to the number four.

"The nurses are willing to all pitch money in for beer if you give him a shower."

"He was just here last week. He can't smell that bad."

"But he'll be back next week and if you shower him today it will save all our noses then."

"You realize you're talking about me getting a *man* in a shower."

Lisa rolled her eyes. "I'm aware."

"Now if the nurses were willing to all pitch in and get in with us..."

"The shower stall isn't that big, Sam."

"Your loss."

"I'm not a nurse."

"You're still invited."

"Thanks, but my fiancé might protest." She rolled her eyes again, but was smiling.

"In that case, I'll talk to Tommie about wet wipes and deodorant." Sam shrugged and tried to look apologetic. Even though he knew Lisa wasn't buying it. "Best I can do."

"You're a prince," Lisa said just before the door bumped shut behind her.

He was chuckling as he dug in his pocket for the seventy-five cents he needed for the vending machine. He glanced at Danika, who was watching him. Oops. The comment about the shower with the nurses had been a joke, but probably not appropriate in front of the woman he was on a kind-of date with. "What?"

"You're amazing."

"Thanks. Why?"

"The sex shop with me and now you're inviting multiple women to shower with you."

He shrugged, now feeling bad. "I was kidding around. I don't date, or sleep with, the women in the ER. Too uncomfortable after things end."

"Got it." She didn't look annoyed or jealous...or in that much pain. Maybe the ibuprofen he'd pilfered from Natalia's kitchen cupboard was helping.

"Dr. Mitchell is in with the guy with the cardiac arrhythmia, Sam," Kaylee told them just then. "It's going to be a while for you."

Sam sighed. He wanted Danika seen, x-rayed and fixed. Now. Dammit.

"How's your pain?" he asked her.

"Not terrible if I don't move it."

"Want to come meet Tommie?"

Danika shrugged. "Why not?"

He liked that about her. That she just went with the flow. He'd prefer to be having her go with it in the sex shop, or bed, or the front seat of his car, but it looked like this night wasn't going to go exactly the way he wanted no matter what. "Let's go."

He took her good hand, wanting, needing to touch her. Stupid as it was. They stopped at the soda machine in the hallway and got a can of Pepsi, then continued to room two.

"Who's Tommie?" Danika asked.

"He's this homeless guy who ends up in the ER about once a week. His injuries are always minor, but they're enough to get him in the doors where he can be fed and fussed over. He's harmless but demanding when he shows up. He only drinks Pepsi, only eats Lorna Doone cookies or orange Jell-O—but preferably both—always wants new socks and only takes advice from me."

She raised an eyebrow. "Wow, what makes you so special?"

"My crew and I found him about a year ago, nearly frozen to death, in front of the library. We wanted to bring him in, but he wouldn't come. Then he saw my empty Pepsi can in the ambulance. He decided I could be trusted and it's lasted. I'm always the one to talk him into going to the shelter."

She smiled at him. "Maybe I can help. I'm a social worker."

"No kidding." Now that she said it, it fit somehow. "Where?"

"Here."

"At St. Anthony's?"

"Yes."

He stopped and stared down at her. "Since when?"

"Two weeks ago."

She'd been here two weeks? Here? Where he spent most of his day, every day? Where he knew everyone? How had he missed her? "Jack is definitely off my Christmas card list."

"Jack?" she repeated.

"Jack Conner. He's a drug counselor on fifth floor. He's supposed to let me know whenever a beautiful woman joins the staff."

He knew that she knew he was teasing her, but she said, "I haven't met him yet."

"What's he been *doing*? Your office has to be right down the hall from his. How could he have missed you for two weeks?"

"I'll make a point of introducing myself on Monday."

"No, don't do that," he said quickly. Jack didn't have Sam's reputation, but he was a single guy who would definitely find Danika attractive. He was straight and had a pulse, after all. Worse, she probably had a lot in common with Jack.

"Why not? We have offices right down the hall from each other," she said with a smile.

"He believes in polygamy."

She snorted. "He does not."

"How do you know?"

"Does he?" She put a hand on her hip.

"Yes. Absolutely. And he hates dogs."

"I'm not a big dog person."

"He spends every weekend at the racetrack."

"I love a man who knows how to take chances."

"He's killed eight people."

"I'm sure he had a good reason."

Sam gave up with a reluctant grin. She was funny. But he couldn't resist one final quip. "He doesn't know anything about orgasms."

She raised an eyebrow. "Something more in common. We'd make a good pair."

Even though they were kidding around, Sam hated that idea. Even though they'd only known each other for a few hours, he hated that idea.

"Hey, Tommie, what's up?" he asked a moment later as he opened the door to Tommie's favorite exam room.

"My hopes, Brad."

Sam chuckled. "Good answer."

Tommie chuckled in return and inexplicably started whistling "The Battle Hymn of the Republic". Which, for Tommie, wasn't anything unusual.

"Brad?" Danika asked from behind him.

Sam turned and grinned at her. "My last name's Bradford. That was the first thing Tommie latched on to when we met. I've been Brad ever since." He crossed the room and put a hand on Tommie's shoulder. "Derek is going to take you over to the shelter."

Derek was one of the social workers that worked the night shift in the ER, one of the more...interesting shifts.

"No," Tommie said simply. Then went back to whistling.

"Just for tonight, buddy."

"No," he said again, switching gears to whistle "I've Been Working on the Railroad".

"It's a good idea, Tommie," Sam said.

Tommie held up a pair of socks. "They're blue." He seemed very pleased.

"Mine too." Sam pulled up a pant leg to show his navy blue socks.

"Good." Tommie seemed even happier with that.

"So how about the shelter?" Sam was used to Tommie trying to distract him from talking about subjects Tommie didn't like. The shelter was one. Showers, shaving and eating anything even remotely resembling vegetables were also on the list.

"No."

"What if Sa...Brad and I take you?" Danika offered.

"No." Then he frowned. "Who are you?"

"This is Danika."

"So?"

"Be nice." Tommie was harmless, and lucid, but was known to say some very inappropriate things when he thought it would get an entertaining reaction.

"What's your last name?" Tommie asked Danika.

Sam had to be thankful to Tommie for that. He was learning more about Danika every second.

"Steffen," she told him.

"I'm thirsty," Tommie announced, looking at Danika as if daring her.

Sam slid closer to her and surreptitiously put the Pepsi in her hand.

"Do you like Pepsi?" she asked without missing a beat. She popped the top of the can open and held it out.

Tommie lit up instantly. He took the Pepsi, tipped it back, took a huge gulp, then grinned. "I like her."

Sam chuckled. He'd decided he liked Danika just about as easily. "So how about the shelter tonight?"

Tommie frowned at Sam for a moment. "They never have Jell-O."

"I'll personally ensure they have Jell-O tonight," Danika said.

"I like the plastic cups."

Danika turned, obviously confused, to Sam.

"He likes those individual cups of Jell-O instead of the boxes that they mix up with water."

"I can do that," she decided.

Tommie considered that. "Okay." He slid to the floor, tucked his new socks into the huge pockets of the long coat he wore, and put his ragged New York Yankees baseball cap back on his head.

"Great." Sam was surprised. Tommie always ended up agreeing with him, but it usually took longer to convince him.

He couldn't blame Tommie. Danika Steffen was having an interesting effect on him as well.

"They have those individual plastic cups of Jell-O in the cafeteria," Danika said. "I'll go get him a couple."

As she turned, Sam grabbed her elbow. "Whoa. You're a patient here too, remember? You're not going to the cafeteria."

"But I promised Tommie." Danika liked the way Sam was looking at her. Protective and worried. Which worried *her*. She hadn't wanted or needed a man for anything for a long time now.

Not that she'd admit it to him, but her wrist did hurt. Talking with Tommie and using the ice pack had helped, but it was throbbing and she was thinking Sam was right about it being broken.

Which was so inconvenient and stupid that she chose not to think about it. Getting Tommie orange Jell-O was a good distraction.

"Lisa will run down there." Sam steered her with one hand and Tommie with the other.

Danika started to reach into her right front pocket for some cash for the Jell-O but stopped instantly, sucking in a breath. She'd tried to reach with her right hand.

"What?" Sam stopped immediately, turning worried eyes on her.

His worry was a lot nicer when her wrist was just aching rather than when it was feeling like someone was trying to rip it free from her arm.

She shook her head. He felt bad enough. It wasn't his fault. "I, um, needed to get some money out of my pocket. But I can't." She held up her hand.

"Oh, I've got..." Sam started to reach for his own pocket. Then a mischievous twinkle entered his eye. "In your pocket?" He let go of Tommie, who stayed right where he was, happily clutching his can of Pepsi to his chest, checking out the junk food selection in the vending machine and whistling "Camp Town Races".

She nodded as Sam moved in closer.

"This pocket?" he asked, hooking the tip of his index finger in the top of her right front pocket.

The throbbing in her wrist seemed to evaporate as she nodded.

"I guess I could help you out with that," he said, his voice dropping and his body taking up every molecule of air around her.

"That would be...helpful," she said softly.

Sam turned his hand so that his palm was flat against her hip. The skirt lay against her body but wasn't at all tight. Still, Sam kept his palm firmly against her as he slid down into the pocket. The heat from his hand instantly heated her skin and she closed her eyes.

He slid back and forth over the area where the band of her panties arced over her hip, covering the lower part of her abdomen.

"I can't seem to find it," he said huskily.

"What are you looking for again?" she breathed.

His mouth curled up. "I can answer that, but it's something other than what I started out trying to find."

She smiled, the warmth from his hand spreading throughout her abdomen and up through her chest. "Whatever the answer, just keep doing that."

"Dr. Mitchell said that if you think she needs an x-ray to go ahead and then he'll see her," Lisa said, interrupting the moment.

Sam didn't jerk his hand free from her pocket. Rather he stayed right where he was, his fingers grasping the edge of the five dollar bill in her pocket and then drawing it out slowly, his hand contacting more of her body than necessary for the simple extraction.

"I'd say get a room, but I already gave you one," Lisa said with a grin.

"Tommie needs some Jell-O from the cafeteria." Sam reached into his own pocket, pulled out another five and handed Lisa the money, not taking his eyes from Danika's face. "Can you send someone?"

She sighed. "Yeah, we have an intern that isn't doing anything."

"Make sure it's orange."

"Of course."

Lisa moved off and Sam said, his eyes suddenly serious, "Tell me you're okay. I know it isn't completely true, but just tell me anyway."

For some reason, Danika felt a lump in her throat. She lifted her uninjured hand to his cheek. "I'm okay. Very okay, in fact."

"Your wrist..."

"Is just one part of my body, and I can assure you that you're making the rest of it feel *very* okay."

His eyes darkened. "I wish, with everything in me, that I

had a chance to make it feel even better than very okay."

"Me too." She hoped that maybe he would have, and take, that chance in the future. But she couldn't say that. This was supposed to be a one-night stand. That was all he signed up for...or whatever he'd done. She couldn't make it into more than that. Even though she hadn't really had everything that a one-night stand entailed.

Tommie's whistling changed to the theme from *Star Wars* and Sam stepped back with a rueful grin. "Let's get him with Derek and then you into x-ray."

Yeah, that was what they should do.

Derek Stevens was at the front desk flirting with Kaylee. Flirting seemed to be something that went on around St. Anthony's a lot.

Derek pushed away from the counter as they approached. "Danika? Hey."

"Hi."

"You know her?" Sam asked, frowning.

"She's new on staff here in our department," Derek said with a friendly smile at her.

"You're off my Christmas card list too," Sam muttered.

"I'm on your Christmas card list?" Derek was clearly confused.

"Not anymore," Sam said shortly.

"Um, okay." Derek evidently decided to talk to someone who would make more sense. "Hey, Tommie, ready to go?"

"Jell-O," Tommie said simply.

"He's waiting on Jell-O," Danika explained. "Someone went to get it."

Tommie wandered off to peruse the selection of the soda machine, pushing the buttons one by one.

Sam shrugged out of his jacket and handed it to Danika. She held it as he pulled his sweatshirt over his head. Danika swallowed and tried to look away as the T-shirt underneath also pulled up, revealing a hard, flat stomach and a line of crisp golden hair down the center, but her eyes simply would not obey. Once the sweatshirt was off, the T-shirt settled back where it was supposed to be and Danika heard Derek say, "Let me know if you have any questions."

She smiled at him. "I will."

"I'm interested in what you think of the project."

Oh, crap. She was going to have to sound intelligent discussing something about which she hadn't heard one word.

"I'm flattered," she said. She meant it too. She always liked it when someone wanted to know what she thought. But she would have meant it even more if she was completely focused on Derek.

The thing was, as long as Sam Bradford was within one hundred feet of her, she would likely never be completely focused on anything else.

He had taken a pair of scissors from a drawer behind the registration desk and had cut a small hole on the back of the right shoulder of his sweatshirt and then used the scissors to fray the cuff around each of the wrists. Finally, he picked up a Styrofoam cup and splashed coffee down the front.

Sam handed the shirt to Derek and took his jacket back from Danika. "Give that to him when it's dry. Tell him some other guy left it here a few days ago." He handed Derek a twenty dollar bill. "And get him a scarf. He lost the other one."

Derek nodded and pocketed the money. "I'll get a blue one."

Sam clapped Derek on the back. "Thanks."

Danika had only one thought at that point. *Uh, oh.*

Sam Bradford was a good guy. That was not going to make it any easier to not want to get to know him.

A young man in a white lab coat appeared from around the corner. "Someone needed Jell-O?"

Derek took the three plastic cups and grabbed a plastic spoon from the coffee cart near the magazine rack. "Time to go, Tommie."

"Okay." Now the man was agreeable. "Let's go."

He was whistling "Auld Lang Syne" as he headed for the door. "Bye, Stephanie!" he called as the doors swished open.

Startled, Danika looked at Sam. "Steffen," he said with a shrug.

Right.

"Bye, Tommie!" she returned.

"Time for x-rays," Sam announced, not waiting even for the doors to shut behind Derek and Tommie.

He escorted her with his hand on her lower back and Danika wished for the hundredth time that they were walking through a romantic, candlelit restaurant instead of a hospital's emergency department. Especially the hospital they both worked for. Everyone would know that she'd been admitted to the ER, for a fractured wrist, with Sam.

That might be interesting to explain on Monday morning.

"Oh, crap!" She stopped short.

"What? Your wrist?"

His concern was sweet. His guilt, not so much. "No, my sisters. I have to let them know what's going on."

She was able to pull her cell phone from the outside pocket of her purse but she did not want to call them. It would be a long, drawn-out conversation which would likely end in one or both of her sisters storming the ER. Especially Carmen, who worked here.

Damn.

"I'm just going to text them and tell them I'm with you," she said.

"You know what they'll think," Sam said, looking amused and not at all concerned.

"It was their idea in the first place."

"They'll just be patting themselves on the back, then?"

"Exactly."

She flipped her phone open with one hand but as soon as she went to push the first button with her right hand, she sucked in a breath. How could that even hurt?

"I'll do it."

She pulled the phone away from Sam. "I've got it." But after two more painful buttons she sighed. "Fine, here."

Sam typed quickly, then handed it back.

"I don't get to read the message?" she asked.

"No need. You know what's going on."

"What did you say?"

"That I'm taking very good care of you."

She smiled, but one glance at his face, and the serious, regretful expression on it, she sobered. "Sam..."

"I lied," he said with a sigh. "You're in the ER for God's sake. Not really good care, is it?"

She gripped his forearm with her good hand and squeezed. "It's *not* your fault."

"Who else was there? Who else tried to kiss you while you

65

weren't looking, while you were standing on top of a table, with nothing to grab onto for balance? Who else—"

"I fell because I had my eyes shut and because you made me literally weak in the knees!" she interrupted.

He did stop. Thank goodness. And stared at her with a goofy expression. "What?"

"It felt so good that I shut my eyes and when you kissed my leg I got wobbly...and fell."

"You fell because it felt good?"

"I was completely overcome with passion," she said, rolling her eyes.

He grinned, just a little. "Seriously?"

"You made me melt into a puddle of lust."

"Wow."

"Feel better now?"

"Your wrist is still broken," he pointed out.

"You don't know that." But she'd be surprised if it wasn't.

"I'll bet you it is."

"What are we betting?"

"Dinner tomorrow night."

She waited for the I'm-just-kidding-grin or the panic at having realized that he'd just turned a one-night stand into a two-night date. But he simply looked at her expectantly.

"What if I win?" she asked.

"What do you want?"

She decided to just say it. After all, what did she have to lose? And it *was* what she wanted. "You, naked in my bed, for eight hours straight."

Heat flared between them instantaneously and Sam moved forward, again into her space. "I think I want to change my bet. Because I'm going to be right."

"You don't want dinner?" She had trouble getting the words out without air in her lungs.

"I can think of a dozen better things to do with my mouth." He lifted his hand and dragged his thumb across her bottom lip.

"I think I can allow one change."

"Thanks."

"For a guy who was so adamant about her getting right in, you're sure taking your sweet time." Kaylee came up behind her, making Danika jump. "How about we x-ray her and *then* you can ...whatever you're thinking about doing."

Sam didn't answer her. Or look embarrassed. He took Danika's left hand and started down the hallway. "Let's get this over with."

"It's definitely fractured." Chad Mitchell was frowning at Danika's x-ray. "In fact, I'd like to call an orthopedic consult. I don't want to cast it without someone else looking at it."

Sam bit back the swear words that he dearly wanted to use. He'd known it was fractured. He'd known it from the first moment. But hearing Mitchell say it, *and* want a specialist, made it all the more real and ugly...and guilt-inducing.

"I don't think that's necessary," Danika protested. "It doesn't even hurt that much."

Mitchell gave her an indulgent smile. "Maybe not right now. You probably still have some adrenaline going. Tomorrow morning is going to be a different story."

Danika sighed and looked at Sam. "You don't have to stay."

He scowled at her. Just where did she think he was going to go? "I'm staying."

"Don't you have to work tomorrow?"

He did, but so what? "Don't worry about me." Because that was what he needed—*her* being concerned about *him.*

"But you'll be exhausted." It was already one in the morning.

"I'll get someone to cover."

"Why don't you just go home? This could take a while."

He moved to stand next to her. Up until now he'd hung back. Chad Mitchell hadn't asked any questions about why Sam was there, or his role in the injury. He'd simply asked Danika to repeat what she'd already told two nurses.

But he knew the drill.

When anyone came in with a suspicious injury, at least three staff members asked for a recount of the injury to be sure that the patient told the same story each time. They also carefully watched the mannerisms of anyone who was with the patient. Women in domestic violence situations would sometimes stumble through their stories, or answer too quickly, or too mechanically. The men with them would often hover, answer questions for the woman, or otherwise give off aggressive vibes.

They hadn't asked him to step out of the room either, but he'd voluntarily left for a few minutes so they could question her alone. The normal routine would have been for staff to ask the male to accompany them to the desk for paperwork, where they would again question him. Sam knew he'd been spared only because they knew him and knew him to be a good guy. In fact, he and his crew had answered more than their share of domestic calls because they were good at defusing situations, or handling the male aggressor if needed.

The problem was, he didn't think he deserved special treatment. He had been the one to cause Danika's injury. Of course it hadn't been on purpose. Of course he felt like shit about it. Of course he'd go back and do it over.

Still, it was his fault.

"We can talk about it later. Let's see what the orthopedic surgeon says." Lord, he hated the idea of a surgeon needing to see her. Not only did that mean the injury was more serious, but also meant potential surgery—obviously. The idea of someone cutting into her, even if it was to help her, made him physically ill.

She shrugged. Maybe she would give up on the idea of him leaving now.

"I'll get the consult on the phone," Dr. Mitchell said. "I think someone is already here tonight. There was a car accident a couple of hours ago and someone was called in."

"Thanks."

Mitchell left and Sam turned to Danika. "Listen. I'm not leaving until you do. I'm taking you home. Period. I'm going to be here for the whole thing. Let's talk about something else."

"Do you like Will Ferrell movies?"

He took a second to process the unexpected question. One, because she dropped it so easily and two, because of the actual question itself. "Yes, I do."

"What's your favorite?"

He didn't even have to think about it. "*Elf.*"

She grinned. "Good one."

"Speaking of good DVDs, are you going to watch the one we

got together when you get home?"

"What... Oh."

He enjoyed watching her blush about the DVD she'd been so enthusiastic about buying. He'd wanted to distract her from the x-ray and confirmed fracture and the pending orthopedic consultation, though truthfully, she didn't seem all that nervous.

"Probably not tonight," she said. Was there a note of regret in her voice? "I'd almost forgotten about it."

"But you will watch it?" Though it was torturous to think about Danika watching an erotic movie and learning about oral sex, he did want to think about it. If he couldn't be there.

Which of course he couldn't.

"Probably." She sighed. "I'm a pretty curious person."

"Is that right?" It wasn't a blatantly sexual thing to say, but he found himself turned-on nonetheless. Danika seemed to have a special talent for that.

"Yes. Sometimes I watch or read things I know I shouldn't, or don't want to deep down, simply because it's something I don't already know."

That sounded interesting. "Like what?"

"Oh, I'll read a news magazine story about children starving in other countries, even though I know I'll hate everything I'm going to learn about the situation. Or I'll see a pop-up ad on the Internet and I'll click on it and learn all about how someone is torturing animals somewhere."

"Not exactly the same type of subject matter as the DVD we bought," he said dryly, his erotic visions abruptly leaving his mind as images of abused animals and dying children tried to intrude.

She grimaced. "No. But it's the same tendency I have to watch or read things if they're available."

"Let's talk about oral sex. I like those images a lot better."

She smiled up at him. "I don't have any images to think about. Until I watch the video."

His eyebrows shot up. "You've never..."

She shook her head. "I told you at Tease that I need to learn."

He coughed before he said any of the twelve inappropriate things to come to mind. All of it was pretty much implied anyway by the fact that almost every time they were within twenty feet of one another the room temperature went up.

Then she frowned. "But I don't know if the video will be enough."

"Oh?"

"I think it's like knitting."

"Did you say *knitting*?"

She nodded.

"Oral sex is like knitting?" Sam repeated. "*This* I've got to hear."

Chapter Four

Danika giggled. It was all so silly. The conversation, the situation, the entire night. And she was loving every minute. Well, except for the moments when her wrist throbbed like there was molten lava inside trying to burst free. But other than that, she was having a great time.

She supposed it said a lot about Sam that he could make the night she broke her wrist one of the most fun she could remember ever having.

"When I wanted to learn to knit, my grandma showed me how she did it. But I didn't get good at it until I tried it myself."

"I'm with you so far." And he sounded vastly amused. "Though I'm not sure your grandmother would appreciate the comparison."

She ignored that. Because he was right. "And I messed up a few times in the beginning before I got good."

"And..." Sam sounded like he was choking. He had to clear his throat and cough before he finally managed, "You don't think you'd be good at oral sex?"

"I haven't practiced." Also true. With the guys in the past it had been pretty...conventional. She'd never *wanted* to do anything else with any guy she knew.

Until now.

"Couldn't you just practice on that blue thing I bought you?" Now Sam sounded disgruntled.

"The blue thing can't tell me how I'm doing."

He swallowed hard. "Did the scarf you knitted tell you how you were doing?"

"With a scarf you just kind of know." She couldn't believe

that she was tempted to smile in the midst of this conversation. She should have been embarrassed, at the very least. But instead, she wanted to laugh.

"So, you're looking for practice and feedback?" he asked.

As she'd previously decided, Sam Bradford was way out of her league. There was no way she was going to perform oral sex on Sam, practice or not. But she was enjoying Sam's reaction to this whole thing. He certainly wasn't nonchalant about it. Which gave her a thrill.

"How can I get good at it without those two things?"

"Right." He muttered something else she couldn't quite hear. Then said, "Think you can wait until we get back to your place?"

She nearly fell off the table. "What?"

"Or do you want to do it right here and now? We probably have time." His hands went to his belt buckle.

"Are you insane?" she demanded, in spite of the fact that her blood was coursing hot and fast through her body in response to his words.

"I assume that you want to get good as quickly as possible."

"You're offering to help me? With oral sex?" Which was a terrible idea. A wonderful, swirling-intense-heat-in-her-stomach terrible idea. "Here? Now?" The last word was more of a squeak.

"Of course."

There was *no way* she was doing...that...with Sam. Not here and now, anyway. "You didn't sound very happy about the whole thing," she pointed out, thinking of all the muttering.

"I have absolutely no protest to helping you with this, Danika," he said sincerely.

The way he was looking at her made her stomach flip.

"Then what was with the grumbling and frowning?" she wanted to know.

He looked at her for several heartbeats, as if trying to decide if he should answer honestly or not. Finally he sighed.

"To borrow your habit of making analogies," he said. "I could never be one of those guys who flip houses. You know the ones that buy an old dilapidated house, go in and make it over and then turn around and sell it again. If I went to all that work of making something so awesome, I would want it for myself."

Danika crossed her arms. "I'm the old dilapidated house in

this example?"

He grinned at her. "Sorry. I thought that was pretty good for thinking on my feet."

"You might want to try sitting down next time."

He chuckled. "Would you rather be a masterpiece painting?"

She narrowed her eyes but motioned for him to go on.

"I could never make a living as a painter, because if I created a gorgeous work of art, I would never be able to sell it. I would want it for myself."

"Better," she acknowledged. "But in both examples you're giving yourself a lot of credit for the final product being awesome."

She should end this conversation right now, Danika thought. This verbal sparring with Sam was fun and she felt herself starting to like him more. Which would lead, inevitably, to her wanting to spend time with him that was not naked time and that would be a disaster.

Sam was simply the first man to get her to almost lose control. Had she given him thirty more seconds in Tease he would have been the first man to make her vulnerable. Liking him and being vulnerable with him might lead to her trusting him and then depending on him and...well, *that* wasn't going to happen.

Sam moved in close, which obliterated all of the thoughts she'd had going.

"You'll have to excuse me for thinking that I might not want you to share what I'm helping you learn with someone else."

The breath Danika had just taken in stuck in her chest. He didn't mean... He couldn't... He wasn't saying that he wanted to keep her all to himself...forever. She shook her head and closed her eyes, trying to break the ridiculous spell Sam seemed to have cast over her.

"No, I'm not excused for not wanting you to get good for another guy?"

"If that bothers you, then you better not be the one that helps me get good."

He frowned. "What do you mean?"

She shrugged. "You don't care when someone buys a painting that someone *else* painted do you?"

His frown deepened. "Um...no."

"Then I'll just find someone else to help with practice and feedback." She hoped she sounded flippant. The awful truth was that she already didn't want anyone else doing any of these things with her. Which was a bad place for her to be and meant that she needed to get away from, and stay away from, Sam Bradford.

"Like hell," he growled.

"It's the only option," she said firmly.

It was for the best.

Even though it definitely sucked. Absolutely no pun intended, she thought with a not-amused-in-the-least little laugh.

"Danika, I—"

"Usually, I don't like getting called in the middle of the night, but I'm glad I'm the one who gets to hear *this* story." Dr. Matt Dawson, the newest addition to the orthopedic surgical team, stepped through the door just then.

Danika was half relieved, half annoyed. She'd like to hear Sam Bradford beg to be the one to teach her about oral sex. Or any kind of sex for that matter. Or probably anything at all, sexual or not.

But if she felt like this after one night in his company, how much harder would it be to walk away after a week, or month, or whatever?

She was *not* going to spend any more time with Sam Bradford after this night was over.

"Hi, Danika." Matt gave her a big grin as he looked up from flipping the first few pages of her chart.

"Hi, Matt."

"You know each other?" Sam asked.

"She's helped with placing a couple of my patients in rehab units."

"Right. I heard that Danika works here," Sam said sardonically.

"About two weeks now," Matt said.

"I know," Sam practically snarled.

"Tell me what happened." Matt said, taking Danika's hand, putting his back to Sam.

She was sure she was wrong, but it looked like Sam's jaw

tightened as he watched Matt take a hold of her.

Danika told the same story she'd told already tonight and Matt continued examining her hand, fingers and wrist. As one of the team members called in when abuse was confirmed, or even suspected, she completely understood and respected the process of questioning. She noticed, however, that the questioning was much less intense and detailed and suspected that it was because Sam Bradford was the man in question. Not that it should make a difference who he was, but she further suspected that the staff was not aware that they were letting up on Sam and that said a lot, in her mind, about him. She knew for a fact, even in only two weeks of work, that this ER staff took their jobs and their patients seriously. One reason was Sam's own sister, Jessica, the ER's Chief Nurse.

"You had her up on a table, huh?" Matt grinned at Sam. "Beds are nice and soft, Sam. Couches, even, if you can't be conventional."

"Very professional," Sam growled.

Matt didn't seem fazed by Sam's obvious displeasure as he crossed to the x-rays.

"I think we can do this with a cast. I don't think it's necessary to pin it. But I want to see you back in the office in two weeks to check that everything is healing up."

"Sounds good to me," she said with relief.

"You're right-handed?"

"Yes."

"This isn't going to be easy," he told her. "With this break, I'm going to want to immobilize from your fingers to your elbow. No movement at all until we repeat the x-rays. You're going to be pretty limited."

Instantly a thousand things she had to do with her right hand went through her mind. "I can't type?"

"Not unless you hunt and peck with the left hand," Matt said.

"No writing?"

"Nope."

"What about driving?"

"I can't clear you for that safely. At least not at first. If things heal correctly, we can cut the cast back next time and let you have some finger movement. Honestly, just take these two weeks off, don't mess around and we'll have a better idea."

"What about..."

"She could make it worse?" Sam inserted.

Matt looked at him for several seconds before answering. Danika could only see the back of Matt's head, but she could see Sam's face. He simply stared, unblinking, waiting for the reply as if there was absolutely no reason why Matt shouldn't have to answer to him.

Finally, Matt said, "Yes. She could make it worse. We might have to pin it if the break doesn't stay stable and aligned. I want it to heal clean. I'll do whatever I have to to make that happen."

He turned back to Danika. "I'm letting you off easy tonight because I trust that you're an intelligent woman who understands why it's important to be compliant. If you're not, and that break shifts, sabotaging the alignment and healing, we'll have to go in and pin it."

She frowned. That didn't sound good. She worked in a hospital and heard lots of jargon. Most of the time she understood it, when she didn't she could still figure out the gist. But now that she was the patient, she wanted it spelled out.

"What does that entail, exactly." She had the fleeting thought that she didn't want to know.

"We do surgery," Matt said simply. "I go in and put pins into the bones to hold them in place."

Yeah, she'd been right about not wanting to know.

Strangely, her wrist started throbbing and she felt a little light-headed.

Stranger still, Sam seemed to notice and moved in next to her, putting his arm around her so that she could lean into him. "Falling off one table per night is the limit," he said, his hand cupping her shoulder.

"You'll be a good patient and not move around too much, not do too much?" Matt said, looking at her seriously.

She nodded. "I'm not sure I'll ever move it again."

He smiled. "You will. If you don't, there's a physical therapist who will move it for you."

She grimaced. She'd seen patients in physical therapy and while she knew it was necessary and the patients ended up very thankful to the people who helped them move normally again, the process wasn't always very fun.

"I'll be good," she promised.

"I'll make sure," Sam said.

Matt looked at him again for several ticks of the clock, then nodded, wrote in the chart and turned to leave. "We'll cast it and get you out of here."

"I can go home then?"

"Under Sam's supervision," Matt agreed.

"Under...*what*?" But the door was already bumping shut behind Matt.

She turned, with eyes narrowed, to Sam. "What did he mean?"

"It's normal," he said. "A lot of times we won't release trauma patients unless they have someone that can take them home and stay with them. Don't worry, the guys will cover me at work for the next few days."

"The next few *days*?" She felt like a parrot. "And I'm not a trauma patient."

"You fractured a bone. You're a trauma patient."

"I was clumsy and fell. That's not like a ten-car pileup or falling off a roof."

"You won't be able to drive and you're going to be on pain pills. You have to be released into someone's care at least for the next twenty-four hours." Sam's tone implied that she was being unreasonable.

She didn't care. "I'll call one of my sisters."

"That's ridiculous. It's the middle of the night, I'm already here and I'm willing."

"You shouldn't have to be responsible for me," she argued. She wasn't sure how she was going to handle having Sam with her constantly for another twenty-four hours. She'd end up completely head over heels for him and the pain pills might make her say or do something stupid.

"I should," he said firmly. "I know you don't want to hear it, and no, I didn't mean for this to happen, but I did have a part in it."

"I'm fine," she insisted. "I'm not in a coma, it's not cancer, I didn't lose a drop of blood. I'm healthy. I'll heal. It's nothing."

"Danika," Sam said with a serious, no-argument tone she wouldn't have even imagined he possessed. "I am *not* leaving your side for the next seventy-two hours. You can call whoever you want, but I'm not asking to stay, I'm *telling* you that I'm staying."

"Seventy-two hours? What happened to twenty-four?"

She wasn't going to call her sisters. It was...well, all of the things Sam pointed out including the middle of the night. Besides, Carmen would come in and take over everything. That meant that Danika's cupboards and closets would be completely cleaned out and reorganized since she wouldn't actually need much care and Carmen would go stir-crazy with nothing to do. Then there was Abi. She'd cry, then come over but be so miserable that Danika would feel worse having her there than putting up with Sam. Abi couldn't handle it when people she loved were anything other than happy and fulfilled and healthy in every way.

Sam, obviously surprised by her sudden lack of argument, put his hand on her head, smoothing her hair. "I'll call them," he said gently. "But I'm not leaving, even if they show up."

"Don't call them." She sighed. It would be worse—for all of them—if Carmen and Abi came. Their husbands would both gladly help out, but couldn't possibly do it without their wives finding out. Her father was in Texas. She had friends, of course, but Sam was here, and not leaving. Why would she drag someone else out of bed at this time of night? "You can take me home."

Sam sighed and it was obvious that he was genuinely relieved. Which made her feel good, even as she knew it shouldn't.

So she now had slinky lingerie, a video about oral sex, a broken wrist and a crush on a guy who was the opposite of everything she was trying to find in a man.

What a night.

Danika lived in a two-story brick duplex only seven blocks from his apartment. Sam rolled his eyes. Not only did she work at the same hospital, but she probably shopped at the same grocery store. Yet he'd never met her.

He had to unlock the door, an awkward movement with a non-dominant hand as it turned out. Just as he'd had to help hook her seatbelt and dig in her purse for her keys.

He was sure in a few days she would have compensated

and would learn to do a lot with her left hand. But it was all new and she was obviously not ambidextrous. Added to that was the weight of the new cast, the lateness of the hour and the pain medication that Matt had insisted she would need to sleep well. Danika was quite clumsy with her left hand and still in the habit of reaching first with her right hand, then having to adjust.

"Here we are." She managed to flip on the front hallway light with her left hand.

"Nice."

"Don't you need to go get some clothes or something?"

"I was thinking about that. I'll run home in the morning. I don't live far."

She shrugged and yawned. "Sorry."

"It's been a long night." A great night, he added silently, but long. It seemed like days ago that he'd met her at Marina's.

"I'll get some sheets for the couch," she said, tossing her purse toward the small table just inside the door. Since she had to use her left hand, it didn't quite make it. "Damn," she said softly.

It was obvious that she was frustrated with her lack of ability and discomfited with him in her house.

She was going to have to get over it.

"You can't put sheets on the couch with one hand."

She went to the first door on the right of the short hallway and pulled out a stack of sheets. She crossed to the couch and dumped them on the cushions. "Yes, I can."

He smiled. He was glad she had some spunk at this point. "Sorry to doubt you."

She sighed. "Sorry I'm being grumpy."

"No problem," he said, meaning it. "You've had a lot happen. Being grumpy is a normal side effect."

She propped her left hand on her hip. "Quit being so nice."

"You want me to be mean?"

"I...don't know."

"You're exhausted. Go to bed. We'll figure everything out in the morning."

She glanced over her shoulder toward what he assumed was her bedroom. "Yeah. I'll just..."

She looked so confused, so tired and so beautiful that he

knew he had to kiss her.

"I need to kiss you."

Her eyes widened and the heat that seemed always just below the surface, flared.

"Is that okay?" he asked. He didn't want to take advantage of her weakened state.

"Of course it's okay," she said.

Something about that made him want her, intensely, all over again. As if she'd said "take me now" or had stripped naked right in front of him. The "of course", the implication that he didn't have to ask permission, that he somehow had a right to kiss her, made him want that kiss more than anything he could remember wanting in a very long time.

He gently took her face in his hands and stroked his thumbs over her cheeks. He looked at her for a long time, wanting to savor the moment. He drank in the look of desire in her eyes, in spite of the fact she'd just come from the ER. He drank in the way she stood there, accepting his touch, letting him look.

Slowly he lowered his head, loving the feel of anticipation, hoping she felt it as well.

When their lips touched, it was like all the other times, with want and longing and passion welling up. But it was also...different. It was gentle. The other times when he'd kissed her he'd wanted to nearly devour her, he'd wanted to push on harder and faster to the ultimate culmination. This time, he wanted to draw it out, to enjoy it, to remember it later. For her to remember it later. He wanted this to be that kiss that brought her fingers to her lips and made her close her eyes to remember.

No pressure at all.

He felt her lift her hands, but while her left hand fisted in the front of his shirt, the cast on her right hand bumped against his chest.

She sighed against his mouth, but it was in frustration.

He lifted his head.

She did stare up at him and she pressed her lips together, which was almost as good as lifting her fingers to her lips. Then she smiled a slow, sweet smile. "That was nice."

"Very," he agreed, his hands still cupping her face.

"I want to touch you, though."

"Touch anything you want."

"I could only do half of what I want." She held up her right hand.

He smiled. "I think half of whatever you would do to me would be better than all of what anyone else would do."

Just then her stomach growled. He laughed. "Maybe we should take care of that first."

"I guess it has been awhile since I ate."

It was two-thirty in the morning.

"I guess it's granola bars," she said, stepping back. "I can't even peel a banana one-handed."

"And you shouldn't even try," Sam reminded her. "The great thing is, I'm here. And I can not only peel bananas, I can make a grilled cheese sandwich that will make you cry."

Her stomach rumbled louder. She laughed. "Except that I don't have any cheese."

"Eggs?"

"Yes."

"Then grilled cheese will have to be another night. It won't be gourmet cooking, but you won't go hungry. And if we exhaust my repertoire then I'll take you out."

She laughed. "I'm not sure anyone could ever fully exhaust your repertoire."

He flipped the lock of hair that fell against her shoulder. "Brat. I'm talking about my kitchen repertoire."

"How big of a repertoire are we talking about?"

He thought about that, mentally counting the things he could make that would turn out edible. "It will get us to Tuesday."

"Five things?" she asked, laughing. "I might be in trouble here."

"Then I can start over at the top, we can order in, we can go out, or I can guilt my sisters into cooking and bringing it over. I think we'll survive."

She was still smiling as she looked at him suspiciously. "What things are on your menu, exactly? Besides grilled cheese and, apparently, some kind of eggs."

"I'll have you know that I can make two kinds of eggs."

"And you're counting them both in the five things?"

"They're two different things," he said with mock affront.

"We've got two kinds of eggs, grilled cheese, and...?"

"Grilled steak."

"Of course."

"Of course?"

"You're definitely a steak kind of guy."

"Thanks." He did consider that a compliment.

"What's the fifth thing?"

"Grilled burgers."

She looked at him, as if waiting for the punch line, then started to laugh. "You can add grilled hotdogs and grilled chicken to your list, since if you can grill a burger you can grill those."

He considered that. "Hey, that's true. We can survive until Thursday."

"Except that I don't have a grill."

He shrugged. "I'll bring mine over."

She frowned slightly. "You'll bring your grill over here?"

"Sure."

"And some clothes, I assume?"

"I know you want to get me naked, but I have to wear clothes when I'm on the patio grilling. I could cause a car accident this close to the road."

She laughed, even as she mentally pictured him naked on her patio. She had a surprisingly easy time doing so too.

"You're picturing me naked, right?" he asked.

She felt her cheeks heat. "Of course not. I'm trying to think about how I can make lasagna with one hand."

He'd moved in close, only inches separating them suddenly. "I'm picturing you using one hand very effectively."

Her inner thighs liked the sounds of that. "Very effectively cooking food?"

"No," he admitted, with a roguish smile.

"Isn't that what we were talking about?"

"Yeah, but it seems that all trains of thought lead back to you and me having sex."

"It does, doesn't it," she said softly.

"I have a feeling that if we follow some of those trains, I won't be thinking much about food," he said, his voice also having dropped.

"*Some* of the trains?"

"I'm here for the next one hundred and forty-four hours, I think we'll have the time."

"What happened to seventy-two hours?"

"I distinctly heard Dr. Dawson say that I should stay for eight days."

"That's more than one hundred and forty-four hours," she pointed out, ignoring how nice it sounded to have Sam all to herself for eight days.

"Right, it's like two hundred and forty hours."

"That's more than eight days."

"Is it? Well, he's the expert. Can't argue with the specialist."

She finally laughed and shook her head. "You're kind-of impossible."

"You'll learn that arguing with me can be very frustrating."

"I have no trouble believing that."

"You might as well not do it."

"Interesting concept."

"Do you want scrambled or fried?"

She must be getting used to the quick changes in topic of conversation with Sam because she answered easily, "Neither. I think I have some deli turkey. We can have sandwiches."

"You can't make a sandwich with one hand."

"I probably could."

"It won't be easy."

"No."

He stood looking at her. "And?"

"And, what?"

"Say it."

"Say what?"

"That you need me. That it's a good thing I'm here. That it's a good idea for me to stay."

She sighed. It was practical. He was here, he was willing, he was able to help her with the things she was going to need in the next few days because of the cast. But more than that, it was appealing. She liked him. But that damage was already done. Why not let Sam Bradford, the sexiest man she'd ever spent time with, wait on her hand and foot for a few days?

"It's a good thing you're here. It's a good idea for you to stay."

He grinned like she'd just announced he'd won an all-expense-paid trip to Hawaii, then pulled her close and kissed her on the top of her head.

"You are a very intelligent woman."

"Thank you," she mumbled against the front of his shirt. She inhaled, pulling in the wonderful scent of him.

"Let's eat," he said, oblivious to how much she was enjoying having her nose against his shoulder.

Sam did well with making the sandwiches, which of course she teased him about. He insisted that making sandwiches didn't count as cooking, since there was no heat involved, but she maintained that this expanded their menu by at least a few more days when all the deli meats and peanut butter were considered.

They'd laughed, teased and talked as they ate, but about nothing too serious. They talked about their work and compared stories about patients they'd treated, without sharing names. But she was truly exhausted and as the food filled her stomach, the weight of fatigue, adrenaline let-down and the sheer lateness of the hour began to pull at her until she felt like holding her head and shoulders up was a contest she was about to concede to gravity.

"Let's go," Sam said, pushing his chair back and standing.

"What?" She blinked up at him.

"I just asked you two questions and you didn't even hear me. Time for bed." He lifted her from the chair with a hand under her elbow.

A few hours before, hearing Sam say "time for bed" would have sent her pulse racing, but it was definitely a sign of complete system shut-down that she barely registered anything other than "bed" and her body's desire to be there...for sleep.

"Sorry," she mumbled as he steered her down the hall.

"Don't apologize, Dani," he said gently. "You're worn out. I'm glad you're ready to sleep. Your body needs it."

She was going to tell him not to call her Dani, but besides the fact that her brain was barely connected to anything, especially her mouth at this point, she also realized that she liked how he said it. It truly sounded like an endearment from him.

Danika stopped by her bed and started to reach the zipper of her skirt. Belatedly she remembered her cast as she whacked it awkwardly against her hip.

"Damn."

"I've got it." Sam turned her and unzipped her.

Vaguely, through the fog of fatigue, she realized that Sam was going to have to help her undress and she was in absolutely no shape to enjoy it.

"Sam, I..."

"I wish this was happening differently too," he said, pressing a quick kiss to her shoulder. "But we've got time."

She liked the sound of that. A lot. And she was way too tired to think about why that was a bad thing.

Sam awoke, pleased when he saw that it was just before eleven and he hadn't heard a peep from Danika's bedroom all night. He'd known she was exhausted and the pain pills would have helped her sleep deep and hard, but he was glad to see she'd managed to sleep long as well. She needed it.

He rolled onto his back on the surprisingly comfortable couch in Danika's living room, letting the sun from the sliding glass door to her porch fall across his stomach in a warm rectangle.

He had never spent the night at a woman's house who he hadn't had sex with. He'd slept on some buddies' couches, but never a woman's. In fact, he tried to make a habit of *not* sleeping over at women's houses, whether he was in a comfortable bed or not. It simply wasn't good to set expectations like that.

With Danika, she had been trying to *not* have him stick around the night before and he found himself wanting her to have some expectations of him. Which should have made him get up, get dressed and get out.

He didn't like being needed. He'd made avoiding being needed an art form. He could have taught classes for college credit on how to avoid being needed.

Yet, here he was. She was hurt and he felt responsible. Staying last night was the right thing to do, no doubt. He didn't like being responsible, but he couldn't seem to help being it anyway a lot of the time.

Staying for the next few days was what he was conflicted about. He hated that she was hurt, he hated that he'd had anything to do with it, and—stupidly—he hated the idea of anyone else taking care of her.

But he shouldn't stay.

That would be the exact opposite of avoiding being responsible and depended upon.

Still...he wanted to.

Down the hall, a door opened and then another shut. Danika had gone from the bedroom to the bathroom.

He smiled, thinking about helping her get undressed last night. She'd unbuttoned the shirt, slowly and clumsily. But she hadn't been able to manage unzipping her skirt with one hand, so he'd unzipped her, pushed her skirt to the floor, unhooked her bra and slipped the nightgown laying draped over the arm of the chair by her bed over her head. He'd stayed behind her, seeing nothing more than her naked back and her butt covered in the silky panties. But, of course, he'd been hard as a rock within two seconds.

Interestingly, he'd enjoyed brushing her hair and then tucking her in almost as much as he would have enjoyed the things that usually went along with undressing a woman by a bed.

Okay, not as much. But he'd still enjoyed it enough to make going back out to the couch alone not miserable.

He waited to hear her come out, thinking that once she was feeling better, that she had something to eat and had promised not to try to do anything for herself, he'd run home for a shower, new clothes and a few things he might need during his two-week stay with her.

Yes, Dawson had said seventy-two hours. So what? Danika wasn't seeing him again for two weeks. Sam was going to stay with her at least until he heard a medical doctor tell him that she was healing.

Ten minutes later, he still heard nothing from the bathroom, but she hadn't come out.

He'd grown up with two sisters. He knew all about bathroom time.

But Danika wasn't putting on make-up or doing her hair, so what was taking so long?

He sat up quickly. At least she'd better not be doing those things. She was still a woman and women had a way of being strangely vain about things like bedhead and being seen with smudged mascara. Maybe she was in there trying to make herself presentable before coming out here to face him. Which meant that she was likely trying to use her right hand.

He was down the hall in seconds, pounding on the door. "Danika! What's going on in there?"

"Geez, you scared the crap out of me!" she shouted through the door.

"Do *not* try curling your hair or something stupid. If you can't use your hand you'll burn yourself and we'll be back in that ER. If you do use your hand you'll mess it all up."

"I'm not trying to curl my hair!"

"Then what are you doing?"

"Nothing!"

He thought about that. That was stupid. "Come do nothing out here, then."

"No."

Yeah, she was doing something. "Put the mascara down."

"I'm not doing my makeup either! Just go away!"

She was definitely doing something. "Danika, open the door."

"No."

"You're doing something."

"No I'm not."

"Prove it."

Several seconds went by, then the door was yanked open. "Fine. The door's open. What do you want?"

He peered into the bathroom over her shoulder. There was no curling iron, blow-dryer, makeup bag, or anything but a toothbrush lying on the counter.

"You brushed your teeth," he accused.

"I can do that one-handed."

"How did you get the toothpaste out?"

"I laid the tube on the counter and pushed on the end with my elbow."

He looked closer and saw there was a glob of toothpaste lying next to the brush.

"How'd you get the cap off?"

"My teeth."

He looked down at her, really seeing her for the first time. Her hair was mussed, her eyes were bloodshot, her cheek had a crease from the pillowcase and she wore only the short, silky nightgown. She looked adorable.

"Morning," he said, smiling at her.

Her eyes instantly welled up, tears spilling over and down her cheeks.

The tears startled him. "What's wrong? Are you hurting?"

She shook her head and sniffed, turning away and whipping a tissue from the box on the counter next to the sink. She wiped her nose, even that looking awkward with her non-dominant hand.

"Need help?"

She glared at him. "I am *not* going to have you wipe my nose."

"I don't want to," he admitted. "But if you need help—"

"Just shut up."

He frowned in surprise. "What's your problem?"

"Nothing."

"You're crying."

"So?"

He sighed. He could be patient, but he wasn't especially good at it. "Come on. What's going on?"

"I hate this."

He knew what she was talking about. She was used to being self-sufficient. She knew how to rewire a ceiling fan. She'd claimed that she made a point of always doing everything for herself.

This had to be hard for her.

But he was enjoying it. Not to the point of being truly happy in the face of her misery, but definitely not upset about the situation that made this sweet, funny, beautiful woman let him hang around for awhile.

"Why were you crying, Dani?"

She sniffed, but met his eyes. "I can't wash my hair."

He thought about that. Yep, that would be tough with one hand. Especially one hand that she could not get wet.

She just looked at him, her eyebrows slowly rising. "You're going to make me say it, aren't you?"

"Say what?"

"That I...need you."

He probably moved a notch closer to "ass" on the jerk scale but he did like hearing those four words from her.

"You need me to wash your hair?"

She nodded, looking royally pissed about the whole thing.

"Um..."

Sam blinked down at her.

Her hair.

It seemed like a simple request. But she was a girl. Which pretty much guaranteed that anything to do with her hair wouldn't be simple.

"You realize that as far as I'm concerned, hair washing involves three steps. Get hair wet, rub shampoo in it, run more water on hair."

She propped her left hand on her hip. "Why are you looking like I just asked you to perform open-heart surgery on me?"

"Well, girl hair involves those twelve additional steps that I don't even know about."

"What twelve additional steps?"

"Whatever it is that ensures no woman can get out of the shower in less than twenty minutes."

"Did it ever occur to you that they were doing more in there than fussing with their hair?"

"Okay, there's soap and other body parts, but come on, twenty minutes?"

She laughed at that. "Sam, there aren't any magic hair-washing steps. There's conditioner, but I know you can handle it."

He watched her face, and felt humble. He sensed that this woman didn't ask people for things often or easily. "You hate that you need help for this, don't you?"

She pressed her lips together and nodded.

"Get over it," he said simply.

She slipped around him and was through her bedroom door before he realized she was moving.

"What are you doing?" he asked her back.

"Getting my swimming suit."

"You don't need—"

"*Yes*," she interrupted. "I do." The door shut in his face.

He grinned. "How are you going to get a swimming suit on by yourself?"

"I'll manage," she called.

He leaned back against the wall across from her bedroom to wait.

Chapter Five

She was desperate. Plain and simple. She *had* to wash her hair or she was going to go crazy and there was absolutely no way she could do it herself.

It was *so* frustrating! To not be able to do the simplest, most normal thing made her want to scream. She didn't want to need Sam, not like this. She was kind of okay with needing him physically, with feeling like she would die if he didn't touch her. At least, she was getting used to it. She wasn't as okay with needing him to make her a sandwich, unzip her dress and wash her hair.

Talk about pathetic.

This was *exactly* the kind of thing she avoided at all costs. She never let other people take care of her. She'd been sick with the flu for almost a week four years ago and it had taken her three days to call Carmen and even tell her and another two before she would let Carmen come over. She hated the feeling of vulnerability, of weakness, of being a burden.

Sam thought this was fun now. He felt responsible now. He was even making it sexy.

How long would any of that last?

Not as long as she would remember being dependent on him for the smallest thing.

She was able to wiggle out of her panties and the nightgown was loose enough that she could pull it over her head one-handed. The swimming suit was more of a challenge. It was a one-piece and she was able to get the bottom of the suit up by pulling one side up, then the other until it was in place. She threaded her casted hand in through the strap and up onto her shoulder, then the other side.

"I'm going to need a plastic bag to put over the cast," she said as she stepped back into the hallway, still pulling her right shoulder strap up.

Sam was standing across from her, leaning back against the wall, but he pushed away as she stepped through the door. His eyes were wide.

"Wow."

She stopped short at the look in his eyes. She might as well have been naked. He was looking at her as if memorizing every curve and prominence.

She tried to ignore the tingles that seemed to erupt everywhere as she realized that he was imagining peeling her swimming suit off of her. It was so clear, in fact, it was like reading his mind. "You going to be able to do this?" she asked.

"Definitely. I'm a little tight in my jeans, but I'm okay."

Her eyes dropped to his fly in spite of her effort to avoid it. He was grinning when she looked back into his eyes.

"Let's do this," she muttered, stepping past him into the bathroom.

"Yes, ma'am."

She looked over her shoulder. "Washing my hair," she clarified.

"Of course."

She narrowed her eyes suspiciously. "The garbage bags are under the sink."

"I'm all over it."

She wanted him all over her. "Garbage bags." She wasn't sure if she said it to try to distract her own thoughts or to again clarify what he was all over.

"Right."

She started the water running while Sam went to retrieve a plastic bag from the kitchen. She knew the moment he was back because the air temperature in the bathroom spiked and she could feel him behind her, checking out her butt.

"Isn't that how we ended up in this mess?" she asked without looking at him.

"Yep," he said unapologetically. "But it isn't my fault. You can't take someone to the edge of the Grand Canyon and expect him not to look."

With the water the right temperature, she turned to frown

at him. "My butt reminds you of the Grand Canyon?"

He held up his hands in surrender. "Again, thinking too fast on my feet. How about you can't take someone to see the Hope Diamond and expect him not to look."

"Again, you're comparing my butt to something that is extraordinarily big."

He chuckled. "I can't think of anything amazingly beautiful, but appropriately trim, firm and *tiny.*"

She tipped her head to one side, considering that. She, of course, didn't think that he'd been insulting her and she couldn't think of any other way to make him squirm so she shrugged. "Forgiven."

She started to step into the tub and he immediately moved forward and took her good hand. Once she was standing in the warm water swirling at the bottom of the tub, he shook the plastic bag and held it out to her. She stuck her hand inside and he smoothed it over her cast, sliding a rubber band over it to hold it tight. It wasn't going to be completely waterproof, but it would keep drops from kicking up onto the plaster. She would still, obviously, have to keep her hand up out of the water.

"Now what?" he asked.

Thankfully, she had a sprayer that could be taken down from the wall and held. "I'll sit and then you'll have to use that to wet my hair."

"Sounds good." For a guy who had been claiming to not know what to do with washing a woman's hair, he certainly sounded confident.

He held onto her as she lowered herself carefully to the bottom of the tub. Then he knelt beside the tub on the fluffy lavender mat. He pulled up on the lever on the faucet that turned the shower on and she held her right hand up in the air.

"Here, rest your hand on my shoulder." He moved so that she could rest her cast on his left shoulder, somehow leaning around to use his right hand to maneuver the sprayer head.

Warm water hit her scalp and coursed over her shoulders and she closed her eyes and tipped her head back at the feel of it, resisting the urge to sigh.

She felt Sam shift the sprayer to his left hand as his elbow rested on the edge of the tub, the spray angled at her feet for the moment. The gentle pressure of his right hand settled on her head, smoothing her hair back, his fingers curling gently into her scalp, massaging and wetting all the strands.

She did sigh then.

He was leaning in so close that she could smell that wonderful smell from him, and she kept her eyes closed, just absorbing the feel of him touching her, his scent and body heat around her.

"You'd better hold this." He moved the handle of the sprayer to her left hand and shifted away.

She opened her eyes and saw him reaching for the shampoo bottle on the ledge. His eyes met hers as he poured some of the shampoo into his hand, then rubbed his hands together in small circles.

"Step two," he said with a smile.

"So far, so good."

He lifted his hands to her head and started a slow massage again, working the soap through her hair. She closed her eyes again. She didn't know if he meant for the shampooing to be sensual, but it certainly was. Of course, this was Sam and it seemed that even the most innocent touch made her want him.

Her long hair was piled on top of her head and his fingers kneaded from her temples to the crown of her head, then down the back, to the base of her skull.

After a few delicious minutes, he reclaimed the sprayer and aimed it at her head, rinsing the bubbles off.

"Now?" he asked.

She thought his voice sounded hoarse, but when she looked at him he was simply watching her.

"Conditioner." She pointed to the other bottle on the same shelf where he'd found the shampoo.

He repeated the pattern without another word, including the rinsing.

She opened her eyes again as she realized the rinsing was more than complete. "Could you..." she started, then stopped, hoping he'd let it go and knowing he wouldn't at the same time.

"Yes, I could."

"You don't even know what I was going to ask."

"Doesn't matter. Whatever you need." He was suddenly so sincere.

Which made her ask hesitantly, "Could you help me wash

my face too? While I'm already here and wet."

At that Sam pulled in a quick, sharp breath, but he nodded. "Sure."

She pointed to the bottle of foaming facial cleanser and he pumped a small amount into his palm and then spread it out with the pads of the fingers on the other hand. He lifted his hands to her face and gently began making circles on her cheeks.

"Here, I can..." she started.

He bumped her un-casted hand out of the way. "I've got it."

It was strange being bathed for the first time in twenty years. Not terrible, but strange.

Sam's fingers circled over her face, spreading cleanser over her forehead, down the bridge of her nose, over her cheeks and along her jaw and chin. He washed her face nearly two minutes longer than she ever had and Danika found it stupidly erotic. She figured Sam was just thinking what a pain in the ass this was all going to be after a few days.

Once the cleanser had been washed off, Danika realized she didn't have any reason to linger in the tub. Other than that she just wanted to, at least.

"What about the rest?" Sam asked.

"The rest of what?"

"Your body. You have to bathe everything at some point."

Of course she would. But...

"Are you offering to help?"

"Absolutely." He grinned.

"If we do that," she said directly, and out loud, "it will lead to much more than simple washing."

"You seem pretty sure of that."

"Completely."

"I realize that there were extenuating circumstances, but I feel like I still need to test to see that you retained some of the knowledge I attempted to impart last night."

Ah, yes, the *examination* he'd said she would need to be sure that she'd learned what she needed to from his instruction. The idea of it last night had excited her and this morning was nothing different.

Sam reached for her bottle of liquid body wash and soaped his hands. Not the bright blue net sponge hanging around the lid of the body wash, but his bare hands.

"You gonna take that swimming suit off?" he asked.

"No."

Evidently her lack of hesitation amused him. He chuckled. "I realize that I have more experience than you do with this, but I figured you knew that naked was part of the sex thing."

She was going to give in. They both knew it. But she still wanted to make him work for it. "It's not a *requirement*, though."

"Makes things easier."

"True. But insisting on naked limits the time and place, doesn't it?"

He grinned and reached for a foot, that he began soaping. It was heavenly and Danika let herself moan in appreciation.

"You're an any-time-any-place girl?"

"I like to have options."

"I like to see what I'm doing." He ran his slippery hand up her calf and back down.

"I figured you'd be good enough by now to find your way around without looking."

He chuckled. "I haven't gotten lost for a long time." He switched to her other foot and calf.

"I'll bet," she muttered. The truth was, Sam was way out of her league. She didn't doubt that she could still stay in control sexually with him, but she wasn't sure she'd want to. Which definitely meant she couldn't even get close.

At least not any closer than letting him soap her thighs.

"Back to the issue of how to know if you learned anything last night..."

"I've been busy, what with the ER and all. I haven't had time to study," she protested, as butterflies kicked up a party in her stomach.

His voice was husky, his eyes hot, as he slid his hand to her inner thigh and ran it from knee to just centimeters short of the crotch of her swimming suit. "This is a pop quiz. No warning or prep time."

She wasn't a bit scared, or even intimidated, by him. Just excited. "All right, I'm ready."

"Okay." He switched his hand to her left arm, running his palm up and down the length from wrist to shoulder. "True or false—you need dildos, gel and videos in order to have an orgasm."

With him? No question. "False."

He leaned in and kissed her. It was unexpected, but very, very good. Slow and deep.

When he lifted his head, she was breathing hard. He ran his hand, and the soap, over the skin on her shoulder, neck and chest that was exposed by the swimming suit.

"True or false—you need sexy underwear to have an orgasm."

She shivered as the left strap of her suit slid off her shoulder.

"False," she said, somehow.

"Very good," he murmured, leaning in and capturing her lips again as his hand brushed over the skin exposed just above her breast.

He ran his hand down, over her breast and ribs to her stomach, dragging soap over the nylon fabric.

Like she cared. Especially when his hand returned to cup her left breast and teased the nipple into a tight, stiff point. She should stop him, she thought as she let her head fall back. In a minute.

"True or false—you need a penis inside of you to have an orgasm." His breath was hot against her ear.

She gasped as his hand rubbed back and forth over her stomach, then slid lower, palm down, to cup her through the swimming suit.

Even with material between them it felt amazing.

Then he slipped under the elastic edge, brushing over her curls.

"Um." She thought hard, trying to remember the question as her mind wanted to simply stop thinking and just feel. "I'm thinking that's also—" She gasped as the pad of his finger brushed over her clitoris. "False," she breathed. "Usually."

His finger stopped moving and she moaned. "What do you mean *usually*?"

She pried her eyes open. Then she shifted, trying to get closer to his finger. But he wouldn't resume the motion.

"What do you mean *usually*, Danika?"

"I mean, it's probably false for most women. I'm not sure

about with me," she managed breathlessly.

Sam chuckled. "You can't be serious."

Her sanity was returning slowly. "*Why* would I joke about that? Especially right now?"

"You are not going to have a problem having an orgasm."

"I have so far."

"But we have something important here."

"Your finger?" she asked, trying to wiggle closer.

He chuckled. "That's not hurting the situation. But I was talking about the heat."

Her heart began pounding again, but it was different this time. *The heat.* Just like her sister had described.

"You feel it, don't you, Dani?" He rubbed his lips back and forth across hers.

She was going to remind him not to call her Dani. It was too tomboyish. Not sexy or feminine. Except when Sam said it.

She nodded. "Yes."

"You feel how your body temperature goes up, your heart starts racing, you can't get a deep breath—all just when I look at you. Because you know that I'm thinking about touching you slow and deep and long..." His finger stroked down and then his finger slipped inside of her, causing them to moan in unison. Sam found his voice again. "Until you're crazy for something only I can give you. And you're body is getting ready. Priming for that moment when you need my body—the motion, the pressure, the friction—more than you need your next breath."

His finger stroked in and out and Danika thought she might possibly cry from the pleasure.

"It's that heat that your body puts off to make my body want to be closer and closer. And deeper and deeper." He stroked again. "It's not your brain, or your heart, it's body heat—pure and simple." He leaned over and sucked on her nipple through the wet fabric of her suit, while his finger slid deep again.

Then he kissed her, his tongue mimicking his finger's motion. Danika's eyes had closed at some point as Sam's lips continued their torture. Maybe it wasn't her brain in the rational-think-it-out-and-make-a-decision way, but it was her imagination and her nerve endings and every one of her five senses. They were all engaged and excited and working overtime.

Sam knew exactly what he was doing. His words in her ear—and her own fantasies—were as powerful as his hands on her body. Combined they were enough to make her feel so *close.* Or at least as close as she'd ever been.

"Sam," she moaned as his finger stroked in and out again. She had to stop him.

"See, you have every potential to be a firecracker in bed. You just need the right spark to start you off."

"Sam..." she started. Then he pressed with perfect, exquisite pressure on *exactly* the right spot. How did he know how to do that?

"Let yourself go," he breathed against her neck. His finger circled again. "Come for me, Dani," he urged. "Let it go." He slipped two fingers into her, his thumb still on her sweet spot.

She wanted to. She wanted Sam to be the one to send her over the edge. Which was crazy and delicious and amazing.

And bad. Really, really bad.

She immediately pushed on Sam's shoulder at the same time she tried to pull her hips away from his.

"Whoa." Her body rejected the idea of moving away from Sam. "Sam, stop," she panted.

His fingers froze. "*What?*"

"Stop. You have to stop." Her mouth was the only part of her body that even understood the word "stop" at that moment.

"You've *got* to be kidding me."

His hand and lips didn't move away from her but they did stop...well, moving.

She dragged in a deep breath and pushed more firmly on his chest. "I'm not kidding."

He moved a finger. "You don't mean it."

She bit back a groan and shook her head vehemently. "I do. You have to stop."

Sam gritted his teeth and slowly—very slowly—removed his hand from under the edge of her suit.

"*Why?*" he asked.

She sat up straighter, concentrating on breathing...and not begging him to put his hand right back.

"I just...can't. I don't even know you that well." It seemed like such a stupid thing to say, considering all the time they'd spent talking.

"You told me when we left the bar that you didn't want to know me."

"Right. I don't."

"So…"

She twisted, trying to get her left hand on the edge of the tub to help her get up. Sam took her by her upper arms and put her on her feet.

Don't look at him, don't look at him. He thinks you're a crazy person. You are a crazy person. Don't look at him.

She looked up, wanting to ask him…something…anything.

Instead, she just stared.

And bit her tongue.

She wanted him. More than she'd ever even imagined a woman could want a man. Almost as bad, she liked him. He was exactly the kind of guy she could fall for. For real.

She didn't want to fall for anyone for real.

She took one last look at Sam's face. Then stepped out of the tub and allowed him to dry her off with her towel. Neither of them spoke. Which helped her avoid asking him when his birthday was, what his favorite pasta was, or any other ridiculous personal thing that would mean she knew something about him other than the fact that he could single-handedly put the clitoral warming gel companies out of business.

It took three Meg Ryan movies in a row, but Sam finally realized Danika was trying to drive him away.

She'd fallen asleep hiding in her bedroom after the bathtub incident and when he'd cracked the door and seen, he'd run home for some clothes and supplies. But he'd come back here to shower, not wanting to leave her longer than necessary.

Ever since she'd come out into the hallway as he stepped from the bathroom with only a towel wrapped around his waist, she'd been trying to get him to leave—to go to work, then to go check on Natalia and the others, and then just to go to the grocery store.

But the harder she pushed to get him out, the more determined he became to stay.

He knew she was scared of him. Not that she thought he

would hurt or endanger her physically, but she was scared that he could make her give in, scared that he *would* make her give in eventually. Because he would.

He didn't know why she'd pulled back from what had been happening in the tub. He had no idea why she would want to avoid that pleasure. She wanted him, he was positive. She even liked him.

Whatever her reason, he would respect it. For now. When he took Danika to that ultimate pinnacle, it would be because she asked him to.

He wasn't leaving until that happened.

In the meantime, she'd tortured him with a marathon of romantic comedies. It wasn't his pick of how to spend eight hours on the couch, but at least he was with Danika. And she wasn't using her casted hand for anything.

The credits were rolling for *French Kiss* when she turned to him. "Aren't you bored?"

He lifted a shoulder. "I'm not a big sitter," he admitted. "Want to take a walk?"

"You should definitely go take a walk." She said it enthusiastically.

Wow, she did want to get rid of him. He held out his hand. "Let's go."

"Oh, I don't feel... I should probably take a nap."

"Are you tired?" She looked great to him.

"Yeah, I guess I am."

"Then I'll wait until you've rested. We can go later."

"No, you go ahead. I'm fine. I'll just go lie down and...I'll call you later."

"How far do you think I'm going to walk?"

She wouldn't look at him. "But I'm feeling so good. There's no reason for you to stay."

"Even if you were just going to eat PB and J, you couldn't get the jelly jar open by yourself."

"I'll order pizza tonight," she answered.

"Sounds great. I'll eat anything, but I like all meat best." He propped a foot on her coffee table and crossed his other ankle over it, settling in. He could be just as stubborn. He'd had plenty of practice in driving his sisters crazy.

Danika didn't really want him to go—he knew that. And she

did need him to stay. There was a lot she couldn't do with only her left hand.

His phone rang in his pocket. One of the guys was finally calling to see why he was taking the week off, no doubt. He never took off this many days in a row and he'd only called his replacement. The guys didn't need to know the reason for his absence. Not that they would see it that way.

It was his little sister's number that showed when he flipped his phone open, though. "Hey, Sara."

"Where are you?"

He glanced at Danika. "A friend's. What's up?"

"I've been trying to find you. Jessica's party's tonight."

Oh, shit. He was in huge trouble.

"And?" he asked, stalling. He'd totally blown off the fact that tonight was his older sister Jessica's birthday. They were having a surprise party for her. In about three hours.

"How about the location of the party?" Sara asked sarcastically. "I need to call Ben to pass the word around and I want to get there and decorate."

The location. Right. His job had been to find a place for the party.

"The center," he answered. Sara was the Director of the David Bradford Youth Center, the youth center founded and named after their father. Sam and his sisters kept it going with the trust they'd established with David's life insurance policy after he'd died.

"The center?" Sara repeated. "That's not very original."

"But it's available, and it will be easy to come up with some reason for Ben to get her there tonight," Sam said, thinking fast. "Besides, the kids would love to be a part of it."

This was just a small example of the way he often disappointed his sisters. He usually fixed it and they always forgave him. Still, it seemed that he had a hard time doing the right thing the first time.

"True," Sara agreed. "You know, there's a bunch here now. I'll get some of them involved in making food, others can decorate, some of them will help with entertainment. They're all so creative. This will be great!"

"We can come over and help," Sam said, feeling guilty for not only forgetting the party today, but for forgetting it in general.

"We?" Sara asked, picking up on his slip instantly.

"The friend I'm with."

"A woman?" his sister asked, in a tone that implied she fully expected the answer to be yes.

"Yes."

"I don't know, Sam. Is that appropriate, bringing one of your women to your sister's birthday party?"

He didn't like the way she said "one of your women" like he had a collection. "She broke her wrist last night and she's going stir crazy. It will be good for her."

Danika was looking at him like *he* was crazy.

"Oh." Sara's tone changed when she heard about the injury. "Well, then. Sure, bring her. What the heck?"

Sara would like Danika. The thing was, he didn't want his sisters and friends meeting Danika like this. Or at all. They would all like her. Which would make this already tangled situation even messier.

But he had to be at the party and Danika couldn't be left alone. She had to be bored and he wanted to be sure she didn't do anything to endanger her hand.

And because if he left, she might not let him back in.

Then he'd have to break down her door, then get it repaired... It would all be much more of a hassle than taking her along to the party and fielding the questions.

Sam hung up and turned to Danika. "We're going to a party."

"A party you were supposed to help plan and forgot about?" she asked.

How had she figured that out? "We need to go down there and help."

"Who's the party for?"

"My sister, Jessica. It's her birthday."

"I'm crashing your *sister's* party?"

"She won't care. She loves to meet new people. And there will be a ton of people there. Jessica is the nursing director of the ER and Ben, her husband, is a trauma surgeon so most of the hospital will be invited anyway. It's fine."

Danika's eyes widened. "I know who your sister is."

"Oh, good."

"My sister works for your sister."

He nodded.

"Carmen will probably be there."

He hadn't thought of that. "Probably."

"I haven't told her about my wrist."

"Then maybe it's better she find out in public where she can't yell at you."

Danika raised an eyebrow. "Have you met Carmen? She has no qualms about doing pretty much anything in public."

Sam laughed. That was a true read on her sister as far as he knew too. "At least there will be cake to cushion the blow."

She sighed. "I can't avoid telling her for two weeks anyway, I guess."

"So go get dressed for a party," he said, holding out his hand and pulling her to her feet. He didn't let her go right away and in fact tugged her closer. "Unless you need help with your zippers."

She swallowed hard and her eyes flickered to his mouth. "Um..."

"We won't make it to the party if we start that now." He turned her and nudged her in the direction of her bedroom. "Let me know if you need me."

Thankfully, his sister's party would be casual, meaning the blue jeans and polo shirt he had on would be acceptable.

Five minutes later, Danika emerged, also in jeans—that made her butt look incredible—and a loose, gauzy purple blouse that had probably been the easiest thing to pull on with her cast.

He had no idea how she'd managed to hook her bra, but she did have one on and he knew asking would take them down a conversational path that would probably only end in frustration for him.

"Let's go."

She was showing up in a cast to a party for a woman she'd never met with a man she shouldn't even be spending time with but who was essentially living with her. Temporarily. Danika found herself looking forward to the party anyway.

They pulled up in front a building that looked like it had

been part of a school at one time. *The David Bradford Youth Center.*

"Bradford?" she asked, turning to Sam.

"Named after my dad," he said softly. "He started it years ago and we named it for him after he died."

"Oh." She wanted to know everything. What had his dad been like? How old had Sam been when he died? How had he died? Was Sam okay? But asking those things was even more personal than asking if Sam liked white or chocolate cake better and she'd been biting her tongue on questions like that all day.

The less she knew about him, the less she could like him, and the less she'd miss him when this was all over with.

They stepped into the empty entryway and Danika greedily looked around, incredibly curious. She was a social worker, she reasoned. She was supposed to be interested in services and organizations that helped the community. It had nothing to do with the man beside her and his link to the place.

To the right was a hallway that appeared to lead to a number of offices. To the left was another short hallway that ended in a set of double doors. From the outside she had identified that end of the building as a school gymnasium. Sam headed in that direction.

The quiet and lack of company ended abruptly.

They'd stepped into a recreation room that filled the space between the entryway and the gym. It was a huge room with a twenty-foot ceiling and wide open space from wall to wall, filled with groupings of mismatched furniture, three ping-pong tables, two pool tables, four TVs—complete with game systems—and various sized tables.

The wall straight ahead was painted bright yellow with black letters across it that read, *"When we treat man as he is, we make him worse than he is; when we treat him as if he already were what he potentially could be, we make him what he should be." —Johann Wolfgang von Goethe.*

"Always do right. This will gratify some people and astonish the rest," —Mark Twain, ran across the bright blue wall to the left and the wall to the right was a pale green and said, *"...to know even one life has breathed easier because you have lived. This is to have succeeded." —Ralph Waldo Emerson.*

The room was also filled with at least thirty teenagers and a variety of activities. Some of the kids were on ladders and chairs hanging balloons and streamers, others were bent over a long table, drawing and decorating a Happy Birthday sign. There was a group of about ten in one corner dressed in costumes and apparently practicing a skit.

A loud crash sounded off to the left, drawing their attention to the two swinging doors that had been propped open.

Sam headed in that direction, tugging Danika along. They stepped into the kitchen and into the argument in progress.

"T-S-P means tablespoon."

"No way. That's teaspoon."

"Is a tablespoon bigger than a teaspoon?"

"Duh."

"How many teaspoons are in a tablespoon?"

"Like, five."

"Then put in a tablespoon and then we for sure have enough."

"What's up in here?" Sam interrupted.

The six girls encircling the center kitchen island turned to face them. They all wore aprons and were huddled around an open book with a plethora of baking utensils strewn about the countertop.

"Is T-S-P tablespoon or teaspoon?" one asked, clearly not shy or overly concerned with who Danika was or why she was there. In fact, the question seemed directed at her.

"Teaspoon," Danika answered.

The girl shot a gloating grin to another.

"We don't have a three-fourths cup," the shortest girl, with curly brown hair said.

"No," Danika agreed. "They don't usually make those. You just use a half cup and a fourth cup."

"Oh."

They all bent their heads back over the book.

"Can I help?"

They looked up, then at one another, then shrugged. "Sure," one said.

Another handed her a wooden spoon.

"This is Danika," Sam said.

"Hi," a couple of the girls answered. The rest were back to business.

"The recipe says baking cocoa."

"All we have is this square stuff."

One lifted a square to her mouth and bit in. A second later she wrinkled her nose, ran to the sink and spit it out. "Ugh. This is *not* right."

"It is," Danika said. "Baking cocoa isn't sweet. And you can convert the amount of powder you need into how many squares to use."

Six pairs of eyes looked at her again. "Come on in." A girl with long blonde hair came over, took Danika's good hand, not even blinking at the cast. "Welcome."

"You okay?" Sam asked, looking worried.

"Completely fine," she answered.

"I'm going to let Sara know I made it and see what else needs done."

"Great." Danika turned her smile to the girls around her. "Chocolate cake, I take it?" She was now front and center with the cookbook.

"Cupcakes."

"Sara thought this would be a good learning experience. Like cooking class." The girl who spoke rolled her eyes.

"How's it going so far?" Danika asked.

"Um." The girls looked around the kitchen, which looked like it had been ransacked and everything from the cupboards and drawers dumped onto the countertops.

"You're in luck," Danika said. "I'm a great cook, a better baker and an excellent teacher. Even with one hand."

The girls all smiled.

"One dozen cupcakes coming up."

"Uh."

The girls looked at one another. "A dozen is twelve, right?" the one with short black hair and a nose ring asked.

"Right."

"We need like..." The girl paused.

"Ten dozen," a blonde-and-pink-haired girl said.

"O-kay." Danika processed that. Wow, that was a lot of cupcakes. "Then we better get started." She glanced through the doorway to see that the sign-makers and streamer-hangers had finished and were now gathering around video games and the pool table. "Maybe some of the guys can come in and help frost. It's going to take a while."

"Those guys won't help."

"Why not?"

"They're guys. They think the girls should cook," the girl told her.

Danika blinked at her. "Then I think this cooking lesson could be a lesson in a lot more than mixing up cupcakes."

"Yeah? Like what?"

"Like the fact that guys can bake just as well as girls. And that if they don't change that attitude they're going to need to be able to cook because no girls are going to be hanging out with them."

"Whoo-hoo."

"You got it."

"That's right."

The reactions included high-fives, bumping hips and lots of grinning.

"Let's just get this first batch of batter done and in the oven," she said, indicating the bowl in front of her. "Then we'll make a plan for getting some testosterone in this room."

She looked at the bowl. It looked like chocolate cake batter. Which was interesting considering they'd been unsure about the cocoa conversion and the measurements. "What still needs to go in?"

The girls all looked around.

"Did you put in the eggs?" one asked.

"I think so," another said.

"How many?"

"How many was I supposed to put in?"

"Two."

"There are two egg shells here," someone offered.

"Then I put in two," the girl decided.

"I put the flour in."

"I did the baking soda."

"I did the cocoa."

"Okay, okay," Danika broke in. "Let's just check it out." She stirred the batter, thinking the consistency seemed about right. Then she dipped a finger in for a taste. "Oh." She pursed her lips and tried to swallow but her body fought her. Finally she forced it down. "Nobody did sugar, I guess."

The girls looked a little deflated.

"That's okay. We'll just start over. And I think we need a process so we know everything goes in with a double check on the measurements."

Within minutes they had divided up the bowls, pans, spoons and measuring cups and ingredients into a logical order. Danika figured it was better to just make ten batches. For one thing, it was probably easier than trying to mess with doubling or tripling recipes at this point. For another, it was a great way for the kids to get ten chances to practice.

"Now we just turn this into an assembly line and we'll be ready to go." They were also running short on time. "Let's get some of the boys in here."

"Good luck," a girl snorted. "Unless there's a football or video game involved they won't be interested."

Danika smiled at her. "How old are you all?"

"Fifteen."

"Fourteen."

"Sixteen, almost seventeen."

"And I assume the boys are the same ages?"

"Pretty much."

"I think there's one thing boys your age are interested in that you didn't mention."

"What's that?"

"Girls your age."

Danika glanced toward the doorway. Then did a double take. Sam was perched on the arm of the couch in front of a video game. "And I have a great idea."

She headed straight for Sam, wiping her hands on her apron, her heart thumping crazily, as it always seemed to do when Sam was involved. "Hi."

"Hi," he grinned at her. "How's it going?"

She loved his grin. "Great."

He glanced over his shoulder at the kitchen. "You didn't have to do that you know."

"It's great. I don't mind."

"Did you use your right hand?" he asked.

"Of course not. But that brings something up." She glanced at the boys sitting in front of the television. "I was thinking maybe you wouldn't mind helping out in there."

He shrugged. "Whatever you need. I missed the balloon-blowing and the sign-hanging so I'd better do something or Sara will chew my ass."

"Great." She stepped around the end of the couch until she was right in front of him, then put her hands on his knees and pushed them apart. Sam didn't resist, in spite of not knowing what he was going along with, welcoming her with hands on her hips when she stepped between his knees. She gave him a wink and raised her voice. "Oh, Sam, it's so great that you're going to help. Guys who can cook are *so* sexy."

She heard the boys turning behind her. She put her arms around Sam's neck, cupped the back of his head with her left hand and pulled him into a kiss.

Sam either caught on immediately or decided to just take advantage of the situation because his hands pulled her up against him and he deepened the kiss.

Chocolate cupcakes—and everything else in the world—were forgotten for a good minute and a half.

When they finally separated, both breathing hard and unable to do anything but stare at each other for several seconds, they had a rapt audience.

Slowly Danika became aware of the fact that all the boys had pivoted to watch and the girls had come out of the kitchen.

"Where do I get an apron?" Sam asked.

She smiled. "You can have mine." She reached behind her, untied the apron that one of the girls had helped tie around her waist, and slipped it off. Then she put her arms around Sam, pressing close again, and held the ends behind him. He reached back and tied the ends.

"Thanks." His voice was husky and his eyes were focused on her lips again.

"You bet. And you know, it'd be great to get some other guys to help. We have a lot to do."

Seven boys scrambled to their feet, jostling and pushing as they raced to be the first to volunteer.

Chapter Six

Soon they had a smooth system going for creating chocolate cupcakes, with good-natured teasing and laughing mixed in.

Danika sighed happily. This was good. She felt productive.

"I can't believe you jumped in to help out like this," Sam said. They were standing at the end of the line, spooning batter into the baking pans, something she could do with one hand as long as Sam held the bowl and the cupcake pan.

She looked at him. He was adorable in the apron.

"Why?"

"It's just...you don't mind walking into a building full of strangers?"

She considered that. "I guess I didn't think of them as strangers."

It had been fun so far, and interesting to see Sam here. The kids obviously liked and looked up to him and he was easy and comfortable talking and joking with them. Of course, Sam was a big kid himself. She was certain that he played video games, basketball, pool and anything else right alongside the teens.

He stopped pouring and looked at her. "That fits, somehow."

"What do you mean?"

"You just look at strangers as people you haven't met yet."

She felt her mouth drop open. That was exactly what she always said when people commented on how friendly she was and what a great job she did putting her patients at ease. People were always amazed how comfortable she was in new social situations. But it never occurred to her to be nervous or self-conscious. "How do you know that?"

He frowned. "It just seems like you."

"But..." They hadn't talked much about work. "You're right. I've always been that way. It used to freak my mother out because I'd talk to anyone. She'd tell me, "Don't talk to strangers" so I'd tell the person my name and get theirs. Then I figured we weren't strangers anymore."

He frowned deeper. "I can see why that would freak her out. Even as an adult you should be more careful. You can't assume everyone you meet is friendly and just wanting to chat about the weather."

"Are you worried about me, Sam?" she teased, sliding a pan into the oven as he held the door open.

"I don't want to be," he said, somewhat under his breath. "You need to use your head."

She laughed. "Thanks for the advice, Dad."

Sam took her arm and turned her to face him. "Seriously, Danika. You're sweet. You want to take care of people and help them out of their bad circumstances. That's nice, but there are people out there who will take advantage of you. Some of them might even hurt you."

She felt her eyes go round. Wow. That was quite a reaction from a guy she'd known about a day. "You don't want me to talk to strangers either?"

"No." He scowled. "You're not taking this seriously."

She was. His concern was touching. But she also felt almost giddy. Sam was worried about her. "Sam, I'm a social worker. Everyone I meet and need to help is a stranger. And it's much easier to do my job if I can talk to them."

"But you do that at the hospital, where there are other staff around, and protective procedures. You need to be careful not to let those tendencies spill over when you're out in public, like in the parking lot, or at the mall, or whatever." He seemed oblivious to the fact that the kids had passed down two more bowls of batter that were now sitting next to him. "In fact, when you're in the ER I think you need to find someone to be there when you do interviews."

"What? Don't be ridiculous."

"I'd do it every time myself, but I might not be on shift when you're there every day."

"You're offering to be my bodyguard? You have a job, Sam."

"Right. A job that has taught me that people do all kinds of stupid, mean things to other people. When I'm not there, I'll have one of the other paramedics ready to help you out."

"That is not in their job descriptions. That's crazy."

"But Dani—"

"And what about the other social workers?"

"What about them?"

"Are you going to arrange to have someone with all of them when they do interviews?"

He frowned as she stumped him.

"I'm very well-trained for what I do. We have procedures and strategies to deal with hostile patients. I'm fine."

"But..."

She waited for him to go on, but he didn't.

He finally gave in with a sigh. "I don't like it."

She felt her heart trip at his words. She lifted a hand to his cheek. "That's sweet of you, though, to want to be sure I'm okay. If I thought of what all you do in a normal shift, I'd be crazy worrying."

Something flashed in his eyes and he leaned in. "You'd worry about me?"

"You report to fires and car accidents and domestic disturbances and a whole bunch of stuff I probably don't even know about. There's an inherent danger in what you do."

He moved an inch closer. "It's true. I'm at risk every day. Each shift could be my last."

She frowned at him. "What is telling me that supposed to accomplish?"

"Maybe I like the idea that you're worried about me."

"Maybe you're hoping I'll offer to nurse you back to health if you ever get shot or something."

"Maybe. I'd probably need a few sponge baths, for instance."

And just like that he went from protective and sweet to hot and intense.

"Sam?"

"Yeah?" His eyes had darkened and he was practically standing on top of her.

"We have cupcakes to make."

"This would be sweeter."

She smiled. "Look to your right."

He did. And realized they were in a roomful of impressionable teenagers. All of whom were watching them with definite interest. He coughed and stepped back, giving them a sheepish grin. "You'll understand one of these days," he said.

The kids were all grinning at him and Danika suspected that they already understood.

A girl stepped forward. "Here, Danika, since you were the one to get us organized, you get to try the first cupcake."

She held out the frosted and decorated treat.

"Here, let me." Sam took it from the girl's fingers and peeled down one side of the paper cup. He held the cake up to Danika's mouth. "How'd we do?"

She recognized the challenge in his eyes. He thought she'd take the cupcake from him to taste it. So she had to step forward and take a bite while Sam still held it. She watched Sam watching as her teeth sunk through the frosting and into the fluffy cake. Her lips closed around the bite and she got the first feedback from her taste buds.

Perfection.

She groaned in appreciation and heard Sam suck in a quick breath. Her eyes held his as she licked frosting remnants from her lips.

His nostrils flared and she felt a rush that went beyond anything sugar could cause.

"They're awesome," she announced, turning to the group. "Good job."

The kids looked very proud of themselves and she felt another little rush.

Everyone returned to mixing and filling more cupcake pans and Sam and Danika were nudged to the side.

"I do think it's sexy when a man can cook," she said.

Sam smiled. "A guy who won't or doesn't cook is one thing, but no man should ever admit that they *can't*."

"Why?"

"If you can read, you can follow a recipe."

"I suppose that's technically true. But there's more to cooking than dumping ingredients together."

"Oh?"

"You don't cook much?

"I eat at the hospital a lot. Or out."

"Or women cook for you," she added, admittedly fishing for information.

"Some," he said without elaboration or excuse.

"And you have two sisters who cook."

"Yeah." He frowned.

"They weren't willing to teach you?" she asked.

"It was never even an option. They just..." He paused. "Jessica always did everything. It wasn't that I refused. She never asked."

It was strange, but Danika got the impression that bothered him.

"What about Sara?"

"She watched Jessica and learned that way, I guess. She was a baby when my mom left and then she was only ten when Dad died. She clung to Jessica pretty hard. I think she learned by osmosis or something."

"If Jessica was in charge of everything and Sara helped her, what were you in charge of?"

He looked at something over her shoulder. "Nothing."

"What do you mean? None of the cooking?"

"No. I wasn't in charge of anything."

"Why not?"

He didn't answer right away and she wondered if perhaps he would change the subject. But finally he said, "Because Jessica took over like she was possessed. And I decided that...well, I'm more like my mom."

"What does that mean?"

"My mom was a free spirit." He smiled but it seemed strained. "She did what she wanted, when she wanted. And didn't worry much about anyone else."

He stopped and Danika barely resisted grabbing the front of his shirt and shaking him to make him go on. She waited patiently. Kind of.

"Jessica was like my dad. Took care of everything, gave one hundred and ten percent, never messed up. I decided that it was better for both of my sisters if they just kept on that path and never got in the habit of depending on me."

Danika raised an eyebrow. "Conveniently."

He met her eyes again and even gave her a half-smile. "It did leave more time for the arcade and batting cage."

She smiled. But she didn't believe him. At least, not completely.

"And girls. Don't forget about flirting with all the girls," she said.

"Right." Then his attempt at joking fell away. He shook his head. "They were devastated by my father's death. It was so sudden. And they needed him and loved him so much. They were lost. I figured I was doing them a favor if they were completely self-sufficient and not reliant on anyone like that again."

It was also clear that he believed he'd done the right thing. Or hoped he had. She didn't like seeing Sam so...sad. It didn't fit him.

"Doing your laundry, cooking, paying your bills was actually a favor to *them*?" she said lightly.

He tried to smile, but it didn't quite make it to his eyes. "I did my own laundry, and made my own sandwiches. I also paid my own bills as much as possible."

"I didn't mean..."

"I know." He put a hand against her cheek. "I love my sisters. I didn't want to make them do it all, but it was the best thing I could do for them."

"Do you think they agree?" she asked softly.

"No, but only because they didn't see it." He smiled. "Jessica prays for me. And lectures me. And worries about me."

"Now Jessica is married. I assume she's pretty attached to Ben."

Sam chuckled, which made her feel better.

"She's attached to Ben," he agreed.

"And she probably depends on him for some things?" she asked gently.

"Definitely."

"But..." She sensed there was a "but".

"But that's his problem now."

"Oh?"

"All I can do is make it so *I'm* not responsible for her being..." He stopped as if he'd suddenly realized what he was revealing about himself and changed his mind.

"Devastated," she filled in.

He pressed his lips together and nodded.

"What about Sara?"

"Sara doesn't depend on me for anything."

"Everyone needs someone sometimes. I think there's even a song or two about it."

"But no one needs *me*," he said. "That's all I can control."

Ah. As long as *his* conscience was clear... "So Sara's Jessica's problem?"

"Yes. At least until some guy comes along to take care of her." He frowned at that thought.

Danika smiled. "You're not totally crazy about that idea?"

"I'm her big brother. No matter how much I'd like to have someone else worry about her, it's weird to think about her with a guy...like that."

"Even though you don't want her to need you, you don't necessarily want her to need anyone else?"

"I wouldn't mind her being more like you, as a matter of fact," he said, meeting her eyes. "Able to take care of herself."

Danika felt a weird twinge in her chest with his words. Not the words themselves, exactly. They were words she herself had used any number of times to describe herself. But that he thought it was the epitome of how a woman, his own sister, should be.

Which was a compliment, wasn't it?

Why did she feel annoyed?

"That's great, but she can't live in a bubble," Danika said. "What about friendship, and conversation?"

"She can have those with other women," he said.

Danika frowned. "Yes, but what about..." *Just being with someone. Having someone make her laugh. The thrill of giving someone the perfect gift.* She couldn't think of anything that wasn't, technically, something she could do with a woman. Except... *Kissing that she can feel clear to her toes, being held just because someone wants to hold her, being looked at like she's the most beautiful woman in the world...* All of which would sound pretty stupid considering that Danika was choosing to not make those things a priority in her own life.

A fact she felt less than wonderful about right now.

Perfect.

"What about what?" Sam asked.

He loved his sisters. No matter what mistakes he might have made holding himself back, he'd done it for noble reasons. She couldn't fault that.

"They're lucky to have you," she finally said.

He chuckled. "So I tell them whenever I have the chance."

Danika allowed him to lighten the mood. She couldn't handle all these realizations anyway. She cared about him. She liked him. It was good to know that he wouldn't allow himself to fall in love because she suspected that she wasn't far from falling for him.

Now she'd be more careful.

All of a sudden Sam was kissing her.

It didn't make sense, but Danika wasn't going to protest. Especially when it was something she wanted so badly. As always.

It wasn't a quick peck on the lips either. It was an all-out, I-want-you-right-now kiss with heat and tongue and his hand buried in the back of her hair.

They didn't come up for air until they heard, "Yep, I think a man's place is definitely in the kitchen," from one of the boys.

Sam grinned down at her, slowly sliding his hand through her hair as he let her go. "See what a great influence I am? The boys are going to be gourmets at this rate."

The party was a huge success.

Sam couldn't help but grin as his brother-in-law attempted to get the kids to guess that he was acting out *Santa Claus*. The impromptu game of charades wasn't going so well for Ben, while Jessica was kicking butt. Sam suspected that the kids were pretending to not get Ben's words since it was Jessica's birthday. He'd done a pretty good job with both *bowling alley* and *campfire*, but no one on his team had guessed either phrase before time ran out.

The timer rang yet again and Ben puffed out a frustrated breath. "Really? Christmas? Toys? Ho, ho, ho?"

"Oh, was it Santa Claus?" one of the girls asked.

"*Yes*." Ben threw up his hands.

The girl nudged the boy next to her. "I guess it was Santa."

The boy laughed and Ben looked at them suspiciously. But Sara kept the game moving.

"Come on, Jess. You're up again. Last word."

Sam snuck a look at Danika. She was on Jessica's team and seemed to be having a ball. She was laughing and high-fiving her teammates—with her left hand only, of course—calling out taunts to the other team and shouting guesses as loud as anyone.

Sam sat by the snack table—as everyone expected—enjoying the whole thing and tossing popcorn into his mouth kernel by kernel.

Jessica's phrase was *Charlotte's Web* and the team got it in under two minutes. They all jumped to their feet, hugging and congratulating each other.

He saw Eric hug Danika. Eric was only seventeen but he was a foot taller than Danika and outweighed her by about eighty pounds. Eric lifted Danika off the ground and she shrieked with laughter, just before Tim, another large, rambunctious boy, got shoved into Eric. Eric stumbled forward, his balance thrown off by the woman in his arms. He stuck out an arm to try to catch himself, but that let Danika slip.

Sam came to his feet as Danika hit the floor and her knee buckled, her ankle twisted and she fell onto her one knee.

He was kneeling next to her three seconds later. "Dani?"

She was wincing and holding her knee, her right hand held carefully against her stomach. "I'm okay." She looked up at Eric and managed a smile. "I'm okay. Honestly." She started to get up by taking Sam's hand, but she grimaced as she stepped on her sore leg.

The leg didn't buckle, the ankle did turn, she didn't gasp, she didn't limp. But the grimace he'd seen was enough.

"Come on." Sam pulled her against his chest and her arm went around his neck naturally. Then he slid his other arm under her knees and lifted her.

"I just bumped it. It will be okay." But she didn't struggle to get down.

"Humor me," he said through gritted teeth.

He couldn't believe how his heart was pounding. It was ridiculous. He knew he had glared at Eric too harshly, was gripping her too hard, and was stomping his feet too loudly to be appropriate for the situation. But he couldn't make himself stop. He couldn't even pull in a deep breath.

Sam strode through the door to the kitchen, kicking it shut behind him. The kitchen had barely been cleaned up before Jessica arrived, with dirty bowls, utensils and pans shoved into the oven and refrigerator so she wouldn't see them. But the countertops had been wiped and Sam deposited Danika on the closest one.

"Sam, I'm—"

"Does it hurt?"

"Well..." He could tell that she thought about lying, but then said, "A little."

Knowing she was hurt, again, made his stomach clench. Eric was just a kid, they'd been playing and Danika was fine. He himself had landed her in the ER. But part of him still wanted to grab Eric and shake him.

He'd like to think he would react the same way no matter who had twisted a knee. If one of the teenagers or one of his sisters had been the one to crumple to the floor he would have felt bad and would have wanted to be sure they were all right. However, he doubted very much that his hands would be shaking as he checked their knee.

But he inched Danika's pant leg up with shaking hands.

He didn't look up at her, knowing she would be watching him with a question in her eyes that he couldn't answer. Why was he freaking out?

Instead, he focused on her knee, prodding the tissue and moving the joint.

"Is any of that painful?"

"No."

He ran his hands down to her ankle and moved it around as well. "How about this?"

"I'm glad I shaved my legs before I hurt my wrist."

At her words he glanced up and saw her smiling at him indulgently.

He couldn't help it—he ran his palm up and down the smooth expanse from ankle to knee again. "And you're fine."

"I'm fine."

He finally pulled in a deep breath and nodded. "Good."

"You better get me some ice, though."

"Ice?"

"If I walk back out there completely fine everyone is going to think you overreacted."

The way she said it, he knew she thought he had too. She was right, of course, but it was one thing for him to realize it and another for everyone else to think it.

"I'll find an ace wrap too," he muttered. He'd acted like a fool. She'd had a minor injury. Very minor. Nothing as bad as her wrist. And he'd carried her off like she'd been shot and fatally wounded. There was a roomful of people waiting for their return, including several co-workers and friends who were never going to let him live this down. He was a paramedic. The best in the city. He didn't overreact to injuries. He was calm and cool and professional no matter what he saw. He'd seen some gruesome things and was known for being able to keep his composure.

Composure was the last thing he'd had with Danika.

"I promise to limp when we go back out there."

One look was enough to confirm that she was teasing him and he tried to smile. "I'll look for crutches in the storage closet."

"Want to use some ketchup to make it look gory?"

Now he smiled for real. "My reaction might have been over-the-top."

"Why do you think that is?" She crossed her uninjured knee over her sore one, bracing her good hand on the edge of the counter.

"Because I wasn't thinking."

"What were you doing?"

"Reacting."

"And now you're regretting it."

"My brother-in-law, two sisters and three best friends are going to find this *very* interesting."

"Why?"

"Because I never act this way."

"With women?"

"At all."

Danika just looked at him.

He'd spilled a lot of personal information in the kitchen earlier while they'd been supervising the cupcake bakers. He was feeling vulnerable and he hated it. He was also feeling serious and introspective and he hated that more. He was the one people wanted around when they wanted to forget the serious stuff, when they wanted to feel good and laugh. He wasn't one for reflection. He was always sincere, but he was never solemn. He was cool under pressure, but never cold in his interactions.

"But especially with women," he said.

"And your friends will think all of this—" she gestured to her knee, "—means something?"

"Yes."

"Does it?"

It was his turn to stare at her for several heartbeats. "It shouldn't."

She took a few seconds. Then nodded. "All right." She slid off the counter to the floor.

"Danika..."

She turned. "Yes?"

"I..." He wasn't sure what he wanted to say, what he was supposed to say. She shouldn't be special to him, that would only cause trouble for them both.

"Don't worry about it, Sam."

Wait. She didn't care that he didn't want a relationship? He didn't like that either.

"Danika..."

"Do we need an ambulance in here or what?" Dooley Miller, one of Sam's best friends, came through the door.

Sam glanced at Danika, whose pant leg was still pulled up past her knee. She quickly took her weight off the leg and leaned against the counter. "I'm doing better."

Dooley was pushed out of the way as another body entered the kitchen. "Anybody naked?" Mac Gordon asked, grinning. "Anything I should cover my eyes for?"

Sam's third friend stepped through the door, more hesitantly than the others. "They might want some privacy. Not that that would have occurred to you two." Kevin Campbell looked at Sam and then Danika apologetically. "I tried to stall them."

"And we let you," Dooley said. "You think I didn't guess "*quarterback* within the first ten seconds?"

"We're paramedics," Mac added. "We can't let someone

suffer without trying to help."

"Who's suffering here, though?" Dooley asked. "Danika or Sam?"

The other two studied him and Sam sighed, feeling very put-upon. His friends often did this and if he tried to divert them from their joking, they would be even more convinced they needed to get to the bottom of whatever was going on. It was best to go along with them and hope they ran out of steam quickly.

"Danika was the one on the floor," Kevin reminded them.

"But Sam's the one looking upset," Dooley said.

"Danika is still fully clothed," Mac pointed out. "That might be some of his frustration."

"Not that your calf isn't gorgeous," Dooley said to Danika. "But that isn't the part I would have exposed first," he said to Sam.

Sam took a deep breath while Danika murmured, "Thank you."

"Maybe she turned him down," Kevin said. "Ever think of that?"

Dooley and Mac looked at one another.

"No."

"Nope."

Sam heard a giggle and turned to look at Danika. She was grinning, watching his friends' banter. Thank goodness she was a good sport.

"I'm quite sure *he* didn't turn *her* down," Kevin said.

Even Sam had to smile at that. Kevin was a born-again Christian and it was always especially funny when he forgot himself and said something like that.

Mac looked Danika up and down. "Of course not."

"Definitely not," Dooley agreed.

"Do you mind not ogling my..."

Everyone grew silent and four pairs of eyes turned to look at him.

Damn.

His what? That's what they were all wondering. Including Sam.

What was Danika to him? What did he want her to be? It should have been an easy answer. She was a one-night stand waiting to happen.

"Ride home," he said, staying with a more immediate answer and stubbornly ignoring that there might be another answer anyway.

But the four people in the room with him knew him. Well. He got three snorts of laughter and one expression that said *That's the best you can do?*

"You know what?" Mac slapped him on the shoulder. "As soon as she's more than your ride home I'll stop ogling her."

"She's definitely ogle-worthy," Dooley agreed. "And as long as you're just friends you don't get to put up anti-ogle rules."

"Anti-ogle rules?" Sam said.

Dooley shrugged. "Not my best effort, but descriptive."

Sam looked at three of the best friends he had in the world. Then he sighed. He wasn't in the habit of warning other guys off women. He generally felt that if he and another guy—even a friend—were interested in the same woman he would let her decide. If she chose him, great. If not, no hard feelings.

Until now. This was Danika.

"Listen, if there are going to be any rules about Danika, I get to make them. And you are all going to abide by them." Sam pointed to each of his friends, one at a time.

Dooley looked at Mac who looked at Kevin who looked at Dooley.

Mac spoke first. "You know us, Sam. We're not exactly rule followers."

He should have expected something like that. He pointed to Kevin. "He is. The Bible is full of rules. Especially the one about coveting your neighbor's things, right Kev?"

Kevin shrugged. "She isn't your wife and she isn't your donkey so that one doesn't apply here."

He couldn't believe this. He turned to Dooley. "Rule number one, no talking about her when I'm not around."

"I thought rule number one was no ogling."

"Fine." Sam gritted his teeth. "No ogling. Then no talking about her."

"What if we say nice things?" Dooley asked.

"*No.*" Sam glared at the guy who had once pretended to be his probation officer to get him out of a bad blind date. "Rule number three, no watching her leave a room."

"Isn't that kind of like ogling?" Mac asked, smirking.

Sam turned his scowl on the guy who had once driven with him sixteen hours straight so he could enter a poker tournament. "Next, no thinking about her after she is out of sight."

"How will we know she's out of sight if we can't watch her leave?"

Sam gave up. These guys were great friends who knew him well. Which meant that this entire conversation was a huge waste of time. He grabbed Danika's wrist and started for the door. "Time to go."

"Careful. What about her knee?" Kevin called.

Danika started limping on cue as the kitchen door swung open.

"You don't have to..." Sam turned and caught the smug, knowing grins on the faces of his three buddies. At least he could try to keep the number of people thinking he was a lovesick idiot to three. He turned and caught Danika under the knees to carry her into the main room.

"Is she all right?" Sara asked, clearly concerned at seeing Danika seemingly unable to walk on her own.

"I'm fine," Danika assured her.

It occurred to Sam that these were the first words Danika had said in several minutes. Of course, with Kevin, Dooley and Mac it was hard to get a word in edgewise, but she hadn't protested or contributed to the conversation in the kitchen.

"But he's carrying you," Sara pointed out.

"Oh, he's—"

"You need to get the kids home," Sam said, bypassing the entire topic of Danika's knee.

Sara's attention was effectively diverted as Mac, Kevin and Dooley surrounded her and hustled her away to divide the kids up between the various adult drivers who would be taking them home.

Whatever else he had to say about those guys, they really did have his back when he needed it.

He carried Danika all the way to the front lobby. They were out of sight of the party as soon as they stepped through the double doors leading into the hallway, but he didn't put her down until they were completely alone by the front door.

He let her feet swing down to the floor, but before he let her go he kissed her, deep and soft.

"I've been wanting to do that for at least an hour now," he said when he finally lifted his head.

"But you've been resisting because your friends will tease you?"

"Nah, if I was worried about them teasing me, I wouldn't have brought you tonight in the first place. With them if it isn't that it will be something else."

She smiled. "They love you."

"Yeah." He knew they did. But being loved by those guys was a pain in the ass sometimes.

"I'm kind of making a scene aren't I? First with being the new girl, then the cast, then falling *again* and then you..."

"Overreacting."

"I was going to say freaking out."

"Okay, that too."

"What was that all about?" she asked.

He sighed, deciding to be honest. "Because I lose my mind around you and act completely out of character."

"Kissing and seducing women is *not* out of character for you, Sam."

He lifted a hand and brushed his fingers along her hair. "Liking it this much is."

She grinned. "*That* is a good answer," she said.

"Let's go home," he said huskily.

"I would love that." She lifted onto her tiptoes and pressed a quick kiss to his lips. "But I think you need to stay. It's your sister's birthday."

"But your knee..."

"Is actually fine. And I'm making things complicated here. It might be better if I go."

"You can't drive yourself home."

"I could—"

"No," he cut in. "You can't."

The door from the rec room banged open and kids spilled into the lobby accompanied by Sam's three best friends and brother-in-law who were providing rides.

"Then one of the guys can give me a ride when they take the kids home."

Sam opened his mouth to protest. Then shut it. Dammit. She was right. One of the guys could run her home and it would make the rest of the evening easier on him.

"I'll be over later."

"You don't have to."

"You have to wash your hair again sometime, don't you?"

Her cheeks turned a very nice shade of pink and he was glad to know that she was remembering a lot more than the shampoo.

"Yeah, I do." Her voice was husky.

They moved to one side, eyes still glued on one another, as the teens and chaperones headed out onto the front sidewalks to pile into cars.

"Mac will take you. Call my cell when you get home."

"Yes, sir."

"And now, I'm going to ogle you." He stepped back and ran his eyes over her from head to toe. "Then I'm going to watch you leave. And then I'm going to think about you like crazy after you're out of sight."

She smiled. "I guess rule number two, talking about me when you're not around, doesn't work does it?"

"No. But I don't intend to talk about you, anyway."

"Oh?" She looked more curious than insulted.

"I'm having a hard time explaining you. And how I feel about you."

That was all he was going to say, to anyone, about that. In fact, it was much more of an admission that he probably should have made to her.

Her cheeks flushed, her eyes went wide and she stammered over the first few words she tried to say. "Th-that's...nice. I mean... I guess..."

Which was gratifying in and of itself.

"Making a woman lose her ability to speak is a big ego stroke." He pushed the front door open and held it for her. "Just so you know."

"You surprised me, is all." She stepped through the door and into the night.

"Why?"

"Because I didn't realize that you have feelings about me to even try to explain." Instead of acting shy she met his eyes

127

directly.

"It's not a situation I'm all that pleased about."

She smiled and put her hand against his cheek. "I'm sorry." Then she turned and went to join Mac and his carload.

He watched her go, wondering if she was sorry for making things in his life so complicated all of a sudden, or if she was sorry that he wasn't pleased about it.

But it didn't matter how Danika felt about it.

He was the one in trouble.

Hell, he'd just given his three best friends rules concerning Danika.

Rules.

To his *best friends.*

They were going to think he'd lost his mind. Over her.

Worst of all, they might be right.

Danika got only to the end of the sidewalk when she heard, "Danika!"

Her sisters had arrived. Two hours late, but they were here.

"Hi."

She'd been surprised that they weren't there earlier, but she wasn't surprised to see them arriving in time to miss the cupcakes but in plenty of time for the margarita machine that was coming out now that the kids were gone.

"What are you doing here?" Carmen asked.

"Sam brought me."

"*Sam?*" Carmen looked alarmed. "But he doesn't take women to—"

"Oh my *God*, what happened?" Abi had seen the cast.

"I took a trip to the ER last night," Danika said. She knew that avoiding this entirely had been unrealistic. "I broke my wrist."

Carmen took a hold of the cast. "How? What happened?"

"I tripped and tried to break my fall with my hands."

"Why didn't you call?"

"I was fine. S-Sam took me to the ER and stayed with me. It was late." She hated that she'd stumbled over his name. It only made her sisters notice it more.

"Sam?" Carmen's eyebrows were nearly in her hairline. "You were with him when you fell?"

She nodded. "He made me go to the hospital. I thought it was fine, but he insisted on an x-ray." She was *not* going to tolerate her sisters blaming Sam.

"Thank goodness he's a paramedic. He probably knew it was broken right away," Carmen said.

"He did."

Abi didn't go so far as to touch the cast, but she leaned in and gave Danika a half hug. "Are you okay?"

"Yes. It doesn't hurt much. It's just a problem because I can't use it for anything."

Abi looked at her closely. "You don't have any makeup on."

"I don't wear much anyway," Danika said. "And it's hard to do with my left hand."

"But your hair looks good."

Danika blushed. She was glad it was dark because Carmen would have definitely noticed and commented. "Thanks."

"How did you do your hair with one hand?" Abi asked.

"I um..." They were the ones that had arranged for Sam to be her one-night stand in the first place. "Sam helped me with it."

"Sam?" Carmen repeated in that disbelieving tone for the third time in as many minutes. "He was there when you got ready for the party?"

"He's been with me since I left Marina's with him."

Abi's smile slowly widened while Carmen's eyes slowly narrowed. "Oh, really."

"He's insisting on staying and taking care of me."

"Oh, really."

"But we didn't...have sex. By the way."

"Oh, really."

"Stop saying that!" Danika snapped.

Carmen was still frowning. "I just think it's interesting."

"Well, keep your thoughts to yourself."

"Sure. I'm good at that," Carmen said.

"Dani? You coming?" Mac called from down the block.

"You're not leaving, are you?" Abi asked, noticing Danika's purse.

"I was."

"Without Sam?" Carmen asked. "I thought he was taking care of you."

She said it sarcastically for some reason and Danika rolled her eyes. "He'll be over later. He can't leave his sister's party early."

"Then why are you leaving?"

Danika thought about that. Because Sam claimed she was driving him crazy. And was making him act like a fool in front of his friends. Which she kind of liked.

"I'm staying after all," she called back to Mac. "But thanks." He waved and got in the car. "Come on," she said to her sisters. "The margaritas should be about ready."

Carmen greeted Jessica and Ben, introduced them to Abi, then the three sisters found some chairs grouped off from the party and settled in with their glasses.

"Why didn't you have sex with him?" Carmen asked without preamble.

"I was busy getting a cast put on my wrist."

"The whole time you were with him?" Carmen said dubiously.

"No. But...I was seriously considering having sex with him most of the night."

"Why didn't you just jump on him the minute you got him alone?"

"Probably should have."

"He was supposed to be the one," Carmen muttered.

"The One?" Danika repeated, stunned.

"Not *The One*," Carmen said, annoyed. "Just the one to finally give you an orgasm."

Danika rolled her eyes. She didn't know a damned thing about any of this. She was good at a lot of things. She could tune up her car, cook a gourmet meal for eight, shoot three kinds of guns and a bow and arrow, and kill any insect no matter how big or how many legs it had. But she didn't know what to do with men.

Her sisters seemed very happy with their husbands, and their boyfriends before that. They were certainly having orgasms anyway. And she didn't think either of them was weak or dependent or needy.

Yet, whenever she started to think that she wanted a

relationship where she let someone have some influence over her life, she would remember her father's perpetual expression of frustration and her mother's daily tears.

Eventually the muscular dystrophy had meant a wheelchair full-time for Ellen Steffen. Ellen would keep a brave, determined face all day, insisting on doing everything she could for herself. The girls' dad, Bill, would be gone at work all day, but even when he was at home she wouldn't let him do a single thing that she could do whether it took her five times as long or not.

When he was home and tried to help, their arguments were loud and redundant.

But at the end of the day, she would be exhausted and depressed and when it was time for bed, the tears would come. Bill Steffen insisted that his wife sleep in the same bed, in the same bedroom, with him as they'd done for their entire marriage. Where he could hold her. Where she could get away from the wheelchair and find relief from reality with blissful unconsciousness and dreams. But she couldn't manage the stairs by herself. The times she had tried had been emotionally and physically painful, for all of them.

So Bill would pick her up and carry her up the stairs, her arms around his neck, her face buried against his neck, tears streaming. And Danika remembered seeing her father trying valiantly to hold back his own tears.

Danika couldn't imagine feeling the way either of them had felt. Her mother felt like a burden, her father felt helpless. Because they were in love, because they'd let the other one matter so much.

"I hate that you set me up like that," Danika said, her throat feeling clogged.

"You weren't doing anything about your sex life, so we did."

Danika knew that her sisters believed that she was uptight. That she'd started bottling her emotions after their mom died. That she didn't want to get close to anyone because she was afraid of losing them.

But that wasn't entirely true.

Her mom's influence was definitely part of her feelings about men, but it wasn't fear of losing someone. It was the fear of losing herself.

And she developed that fear long before her mother's death.

She also knew that her sisters thought that she needed an emotional breakthrough to get over her aversion to falling in love. They thought a great sexual experience would do it. Or, at least, they hoped so.

They were probably right that she couldn't get close enough to a guy to fall in love if she wouldn't get close enough to anyone to fully let go sexually. Fabulous sex required trust and the willingness to be vulnerable with another person. Falling in love required the same things.

Carmen and Abi didn't know what held her back from that trust and vulnerability, why she was so determined to stay independent and unattached to a man.

When their mom got sick, Carmen took over everything from laundry to bill paying to keeping the schedule of doctor's appointments and piano lessons. It kept her too busy and preoccupied to deal with what was happening to Ellen. Abi, the youngest and least able to deal with their mother's illness, spent as much time away from home as she could with school, a crazy work schedule and a packed social calendar.

Danika had spent time with their mom.

They'd watched movies, played cards, read and talked. Sometimes Danika thought that she'd received three times the amount of motherly advice and influence since she'd been the only one there to listen.

And when Ellen passed away, Danika felt the loss the most. Her free time was suddenly truly free...and empty.

But she wouldn't have traded that time for anything. Even though she knew that her mother's insistence that she be fully independent, know everything she could possibly know and that she enjoy every moment, every activity where she was her own person, had jaded her in a number of ways.

Her sisters might understand, if she explained it, but it would also make them sad. So she kept it to herself.

She had to make them think she was trying to find what they had both found, what they wanted for her. "Sam's staying with me for a few more days, so—"

"No." Carmen was shaking her head before Danika even finished. "You can stay with me and Luke."

"No." Danika wasn't going to live with her sister, the fusser and worrier. That was ridiculous. "It's worked out fine with Sam so far."

Carmen sighed and looked at Abi. "Great. So there you go." She sounded mad.

"What?" Danika asked.

"I told him *one night.* I made it very clear," Carmen said to Abi.

"I know." Abi looked at Danika, worriedly. "But it wasn't his fault. He did the right thing by staying with her."

"Bullshit." Carmen took a drink of her margarita and angrily chewed an ice cube. "He should have just nailed her in the car and then dropped her off at home."

"Wow, *that's* nice," Danika said, scowling at her older sister. "What is your problem?"

She turned to look at Danika. "I asked Sam to do one thing—give you an orgasm. I didn't ask him to take you out on the town, or nurse you back to health, or hang out with you all afternoon. I didn't want him to be your boyfriend."

"He's not my boyfriend." Danika sat forward in her seat, lowering her voice and hoping her sister would take the hint. "Last night was a series of unexpected, uncontrollable events. Sam is a good guy. He's sweet and considerate and—"

"Shit." Carmen sat back in her seat, her margarita forgotten on the table. She was positively glowering. "That's just great."

"*What?*" Danika demanded.

Carmen looked at her seriously. "You're falling for him."

"What do you mean? I barely know him." Danika felt sick to her stomach and set her mostly full glass back on the table.

"This was the one problem with picking Sam," Carmen muttered.

"So you did set me up with Sam," Danika said.

"It was him, or one of two others. The other two were...less of a risk."

Danika sat forward. "In what way?"

Carmen glanced at Abi. "Any of the three guys I picked out would have accomplished *the goal.* I knew that you'd be safe with any of them, but you'd have the most fun with Sam. He's funny and charming and a big kid. Unfortunately, he's also a great guy. I just didn't want you to find that out. I hoped that he'd...do his duty...then leave you the hell alone."

"I... But... I didn't... *What?*" Danika knew she sounded like an idiot. But Carmen's words weren't making sense. Or rather, they were making sense and Danika didn't like any of them.

"Sam Bradford has more women in love with him than he does hairs on his head," Carmen said. "He's got it all. Looks, charm, brains, interests, heart. For you, he'd be a rare find. But for him, you're...one of the crowd."

Ouch. Danika flinched. She knew that Carmen didn't mean that Danika wasn't special. She did, however, mean that she wasn't special to Sam. And it was probably a good thing to point out, no matter how much it hurt.

Because until she'd heard it like that, Danika hadn't even been aware that she wanted to be special to Sam.

"There he is." Carmen stood up. "I need to have a talk with Sam Bradford."

Danika managed to grab the hem of her sister's dress. "You are not going over there to talk to him," Danika said, pulling on Carmen's skirt until Carmen sat. Then Danika stood and smoothed the front of her shirt, flipped her hair over her shoulder and wet her lips. "*I'll* go talk to him."

Fine. She was one of the crowd. It wasn't Sam's fault, exactly, that women fell in love with him easily, all the time, apparently in droves. But she had her pride. Carmen was right. The less time she spent with Sam, the better.

But as long as she wasn't going to fall in love with him, wasn't going to spend her life with him, then what difference did it make if she lost control with him just one time?

"Danika, are you..."

"I've got this," she told her sisters. "I'm all over it."

Chapter Seven

"Danika's great," Sara said, looking over his shoulder to where Danika was sitting with her sisters.

Sam didn't look, though he wanted to. He'd seen her sisters intercept her on the front walk outside of the center and figured they'd either take her home, or talk her into coming back in.

He just hoped they weren't taking her home and then planning on staying to take care of her.

Because that was his job.

As he would inform them, if needed.

Carmen was a formidable character though. His sister Jessica, Carmen's superior, was called the little general in the ER, but Carmen was her first lieutenant. For good reason. Carmen didn't take any crap.

"She is," he agreed, tipping back a swallow of beer from the bottle Mac had given him as a sort-of apology for giving him a hard time earlier in the kitchen.

"The party came together," Sara said.

"It did."

"In spite of the fact that you didn't have a place for it until I called."

Sam swiveled on his seat. "How did you—"

"Come on, Sam." She laughed and sipped her wine. "I've known you for a long time."

"So I'm a fuck-up?"

"No, you're...you."

He raised an eyebrow at her. "Which means what? That you don't spend just as much time as Jessica wondering what I'm up to and worrying about it?"

Sara smiled. "I don't think anyone spends as much time as Jessica on that."

"But you do think I'm irresponsible."

She looked taken aback at the serious turn to the conversation. "But it's on purpose so it's not like it's a character flaw. It's a choice."

Sam looked at his little sister in surprise. "How do you know that?"

"Because I remember how you were before..." She trailed off. "This is a serious conversation for a birthday party."

"Yeah, well, it's not your birthday, or mine." He reached for the wine bottle on the table in front of them and filled his sister's glass. He couldn't say why, but he wanted a serious conversation. A conversation with someone who loved him, about why he did the things he did. Because for the past twenty-four hours or so he had no idea what was motivating him to act so out of character. "Okay, go."

She sighed and turned to him. "I remember how you were before Dad died."

"How was I?"

"Like you are now. Funny, sweet, good-hearted. But you were more accountable. You were more concerned with other people."

"Now I'm a jerk?"

"No." Sara shook her head emphatically. "Now you're careful."

"What do you mean?" He couldn't explain why this was so important right this second. He also didn't know why he and Sara had never discussed any of this before. What he did know was that he wasn't leaving, and neither was Sara, until she told him what she was talking about.

She took a sip of her wine. "You were only five when Mom left, so maybe that didn't affect you as much, but when Dad was suddenly gone you changed. You still seemed happy and were fun to be around, but it was like you stopped being *there* as much."

He frowned. "I was there."

"But you stopped being—I don't know—supportive and helpful." Sara shrugged. "I don't know how to describe it."

"Try," he said shortly.

She set her glass down. "I was in junior high. I wanted to try out for cheerleading but you wouldn't help me practice."

"I wasn't a cheerleader. How could I have helped?" But his stomach felt queasy.

"You helped me when I wanted to learn to make my own candles in 4-H when I was seven. You'd never made candles before either, but you helped me with that." Her voice dropped and she looked at the top of the table, running her thumbnail along the bottom of her glass, instead of looking at him. "You used to help me with anything I needed."

Sam scowled at the half-inch of beer left in the bottom of his bottle. It wasn't enough and the queasiness increased. "You were getting older. You needed to do more on your own."

Sara's eyes were sad when she looked up at him again. "You were home with me when he went over to Jessica's apartment that afternoon. Do you remember what he said when he left?"

Vividly. Sam could still see his dad standing in the doorway after instructing him to look after Sara while he went over to Jessica's. Jessica had been living in a not-so-nice part of town in her first apartment on her own. David hadn't wanted to take his younger children over because of the neighborhood, but also because he and his oldest daughter were in the very tenuous first stages of mending a four-year-old rift.

Sam and Sara had never talked about that evening. He'd never talked to anyone about it. He'd been fifteen and Sara had been ten.

"I'll be right back," Sam said hoarsely. He swallowed hard against the tightness in his throat. "He said, 'I'll be right back'."

"Do you remember how worried and then scared we got when he didn't come and didn't come? You tried to keep me distracted. We played five hands of UNO, which you hated. That's how I knew you were worried and trying to keep me from asking about Dad. Then you made dinner—mac and cheese, my favorite—and then put me to bed."

Sam remembered all of that, but was amazed Sara did. He remembered feeling so terrible that mac and cheese was the best he could do for her on what he had grown more and more certain was going to be the worst night of her life. He'd forced himself to eat the macaroni with her. His stomach still churned at the memory and he didn't eat mac and cheese to this day.

"But I remember getting out of bed and coming downstairs and sitting with you on the couch. You agreed to read to me. You never read to me and that night you read me four books. That made me even more sure something was wrong."

Sam felt sick. God, he remembered that night. The fear had felt like it was acid, eating him up from the inside. As the minutes and hours had gone by, he'd become more and more sure that something terrible had happened and he remembered being petrified about what that meant to him and his sisters. He hadn't known if Jessica was okay, either. He remembered being unable to breathe, thinking that maybe he was all Sara had left. What were they going to do without their dad? How could they live? Who would make sure that Sara ate something other than mac and cheese?

By the time Jessica had come to the house, Sam had already known that he'd never see his father again. The misery over losing his father had sunk in slowly over the hours and he was nearly numb to it at that point. But he'd nearly fallen to his knees with relief at seeing his twenty-year-old sister, seeing that she was alright and realizing that she was someone able to step in and take care of things.

That night had left a hole in his heart that had never fully healed.

He never wanted to be responsible for that in someone else. Ever.

"You never make promises. Not even ones that you can definitely keep. Did you realize that?"

Sam just stared at her.

"And it's not that you always keep your promises. You never make them. Not ever. You never promise to call, you never promise to be anywhere at any certain time...nothing."

She was absolutely right. He was surprised only that she'd realized it.

"Of course, I know why. You remember what it felt like to have a promise not be kept. Dad said he'd be right back, and he wasn't. And you realize that it wasn't his fault, but it still turned your world upside down. All of our worlds. So you never make promises, because you don't want to not be able to keep them."

It certainly didn't sound like she was realizing all of this right now. This was a topic she'd given some thought to before this moment. Of course, she had a master's degree in social work. She'd taken counseling and psychology classes and had made helping people her career. It probably shouldn't surprise him that the huge, sudden change in their family dynamics had been a topic of consideration.

"Sounds like you know what you're talking about," he said gruffly.

She smiled. "I got an A-minus on the paper."

"The paper?"

"The paper I wrote about you in grad school."

"You wrote a paper about me?"

"I changed your name."

"Thanks," he muttered. As if that had been his first thought about the paper. Then he downed the rest of his beer. "You probably should have gotten an A-plus."

Her eyes widened and she grinned. "I'm that close?"

"Pretty much right on," Sam admitted in a rare moment of raw honesty.

His dad had literally taken a bullet for Jessica. That was David Bradford. He would have taken a bullet for anyone, but especially one of his children. Marisa Bradford, their mom, had been the exact opposite. Free-spirited, even selfish to hear their aunts and uncles tell it. She'd never been there for her kids, but she'd never agreed to be. From the beginning, having a family had been David's idea and when it turned into more than she wanted to handle, she'd walked away. And no one had been surprised, or blamed her. Because she'd never claimed to be good at being a mother, nor had she promised to try.

Sam sighed. He didn't defend his mother's choice, even in his own mind, but he understood her to an extent. What she'd chosen had been a lot easier than what David had chosen. Being everyone's hero meant that everyone expected you to be heroic all the time. There was no margin for error or room for mistakes. Being selfish and irresponsible, on the other hand, meant never disappointing anyone.

When choosing whose example to follow, it hadn't been a hard decision as far as Sam was concerned.

"I might need you to write a letter to that professor," Sara said with a small laugh. "He thought I was being too harsh in my analysis of your motivations, making you too egotistical in your thinking you could be that important to someone."

Sam smiled. "I know first-hand that people *can* be that important to other people."

"Because of Dad," Sara said.

"And because of you and Jess."

Sara's eyes glistened and Sam realized she was choked up. He leaned over and pulled her up against his side in a hug.

"I always figured you'd turn into the smartest one of us."

"Of course." She sniffed and hugged him back. "Good thing for you."

He stood. He wanted to find Danika and take her home. And to bed, if possible. But at least away from here where it seemed that every one of his emotions and character traits was obvious to everyone.

"Sam, I need to talk to you. Right now."

He turned to face Danika. Looking beautiful and determined...about something.

"You ready to go home?"

She shook her head, wet her lips and looked straight at his mouth. "Not yet."

"Do you feel okay?"

"Not really."

"Are you sick?" he asked with concern. "In pain?"

"No."

"Drunk?"

She frowned at that. "No. Definitely not."

"Then..."

"Can we go somewhere private?"

"Use my office," Sara offered. "I already grabbed my purse. It's not locked."

Danika took his hand and started toward the doors. He shrugged helplessly at Sara and waved to Jessica as they passed her and Ben. He had no idea what Danika needed to talk about, but going somewhere alone with her was not an idea he was inclined to fight.

"First one on the right," he said as they crossed the entryway where a few people stood around chatting as others came and went through the front doors.

Danika said nothing until she had pushed him into Sara's office ahead of her and shut the door behind her.

His sister had made her office into a classy, comfortable

space. The walls were painted a deep red with white baseboards and trim around the windows and door, the floor was a light pseudo-wood flooring and the desk, the round table and two chairs and the coffee table in front of the long couch by the window were all black. She had a tall floor lamp in the corner and a small desk lamp connected to the switch by the door instead of overhead lighting. The modern prints on the walls and the area rug under the desk had bold squares of black, red, brown, and orange, with hints of green.

"Danika, what's going on?"

"I need you to give me an orgasm."

Well, *that* was unexpected.

His body understood what she'd said a few seconds before his brain did and he had an erection, elevated blood pressure and heat tingling through his body as he realized that she was coming toward him, lifting the bottom of her shirt.

"Let's go home," he said roughly. "I'll take care of you, honey."

"No. Here. Now."

She somehow managed to pull the shirt off with one hand and tossed it away, standing before him in her bra and jeans. The bra they'd bought together the night before at Tease.

"Well, if you insist." He reached for her and caught the waistband of her jeans with his index finger. He pulled her forward, then turned her and walked her back until she was up against the wall next to the lamp. Here he'd be able to see everything.

He leaned in and put his lips against hers, simply because he couldn't *not* do it another second. But it wasn't really a kiss. It was more a shared awareness, a glimpse of what was to come. "What brought this on?" he murmured against her mouth.

"It's been coming on since we met," she breathed. She didn't press closer, or pull back, but seemed suspended, waiting for his next action.

He pressed his lips against hers in a light kiss, then lessened the pressure, but maintained the barest contact. He lifted his hand to her rib cage and reveled in her quick intake of air. He slid up and down the curve of her waist to her hip then slid higher, cupping her breast. She sighed. He smiled. "You wouldn't wear this bra without the matching panties, right?" he asked, rubbing lazily over her nipple, which stiffened instantly.

"Right," she whispered.

He'd suspected as much but he still paused at her admission. She had on the almost-see-through black bra and panties. Lord, have mercy.

"Do they make you feel sexy?" he asked.

She nodded, which moved her lips against his.

"They should. I want you more than I've ever wanted anything."

Sam willed his eyes to stay on her face, not wanting to look until he could see it all. He slipped a hand down, popped the button on her jeans open and pulled the zipper down, sliding the denim off her hips and pushing it to the floor in one movement.

"Kick them off," he ordered.

Her left hand stayed palm flat against the wall next to her hips and her right hand with the cast hung at her side, but she kicked her feet free of the jeans.

Sam held her gaze as he stepped back. Then he took a deep breath and let his eyes drop. Danika stood before him in a mostly see-through bra that cupped her breasts from underneath, the top just barely covering her nipples, and the scrap of material that was supposed to be panties. The triangle that was outlined in black satin acted like an arrow pointing him right to where he wanted to be. Her stomach was flat, her waist narrow, her hips flared gently and her legs were long and smooth.

"Holy..." He trailed off, not wanting profanity to mar the moment, but feeling that invoking the Lord's name at that moment would be more in prayer. Of thanksgiving.

She smiled at him, but seemed nervous.

Sam stepped forward quickly, realizing that she needed more than words.

His hand went to the back of her head, pulling her into a deep, hot kiss, while his other hand again lifted to her breast. The bra cup was easily pulled down, letting her nipple press into the center of his palm, hot and insistent. He tugged and rolled the tip, making her moan, then pulled his lips from hers to dip his knees and take the firm point into his mouth.

Her hand tangled in his hair, the pads of her fingers

pressing into his scalp and he heard a whispered, "*Yes.*"

He licked, sucked hard once then gave the other side the same attention, before kneeling on one knee to allow his lips to move down to the top of the thong.

"Oh," she moaned. Her eyes closed and her head bumped back against the wall.

He kissed his way down the front of the see-through silk, then licked, pressing his tongue against the spot where he knew she needed him most.

She cried out and her back arched, bringing her more fully against his mouth. He pulled the thong down, baring her to him and tasted her, tongue on flesh, holding her hips firmly so that she wouldn't fall as she bucked. She gasped and her hand clutched his head. "More," she whispered.

Sam stood, whipped the thong down completely, then kissed her as he circled her clitoris, dipped his finger inside, then repeated the pattern. Over and over. Until she was panting and he felt her inner muscles begin tightening. He slid another finger into her and increased the rhythm. That was when he felt her touch him.

Her hand cupped him, stroking up and down his erection and Sam knew he was seconds away from embarrassing himself like he hadn't done since he was a preteen.

"Dani," he moaned against her neck, trying to move his hips away from her hand, while not moving his hand away from her.

"*Sam.*"

"Come for me, sweetheart. Come on."

And she did. Calling his name in a way that made him want to hear it over and over again.

Thankfully, it happened before he got too close himself. He pulled his hips away from her as her inner muscles milked his fingers and her orgasm distracted her enough to drop her hand from his fly.

As her climax quieted, Sam rested his forehead against hers.

"Amazing," he said sincerely. He'd never enjoyed giving a woman pleasure as much as he'd enjoyed giving it to Danika.

"You are so good at that," she said with a happy sigh.

He lifted his head and smiled down at her. "I'm not sure it

had to do with my talents so much as it did with you." The realization had just occurred to him.

Her eyes widened. "What do you mean?"

"Have you ever pulled another guy into an empty office spontaneously and asked him to give you an orgasm?"

"No."

"Dani, it wasn't so much that I gave you an orgasm as it was you *let* me give you an orgasm."

She was shocked. It was clear. He'd hit on the truth, or very, very close to it anyway. She'd wanted this with Sam more than she'd wanted it with any other man.

Yeah, he felt pretty good about that.

"Sam?" she asked a moment later.

"Uh, huh?"

"Are you still coming home with me tonight?"

"Of course."

"Don't worry about putting sheets on the couch tonight."

He swallowed hard. Danika was asking him to spend the night in her bed.

"Because you feel guilty about my lumbar spine?" he asked, trying to keep his head.

"Sam," she said, looking him directly in the eye. "Your lumbar spine is the last thing I'm thinking about in regard to your body. In fact, I don't care about anything other than you making me moan."

He couldn't breathe. He couldn't. His lungs and diaphragm had no input from his brain because all his brain could do was repeat over and over *make me moan, make me moan, make me moan.*

Finally, his body's demand for oxygen overpowered the intense lust that roared through his body and his brain kicked in again.

"I will," he finally said. "But," he added at the look of desire and relief on her face. "I want to be upfront with you about something."

"That's...great." She looked uneasy, though.

This was important. He had to say it, had to put it between them, because it was the only thing that might save him from making an exception for Danika and then having to push her away later, when it would be more difficult.

"I only sleep with a woman once. If it's tonight, it's only tonight." Sam didn't have a lot of rules and standards, but the ones he did have served him well and had been tested over time. "You need to know that ahead of time."

The very fact that he was considering making an exception made him sure he couldn't mess with Danika. He didn't want to break her heart. He didn't want to have his own heart broken. He wasn't single, and determined to stay that way, because he didn't think he could fall for someone. It was the opposite. He knew he could fall in love. But he also knew he couldn't be responsible for someone else, for their happiness—or worse, for their unhappiness.

So he'd made a decision—falling in love wasn't an option. He'd learned to accept it, to not think about it much, and to not get close enough to anyone to let it turn into anything stronger than desire.

He was living a life that many men envied. He was happy with that. Most of the time.

What he was going to give Danika tonight was all he had to offer a woman. That was the reason that he was determined to be the best a woman ever had. He supposed he could open stuck jar lids, mow the lawn and explain the West Coast football offense. But he knew that none of that made him special, or unforgettable. What he could do in the bedroom did.

Which was fine for short-term situations, but couldn't sustain 'til death do us part.

He liked Danika and he wanted her more than he could remember ever wanting anything. He was already at risk for being way too involved with this woman.

So it would be one night. Only one night. One hopefully very long night.

Then he'd get away before he could disappoint her.

Danika finally nodded. "That's probably a good idea."

"It is," he assured her, though he didn't think he sounded as convincing as usual.

"Okay." She bent to retrieve her clothes and quickly pulled her shirt and jeans back on. Then she ran her fingers through her hair, took a deep breath and grabbed his hand. "Let's go."

They were only halfway across the entryway when they heard a deep voice say, "There you are."

Sam turned to find Danika face to face with Matt Dawson

and his charming grin.

"H-Hi, Matt," Danika stammered.

Sam frowned. She'd never stammered around him.

"Ben said you were here. How's the wrist?"

Damn, Ben was some supposed friend, Sam thought as he watched Matt look at Danika. If that was the way the man generally looked at his patients, he would have been turned into the Board of Medicine a long time ago for sexual harassment.

Matt was looking at Danika, and holding her injured wrist in his hand, like he wanted to make a house call.

With Sam standing right there. Holding her uncovered hand. With her cheeks flushed, her hair mussed and the definite look of a woman who'd just been majorly making out.

"The wrist is fine...good. Doing fine." She stammered again.

Sam frowned harder. Why was she tripping over her tongue?

"Good. You're being careful?" Matt asked.

"Very," Danika promised. "Thanks to Sam, I haven't done anything more than lift a margarita glass."

Matt grinned at her. "Glad to hear it. I'd hate to have to give you a scar."

Danika smiled. "I appreciate that." She seemed to relax.

Sam wasn't sure if he preferred her nervous or at ease around Dawson.

He preferred her to not be around Dawson at all.

"You're still staying with her?" Matt asked, finally acknowledging that Sam was there.

"Absolutely." He pulled Danika closer to his side in a juvenile, but absolutely necessary show of possessiveness.

"Good. Keep her out of trouble. Nothing wild." The smile Matt gave him made Sam grit his teeth. "Doctor's orders," he added.

"Right." Sam didn't smile and he was quite sure that Matt understood he was *not* amused.

Unfortunately, Matt's words reminded Sam that he was supposed to be staying at Danika's house. For thirteen more days. Twelve nights. Until she was healed.

That changed what was going to happen at her house tonight a lot. He wished he could blame Matt for that, but the truth was, he should be grateful Dawson had reminded him of his prolonged stay at Danika's.

He couldn't possibly sleep with her tonight and then leave her alone for the next twelve. Yes, he wanted her. It was almost making him insane. But it was much easier to avoid a drug before getting it into his system. If he made love to Danika, he would want to again, and again. Which would make her the first woman he'd had sex with more than once since college.

Leaving to go home would help with that. Staying away from her might work. Never seeing her again would possibly make it bearable. Being in her home, sharing a shower, a kitchen, a life—however temporary—would make it torturous.

"We were on our way out," Danika said, tugging on his hand and starting for the doors. "I'll see you in a couple of weeks for the good news that my wrist is fine."

Matt grinned. "See you then."

They stepped out into the night and Danika made a beeline for her car. Sam wanted to appreciate her obvious eagerness to be with him. It sucked that he was going to have to come up with some reason for them to not have sex. Other than the truth, of course. He couldn't tell her that he was about to break every personal rule he'd ever made in regard to women for her. That would be too much information.

She'd wanted an orgasm. He'd wanted to be the first to give her one. Mission accomplished. They were both happy.

Then why did he feel so antsy?

He could certainly give her another orgasm. Or two. Or twenty-six.

He wouldn't mind.

He hadn't ever done that with a woman where that was all it was going to be. It was always foreplay, a part of the whole package. In fact, it had never occurred to him to stop with that. He would have felt unsatisfied, surely.

But while he would gladly give his next year's paycheck to plunge into Danika's hot, wet, willing body, there was a definite satisfaction in simply giving her pleasure.

That could be the plan. Give her multiple orgasms in every way he knew except *the* way for the next eleven nights, then make love to her the final night he would be living with her.

And somehow find a way to walk away afterward. For good.

That was officially the plan.

Danika didn't seem to agree. She wouldn't stop touching him. Her unrestrained hand stroked repeatedly over his thigh as he drove. He shifted away whenever she got too close to exactly where he wanted her touch the most, but he couldn't keep her hand from rubbing across his stomach, up his arm to his shoulder, or her lips from pressing against the side of his neck, then his cheek. It was like she couldn't get enough.

He knew the feeling.

They didn't talk. Even when he pulled up in front of her duplex, she didn't give him any space. In fact, as soon as he had the car shut off he had a lap full of warm, wiggling woman.

She straddled him, kissing him deep and hard, cupping the back of his head with one hand. His hands went to her hips, holding her in place and pressing his straining erection up against her.

Several minutes later, Danika pulled back. "Take me inside, Sam."

"Absolutely."

She took off at a run across the courtyard and up the steps to her door. The minute the door was unlocked, he was inside and practically on top of her. He kissed her, dipping his tongue deep and stroking her mouth the way he wanted to stroke the rest of her. He lifted her, fitting her pelvis against his. She wrapped her legs around his waist and he turned, pressing her against the wall.

She moaned, he moaned, and he quickly stripped her blouse off followed by her bra. Her breast fit perfectly in his hand, her nipple distended, waiting for the brush of his thumb.

He knew he couldn't make love to her. He couldn't recall any of the reasons at the moment, but he knew there were several. Still, he could make her call his name again in that way that he was pretty sure he was now addicted to.

He sucked on one nipple as he rolled the other between his thumb and forefinger. She was panting and rubbing against him like a cat, making beautiful aroused sounds in the back of her throat.

Then he let her slide to the floor. "Take them off," he said, gesturing to her jeans.

She did, but not without saying, "You too."

He crossed his arms, watching, and shook his head. "Just you, sweetheart."

"But..."

"Danika, you have to trust me."

She paused with her thumbs hooked in the straps of her thong. She pressed her lips together and took a deep breath. Then proceeded to strip her panties off.

Sam leaned over and locked her front door. "Bedroom. Now."

She looked like she wanted to argue, but she took another deep breath, turned and headed down the hall to her bedroom. Bare naked.

He was right behind her.

"I know that you have a DVD," he said, stepping across the threshold. "But I was thinking maybe you wouldn't mind an in person demonstration."

"Of..." Her eyes widened as she realized what he was saying. "Yes," she said enthusiastically. "Take your pants off."

He wanted to. Badly. Painfully. In fact, he was incredibly proud of the fact that he resisted stripping his pants off and letting her have her way with him.

He supposed that didn't actually constitute sex, which was all he had decided that he wouldn't do. But he was *quite* sure that he would be just as addicted to Danika's mouth on him as he would be to being inside of her.

"Ladies first."

"Meaning, you're going to..."

"Absolutely." He advanced on her, loving the way her breathing quickened.

"But the DVD was for *me* to learn how to do that to someone else."

He felt his erection pulse at her words. "I'm guessing that DVD has some of this too." He ran his hands from her shoulders to her fingertips, then slid to her thighs and traveled up over her hips and waist to cup both breasts. "Lie down," he said hoarsely. "Let me do this."

For Danika to let him pleasure her this way would take complete trust. In many ways, this was even more intimate than straightforward sex.

She sat on the edge of the bed, her un-casted arm crossed over her breasts.

"Lie back." He moved to stand in front of her, knees

touching.

"I um…" She licked her lips.

"Quit thinking so hard." He lifted a hand and brushed his thumb over her lips. "Quit using your brain altogether. Just feel."

She kept her eyes on his as she lay back onto one elbow.

"Uncover, honey. Let me see." He leaned over, bracing his arm on the mattress by her hip.

She moved her arm. She looked so gorgeous, propped on her elbows, breasts bared, nipples stiff, that Sam couldn't swallow for a moment.

Then he cupped her cheek and leaned in to kiss her. He wanted to show her how beautiful she was, how grateful he was that she was letting him be the guy to fully appreciate her. But Danika grabbed the back of his head and pulled him in for a deeper kiss, opening her mouth and drinking him in.

He was only human. Danika was naked beneath him on a bed and very, very willing.

His hand that wasn't holding him up reached up to cover her breast, capturing her nipple between his index finger and thumb. She arched against him and he broke the kiss to take her nipple in his mouth instead.

Then he continued kissing and sucking and licking his way to the valley between her breasts, to her other nipple, then down to her ribs, flicking each with his tongue as he stair-stepped down to her belly, dipping his tongue into her belly button. She tangled her fingers in his hair, groaning and arching her back.

He lifted his head, staring down at her. Her head was pressed into the mattress, her eyes closed, her chest rising and falling rapidly with her breathing.

A wave of possessiveness swept over him. He wanted to know she *chose* him, that she trusted him, that she fully understood what was about to happen and that she wanted it. He also wanted to be the only one to ever see or have her this way.

"Dani, open your eyes."

She did, though she looked as if she was having trouble focusing.

"Spread your legs, sweetheart."

She hesitated. He saw it and waited, stroking his palm over her hip, wanting her to want this, but not willing to do anything more to convince her. This had to be her decision.

His breath caught when he felt her shift. He leaned to the left, and her knees parted.

"You're gorgeous," he whispered, pressing a kiss to her lips.

"Just keep the sweet talk coming," she said breathlessly.

"No problem." He stroked his hands over the inside of her thighs. "You are the most beautiful, passionate, delicious woman I've ever met."

"Delicious?" she asked with a laugh.

"You definitely taste great here." He licked her right nipple.

She groaned.

"And here." He kissed just above her belly button.

She wiggled.

"And here." He pressed his lips to the inside of her left thigh.

Her legs moved restlessly, parting further.

"Where else?" she asked.

"Big toe?" he teased.

She shook her head. "Higher."

"Right knee."

"Higher."

He licked along the crease of her left hip.

"To the right," she gasped.

"Show me," he said huskily.

She wet her lips and moved her left hand from the mattress to her stomach. Then slid it slowly downward, until her fingertips touched the soft curls right in front of him.

But she didn't move any further.

He placed a kiss on top of her mound right at her fingertips, then lifted his head and waited.

"More," she encouraged.

"Where?"

She slid her fingers a little farther. "Here," she whispered.

"Show me, Dani. Show me where you want me."

His heart almost stopped when she pulled her right knee up, let it fall open, then moved her hand, parting the soft, pink folds.

His mouth went dry. He was the luckiest son of a bitch ever.

"God, Dani," he said with true reverence.

"Now *you* show me," she said.

He didn't need to be told twice. He lowered his head and kissed her. The answering moan seemed to vibrate clear to his bones and he wanted nothing more than to make her sound like that again. He licked up and down along the folds on either side, holding her hips still so that she didn't buck him off. Then he flicked his tongue over her clitoris.

"*Sam.*" Her fingers tensed in his hair.

He licked again and again over the sweet spot, then looked up when he felt her hold on his head give. Her eyes were shut, her breathing erratic and she had moved her hand to her left breast. She squeezed her nipple and he thought he might happily stay right here for the rest of his life.

But then she moved her hand to the headboard, pushing up against the wood, causing her body to press down against him and he rewarded her by sucking her clitoris into his mouth.

"*Sam,*" she cried.

He wanted to take her over the edge. More than anything. He slipped first one finger, then another into her as he sucked again and a moment later the orgasm crashed over her. She called out his name yet again and Sam didn't think he'd ever felt quite so good.

"You are my favorite person in the world," she said nearly a minute later, her whole body limp, her eyes shut.

He crawled up her body, thinking he'd never seen anything as beautiful as Danika sexually sated.

"Thank you," he said, kissing her.

She chuckled. "I could say the same."

"No need. I hardly consider that a favor."

She rolled to her side. "Now what?" She put her hand on his hip, then slid it around and stroked it along his erection.

He almost jumped off of the bed.

"Um, I..." He scrambled to the foot of the bed and pushed himself to standing. "I need to, um...go to the bathroom."

He wanted to plunge into her. Over and over. Again and again. In every position he could think of.

Then he might as well marry her, because he'd never want

to leave.

And if he married her, then he might as well get a divorce lawyer on retainer for her because he'd disappoint her, or forget something important, or make a promise he couldn't keep within a few months and she'd want out.

He did *not* want to pay a divorce lawyer a retainer for his inevitable screwup.

So he was *not* going to take his pants off in Danika's bedroom.

He escaped to the bathroom and locked the door.

Going home would make more sense. But he couldn't. He didn't want to, but he *couldn't*. She was hurt.

Right this minute he doubted she even remembered she had a wrist, not to mention a fracture or a cast. But as soon as she tried to do anything she'd be stuck.

He had to get control. Somehow.

A moment later, he stepped into the shower, turned much colder than he generally liked it. He soaped up and then stood under the spray, his head resting on his forearm braced on the cool tile.

He tried thinking about football, his work schedule, his sister's birthday party, what he had going on that weekend, but nothing could keep his mind from Danika. Not when the soap, the shower stall, the very bathroom smelled like her.

There was only one solution to his problem.

It was easy enough to conjure up the mental picture of Danika, lying back on the bed, her body open and willing, giving herself to him. Within minutes he'd taken care of the worst of his problem and was able to dry off without feeling like he was about to explode.

He knew it wouldn't last. But at least he would be able to face her without doing something that would alter both their lives forever.

Sam rolled his eyes. He was probably overreacting. He was definitely being melodramatic. This was crazy. But he knew the problem. He didn't just want her. He didn't just desire her. He *liked* her.

Dammit. He liked helping her, liked being the one to take care of her, liked being the one to completely satisfy her.

Liking women was always dangerous.

Wanting them, he could handle. Enjoying them, he could deal with. Admiring them, he could even allow.

But liking them was nothing but trouble.

Danika lay in bed, growing more and more confused and irritated.

At first, she'd barely been able to move, feeling like a limp noodle, every cell in her body humming with a mixture of contentment and anticipation.

Sam had made her feel things she would have never believed possible if someone had described it to her. But she knew there was more and if Sam was even half as good at that part, she wasn't going to be moving for days.

But she'd listened to the shower run. Which made no sense. They hadn't done anything...dirty. Yet.

Then she heard him go out into the kitchen.

He was hungry. Okay, she could live with that. He needed to keep his energy up.

But fifteen minutes later he still wasn't back in the bedroom and her body had recovered enough that she could get upright. She headed for the kitchen, but when she stepped into the hallway there were no lights on.

She proceeded into the living room with a frown. The light from outside shone in through the sliding glass door illuminating the form lying on her couch.

Sam's form. On the couch. Instead of with her.

What was going on?

She started across the room, trying to decide if she was going to shake him awake or wake him up by arousing him. There was one part of him that she did understand and knew how to interact with.

Did he think she was done with him?

But just as she skirted the coffee table she thought about what Carmen had said—she was one of the crowd to Sam.

Danika came up short and stared at the lump on her couch.

He evidently felt he was done with her.

Not only was she one of many, apparently she wasn't even special enough to take his pants off for.

He'd practically run from her bedroom when she'd tried to continue their love-making.

More than hurt, she was...offended. It wasn't like he would have had to *endure* having sex with her. She was fairly certain that he wasn't faking that erection she'd felt.

Even so, it was more than obvious that she wasn't tempting him into losing his mind as he was her. He was fast asleep on the couch while she was naked in the bed in the next room, for heaven's sake!

Admittedly feeling a bit humiliated, she turned back for the bedroom, choosing to *not* demand to know why Sam didn't want more of her. She wasn't sure she wanted the answer.

On her way back to bed, a terrible thought struck that literally stopped her—maybe she was a vanilla cupcake to Sam.

Good, but not great. Fine, but not worth indulging in.

She stomped to the bed, yanked the blanket back and threw, quite literally, the decorative pillows out of the way.

No. Sam didn't think she was vanilla. Unless he really liked vanilla.

But then why had he left? If she was his favorite flavor there was no way...

Her cheeks heated at the memory of how well Sam knew the taste of her.

He definitely hadn't acted repulsed or like he was forcing himself through the act.

He'd been as crazy for her as she had been for him.

Then again, he hadn't unbuttoned even a single button.

She pulled a T-shirt out of her dresser, slamming the drawer shut, not caring if she woke Sam up. In fact, if she did, she had a few things she'd like to say to him.

About how rude it was to leave in the midst of her seduction. About how inconsiderate it was to make someone question their appeal *after* making her as vulnerable as she'd ever been. About how unfair it was that she hadn't had the same chance he had to look, and touch, and taste.

He'd been great about what *she* needed. But he evidently didn't need anything in return.

How selfish.

He'd made her want him, made her let him do all kinds of things she should have fought, and then went to sleep like she was just another boring dessert, forgettable after that first taste.

Jerk.

Fine. She wasn't a fudge brownie to Sam. He was stuck with her for a few more days whether he had a craving for sweets or not.

And if she wasn't going to get sex, then he was going to have to make himself useful in some other way.

Chapter Eight

Sam awoke to a terrible crashing and pounding in the front hallway. He rolled over and groaned. He hadn't slept well, haunted by dreams of Danika—in which he did all of the things he'd wanted to do the night before, but had resisted.

He pushed himself to his feet and went to investigate the ruckus. He was met by the delectable sight of Danika on hands and knees, butt toward him. Well, hand—singular—and knees. She was dressed in a pair of faded gray cotton shorts and a light blue T-shirt. It wasn't anything unusual or sexy at all, yet he found his libido roaring to life anyway. It was Danika. That was all it took.

She looked to be attempting to pull up the edge of the linoleum in the corner near the front door and she certainly wasn't trying to be quiet about it. She tossed the heavy wrench she'd been using into the metal toolbox from three feet away, causing a grand crash. Then she took the claw of a hammer to the area. That also didn't work, so she tossed the hammer back into the toolbox as well. Finally, the screwdriver she picked up seemed to be satisfactory and she was able to wedge the tip under the edge of the linoleum. But as she tried to pry the tile up, her hand slipped, banging her knuckles into the baseboard. That resulted in a loud string of cursing.

She definitely wasn't trying to keep quiet so that he could sleep in.

Sam propped his shoulder against the wall and crossed his arms, careful not to grin in case she looked back at him.

He guessed she was upset about the fact that he hadn't come back to bed.

Which was good. She'd wanted him to come back.

"Damn son-of-a-bitch shitting thing." She pushed back until she was balanced on the balls of her feet and didn't just toss the screwdriver into the toolbox, but *threw* it in with more than enough force to propel it the distance needed.

"Need some help?"

She whirled around to face him, coming to her feet. "Yes." She didn't apologize for the noise, or ask how he'd slept, or thank him again for the night before, or even say please.

"With what exactly?"

"I was planning to redo this floor this week." She stood with her hands on her hips and Sam instantly noticed that she wasn't wearing a bra.

Terrific. That would make everything so much easier.

"Redo?" he repeated. "As in pull the linoleum up and put something else down?"

"Right."

"You can't do that with one hand," he pointed out unnecessarily.

She raised an eyebrow. "No kidding."

"I suppose I could do it."

She shrugged. "I suppose."

"I've never redone a floor." He looked at the linoleum with a critical eye. "Sounds hard."

"I'll coach you." She headed for the kitchen while he stood studying the floor and the tool box.

He got the general idea. The linoleum had to be removed—somehow—and new linoleum—or something—had to be installed—somehow.

He was going to need major coaching.

Two minutes later, Danika returned with a glass of orange juice, a magazine and an iPod in hand. She opened the closet door just off the entryway and pulled out a lawn chair, which she unfolded and set in the doorway between the front hall and the living room. She set the glass on the floor next to her, inserted the ear piece in one ear, pushed the play button and flipped open her magazine.

He couldn't help the grin. He also couldn't help but notice that the magazine pulled down on the front of her shirt, making the material tighter across her braless breasts.

"What's first, boss?" he asked.

"Tear that linoleum up," she said without looking up.

"With what?"

"Whatever you can find."

There was a utility knife and a crowbar in the bottom of her toolbox and Sam went to work loosening the tile and prying it off of the subfloor. Eventually his stomach would demand he pay attention to it, but for now he'd let Danika play foreman. He did, however, pause long enough to peel his T-shirt off. He was likely to get sweaty doing this work, after all. A glance in her direction showed her still focused on the magazine article in front of her, but her lips were pressed together in a thin line. She'd noticed.

Since he didn't have an iPod, he decided that he'd have to entertain himself. He started humming the first song that came to mind. "Camp Town Races". He was sure that he could thank Tommie from the ER for that one. Still, it made him smile.

The linoleum proved easier to remove than he'd expected and he soon had it peeled back from the door to the front leg of Danika's chair. He was on to humming "You Give Love A Bad Name" by Bon Jovi. He was also nearly up against Danika's leg with his bare shoulder.

He brushed against her a moment later, appreciating the silky smoothness of the leg she had crossed over the other.

"Do you have to hum?" she snapped as soon as their skin touched.

"Yep," he said without looking up.

"Why?" She sounded very irritated.

"Because I don't have any music and you're not talking, so I need something to keep me going while I slave away down here."

"You want me to talk?"

"Sure."

"About what?"

"Anything. How about telling me how you know enough to even consider doing this floor by yourself before you got hurt?"

She sighed and laid the magazine down on her lap. Sam noticed that it was open to the same page it had been when she sat down. Interesting.

"I told you the other night that I make a point of knowing how to do all kinds of things. Especially things that I might need done someday."

"How did you learn this?"

"I read about it, looked it up online, and talked to the guys at the flooring store where I bought the new stuff."

"This linoleum doesn't look that bad," he said. "Why go to all this work? You rent here anyway, don't you?"

"Yes. I got permission from my landlord to do it. He knows I do a good job because of all the other projects I've done."

Sam looked up at her. She didn't seem too upset about conversing instead of reading. She'd even pulled the earpiece out from her ear.

"What other projects?"

"I started with my own stuff. I recovered my couch and a chair. I refinished the coffee table. But then I wanted to redo some stuff that was a part of the duplex. He let me redo the light fixtures and then I installed a new sink and faucet in the bathroom. Ever since that, he'll let me do just about anything."

Sam had stopped working and knelt in front of her, staring. "You did all of that by yourself? Just teaching yourself all of it as you went along?"

"Yes." She looked at him warily as if waiting for him to tell her she was nuts.

"That's amazing." He meant it. He admired people who stepped outside the box, who wanted to learn and try new things. That wasn't something he was particularly good at. He liked things to stay the same, stable, predictable. It seemed that it was just easier to handle life when it went according to plan. But he often thought about trying something new, living someplace else, taking up a new hobby.

"Thanks." She smiled. "I started teaching myself stuff in college. That's how I learned to cook and bake, how I learned to speak French, and how to play the guitar. But then I realized that I needed to learn practical things. So I started out with automotive stuff. I took a class at a community college. And I loved it."

Her eyes glowed when she talked about it and Sam made himself return to the floor lest he grab her and kiss her. Which would lead to all kinds of other things that he was still determined to avoid. For ten more nights.

"Then I started teaching it to other women and that forced me to keep learning new things. Which I love."

"You teach this stuff to other women?" he asked.

"I went to grad school in Kansas City and some fellow students and I started a women's group. It was part-support, part-educational. I took the education part. I taught them all the stuff I knew about cars, plumbing, electrical wiring...everything. I've been in Omaha for over a year now and I miss it, so I'm getting another group started."

He stopped and looked up at her. It was strange. It didn't bother him that Danika knew more about plumbing than he did. In fact, he thought it was cool that she could probably hot-wire a car. But he had to ask, "Why?"

She sat up straighter. "To teach women that they don't need men."

He frowned, annoyed. "Do you burn bras too?"

She frowned right back. "It's a group where women learn to do things for themselves so that if they *are* in a relationship, it's purely about the relationship instead of because the man has something the woman thinks she needs. We talk about finances, parenting, health and wellness, along with all of this stuff I teach them. A lot of the women had been in abusive relationships. Two of them are widows. A couple others simply have always felt that they needed a man around and are trying to escape that. I'm going to give them every chance to do that."

He didn't say anything in answer to that. Instead he went back to pulling up linoleum with renewed vigor. Danika taught a group of women not to need men. Wasn't that just...something. He should probably like it. The more independent she was, the less she'd be looking for him to move in and open her pickle jars. Hell, he should sign Sara up for one of her classes.

But he didn't like it. At all.

"Why are you so against men?" he asked. Hey, he was doing manual labor here. She could answer a few questions from her lawn chair.

"I'm not against men. I just think that it's good for women to be able to take care of themselves."

"Was your mom one of those liberated types or something?" he asked, prying up hard on a particularly stubborn spot.

"No." Danika's voice was quiet. "Not exactly. She wanted to be, but..."

He looked up at her. She was slumped back in her chair,

the magazine tossed on the floor next to her, staring down at her hands.

"But, what?" he asked. He wanted to know about her mom. Weird. He assumed most of the women he dated had mothers, but he'd certainly never thought about any of them, not to mention asking about them.

Danika raised her eyes and swallowed. "She was in a wheelchair. Which she hated every single day. She had been this amazing, active, self-sufficient woman. But the..." She stopped and took a deep breath. "Sometimes I think if it had been sudden, like a car accident or an injury when she was skiing or something, it would have been easier. She could have looked at it as something she risked to do the things she loved. But it was slow. Progressive. Things just got harder and harder, and more and more frustrating. Things changed in little increments. Like it was teasing her."

Danika gripped her hands tightly together, her knuckles white.

"If she'd had an accident and ended up in a wheelchair, she would have still hated it but she would have known that there were things she could no longer do and she would have dealt with it all at once. Instead, she never knew until she tried something if it would work. So she would go for a bike ride, and then not be able to go as far or fast. Or she'd want to go swimming, and find herself unable to breathe after just a few laps. Then afterward she'd be stiff, the muscle spasms would be terrible. It was always a gamble. And most times she lost." Danika put a hand to her head and rubbed her middle finger up and down the center of her forehead as if it was aching.

A moment passed before she continued. "She saw it getting worse and worse and there was nothing she could do. But she was determined to do as much as she could as long as she could. So it was a constant struggle. A constant contest between her and the disease to see how far she could go, or how long she could go, or how well she could do something. She'd push until she was just exhausted and depressed."

"What was it?" he asked.

"Myotonic Muscular Dystrophy."

Sam flinched. He'd certainly heard of muscular dystrophy. He knew it was a progressive disease where the muscles wasted away and caused a lot of disability in some cases. But he didn't know many details. He had no idea what do say.

"She was diagnosed when I was nine and had a pretty aggressive form. Things got worse steadily, but she wasn't wheelchair-confined full-time until I was twelve." Danika drew a deep, shaky breath. "And I had to watch my dad deteriorate too, in a way. He wasn't the same guy after a while. He used to laugh and joke and always wanted to have people over. That changed pretty quickly. Mom hated needing someone, but she did. It just became a fact. So he ended up having to fight with her about everything—letting him help her, letting him do things she used to do. It was awful for him."

Danika swiped at the one tear that finally escaped. "She died when I was nineteen. Respiratory and cardiac complications."

This was new territory for Sam. He had nothing. No previous experience, no words of wisdom, no fricking idea what to do. So he sat there like a dumbass, holding a crowbar and thinking that he could sit and listen to and talk to Danika Steffen for days and not want it to end. Even the stuff like this.

And if that wasn't a sign he was getting in too deep, he didn't know what was.

She suddenly stood up as if she'd been poked in the butt with a needle.

"You want some breakfast?" She was already heading for the kitchen with her half-empty glass.

"Sure." She needed a break. Fine. He'd let her cook for him...

No he wouldn't. She only had one hand.

"I'll do it," he called, pushing to his feet. "You can't..."

"I've got granola bars," she called back. "Just stay there."

Sam stayed. Mostly because he still didn't know what to do or say. *This* was why he couldn't have a lasting relationship. He sucked at it. Should he try to comfort her? Hug her? Smooth her hair? Or make her laugh? Or pretend they hadn't talked about her mom at all?

Hell if he knew. The last female he'd comforted had been Sara and she'd been comforted by Velveeta pasta shells and playing cards. If either of those would have worked for Danika he would have gladly done them.

Instead, he finished pulling up her linoleum.

By the time she came back with a glass of milk and three granola bars for him, he had tossed the six-by-six-foot piece of linoleum into the hallway and stood surveying his work.

It felt good to have done that. With his own bare hands.

He was feeling very manly.

"Nice work. For a paramedic," she said, standing on the other side of the now linoleum-less floor.

"Thanks." He grinned and tore open the wrapper to one of the granola bars.

He was going to take her out for dinner, he decided, watching her as he chewed. She couldn't cook and he didn't want to. But he definitely wanted to be with her. He could go get takeout, he supposed, but going out to a restaurant sounded nice. It would be like a...date.

He almost couldn't swallow the chocolate-covered granola.

Great. Now he was planning to *date* her.

He was in so much trouble.

"Special delivery for a Danika Steffen," a loud voice boomed from the stairwell.

Sam pivoted to find Mac coming down the hall toward him. "What are you doing here?" He had never been so glad to see his friend in his life. With Mac here, Sam wouldn't drop to his knees and propose to Danika as he was, evidently, subconsciously thinking about doing.

Dinner. In a restaurant. Holding her hand, touching her hair, kissing her every chance he got.

Nothing but trouble.

He'd probably go into the first jewelry store he saw and buy the biggest engagement ring he could find if he kept on this track.

"I'm bringing over Danika's care package," Mac said, stopping outside the door. "What the hell happened here?"

"I pulled up the linoleum," Sam said with some pride.

Mac looked at him like he'd just announced he was going to be the next inhabitant of the International Space Station. "You did it?" he asked simply.

"Yeah."

"Why?"

"Danika wanted it done. She can't do it with one hand. So I did it."

"And now what?"

"I'm putting a new floor in."

"You are?" Now Mac looked like Sam had asked him to accompany him to the Space Station.

Sam frowned at his friend's obvious disbelief. "Why not?"

"You'll probably have to use tools," Mac said, looking at the floor.

"No shit."

"Not like a screwdriver or something, but *real* tools."

"Shut up."

Okay, so Sam did a lot more heavy-lifting and cleaning types of things when he and the guys checked on Natalia and the other ladies. The other guys had more experience with tools. But what did they expect? He was the middle sibling between two girls, the son of a man who used his free time to start a youth center and raise money and awareness for underprivileged kids. David Bradford hadn't been building go-carts in the garage with his son on the weekends, that was for sure.

Jessica had been a rebel and a partier, usually in conflict with their father and almost never home when Sam was growing up. Then after their dad died she'd stormed in like the little general she was in the ER and took over the parental role as best she could. Sara was the princess, spoiled and protected by everyone. She hadn't ever picked up a hammer and Sam bet that she never would. If for no other reason than the fact that she'd always have some smitten guy nearby to do it for her.

So power tools weren't Sam's thing.

"Did you say you had something for Danika?" Sam asked, changing the subject of his less-than-testosterone-filled experiences with flooring.

"Yeah." Mac had a big green box in his hands tied with a huge white bow. "A get-well present."

"From you?" Sam didn't like the idea of other men giving Danika gifts.

"And everyone else." Mac turned sideways to fit through the doorway past Sam.

"Everyone else?"

"Dooley, Kevin, Sara, Ben and Jessica."

He followed Mac in, wondering where Danika had

disappeared to. Hopefully to find a bra. "What's in it?"

"It's not for you." Mac set the box on the kitchen table and turned toward the fridge. "You'll have to wait until she opens it."

Sam heard the bedroom door open and then the bathroom door—which squeaked slightly—shut. She'd better just be brushing her hair and teeth and not trying to shower or he'd be in there in a heartbeat.

Mac found a bottle of Pepsi and swung the fridge door shut, leaning back against the counter. "You did good, Sam."

"I just tore it up. Let's see how it goes back in."

Mac chuckled. "Not with the floor, with the girl."

"What do you mean?"

"We all like her. We're glad you waited to introduce us to a girlfriend until it was Danika." Mac took a long swig of cola.

"I didn't introduce you...it wasn't like that," Sam protested. "I had to go to Jessica's party and I had to keep an eye on Danika. It just happened like that."

"It's not like she's hooked up to a ventilator," Mac said, looking at him strangely. "What do you mean you had to keep an eye on her?"

"If I left her here alone she might have..." He almost said, *tried to use her curling iron,* but he knew that sounded stupid. Because it was. Danika wouldn't have done that. She was smarter than that. Besides, it was ridiculous that he was policing a woman's use of her beauty implements.

Mac didn't call him on the unfinished sentence, just took another drink and looked around the kitchen.

"Maybe you didn't mean to introduce us, but you're breaking other rules for her. And I think it's about damned time."

Sam didn't need this. He hadn't invited Mac over. "I'm not breaking rules for her." In fact, he'd had a pretty uncomfortable night because he wasn't breaking rules for her.

"Oh? How many nights have you spent here?" Mac asked.

Sam scowled. "Two. But nothing's happened."

"Nothing?" It was quite clear that Mac wasn't buying that for a second. "If that's true, then you are an idiot."

"She broke her wrist."

"And she feels great. She told me so last night. Matt said it should heal clean."

"So?"

"What's with the big 'she needs my help' story if not a good reason to stay here with her?"

"I'm helping her out. Period."

"Right. Another rule down the drain. You never go out of your way for women, in case they get the wrong idea."

"Did you bring liquor in that care package?" Sam asked, hating that his friend was not only right, but knew him so well.

Mac chuckled. "It's not a care package for you."

"Maybe I need one."

"It's sure sounding like it," Mac agreed, tipping his bottle back again. "Why haven't you slept with her?" he asked after swallowing.

Sam sighed. "It's complicated.

"Uh-huh."

"What?"

"You're allergic to complicated."

"I know." Sam scratched an itchy spot on his shoulder.

"You know, maybe you should let it be complicated," Mac said.

"Not with her."

"Why not her? She's great. She's beautiful, sexy, smart, funny. What else do you want?"

Danika. Nothing else. But he could barely admit that to himself.

"*Not her,*" he repeated.

"No attraction?" Mac said it with thick sarcasm.

"Insane attraction," Sam admitted.

"Then what's the problem?"

Sam regarded his friend. He'd known Mac for ten years. There was very little humiliation that Sam had suffered without Mac's witness. "I like her." He said it as if confessing a gruesome crime.

Mac looked intrigued. "As in you could see yourself spending time with her during which she remained completely clothed? Doing things like picking out furniture and actually caring? Looking forward to seeing her even if it's to go to a retirement party for her boss?"

"Yeah."

Mac chuckled. "Oh, man, you are totally screwed."

"Yeah." Sam knew it. Hearing his friend confirm it did nothing to make him feel better about it.

They stood in silence, thinking about this new development.

Finally, Mac straightened. "Listen, man, just for the record, you've never let me down."

Sam scoffed.

"Seriously. Sure you're late sometimes and you blow things off once in a while, but you never miss anything important."

"What about your big Labor Day bash?"

Mac had thrown the party to celebrate finishing his deck off the back of his house.

"Important things," Mac said. "To some people that would have been important, but to me it was just fun. And you knew it. Or you would have been there. You were at your sister's birthday party because you knew it mattered to her."

Sam had been psychoanalyzed more in the past couple of days than ever in his life and he was growing impatient with it—and with realizing that the people around him had rarely, if ever, been fooled by his plot to seem the carefree, fun guy in the group, not to be depended on, but liked and included anyway.

That was the bottom line—he wanted to be part of the group, just not the heart, without whom the entire thing would fall apart. He couldn't carry that burden.

"That doesn't mean I'm ready for a grown-up relationship with a grown-up woman like Danika."

Mac tipped his soda bottle in acknowledgement. "You might be right. Then again, you're the first person I'd call if I ever needed anything. Whether you like it or not."

Sam didn't know if he did like it or not. So he changed the subject—kind of.

"Listen," Sam said, abandoning all hope of salvaging his pride with Mac. "You have to stay and help me with the floor."

Mac coughed. "What?"

"Call the guys. Get them over here. Ben too." Sam shoved away from the counter he was leaning on. "I'll do steaks on the grill and buy the beer after."

"Why?" Mac asked. "It's what? Ten by ten?"

"Six by six."

"We won't even all fit in there."

"You have to help me."

"With what exactly?" Mac asked. "Because it's just a floor. Even you'll be able to figure that out."

Sam had never seen Mac crazy for a woman. But he had to hope that at some point in Mac's thirty-seven years, it had happened.

"I need a buffer and some distraction, okay?" he admitted, his voice low. He hadn't heard Danika come out of the bathroom yet, but he wasn't taking chances. The fewer people who heard this confession, the better.

"You want me to spend the night? Take a shift for you?" Mac asked, one corner of his mouth trying to pull upward.

"No." Sam frowned, even though he knew his friend was joking.

"Hey, we're all paramedics, as qualified as you are to take care of her. We could take turns."

"*No.*" The biggest problem with Mac's suggestion was that it was true that his friends were as qualified as he was to take care of Danika. Mac and Dooley didn't have the reputation that Sam did, but they were no slouches in the woman-pleasing department. In fact, while Mac couldn't compete for volume, he made up for it with a wildness that made Sam's eyes go wide at times. Even Kevin, before he'd found the Lord, had been with his share of satisfied women.

Mac chuckled but said, "You think having us help with the floor will help avoid complications with Danika?"

"Yes."

"You're an idiot."

"Very, very likely."

"I'll call the guys." He pulled out his cell phone.

Danika wasn't sure how or why, but within twenty minutes of emerging dressed more appropriately and with her hair untangled, her house was full of men. They'd started filling her front entryway, but the space was simply too small for the five guys who all had an opinion about her new floor, so they were spilling into her living room and even the doorway of her bedroom.

Goodness, her bedroom hadn't seen that much testosterone

in...ever.

Her kitchen had also been taken over. Her fridge was full of steak and brats, her countertop was covered with potatoes and ears of corn and her kitchen table held a huge cooler of soda and beer.

Now she'd just overheard Ben say that Jessica and Sara were on their way over with dessert.

Danika had intended to make Sam work for his penance for sleeping on the couch last night instead of keeping her awake in her bed. Instead, he'd turned it into a party.

Typical.

But she couldn't bring herself to mind. For one, some buffer between her and Sam seemed to be a good idea. She couldn't believe how she'd dumped on him earlier about her mom. She hadn't talked to anyone about her mom for a long time. Her sisters didn't like to talk about anything other than the time before their mom got sick, her father refused to talk about it at all, and very few of her adult friends knew more than the fact that her mom had passed away when Danika was a teen.

She also enjoyed seeing Sam interact with his friends and brother-in-law and was looking forward to getting to know his sisters better. Besides, they had made her a care package. Which touched her.

The package itself was as unusual as the fact she'd even received it.

Each thing had a sticky note on top with a message and signed by the person the item was from.

Sara had sent her a box of gourmet truffles, and Jessica had added two romance novels by Susan Elizabeth Phillips, one of Danika's favorite authors. A Ziploc bag held a small bottle of ibuprofen, an ice pack and an ace wrap from Ben, the doctor. And Sam's friends had each added their own flair. There was a book of puzzles and games from Kevin, the Guinness Book of World Records from Mac and an erotic stories magazine from Dooley.

Plenty of stuff to occupy her time, that was for sure.

She'd smiled and rolled her eyes the whole time she was opening it. A lot like the time she'd spent with Sam so far.

She wondered what Sam thought of his people giving her a gift.

"I'm going to start the grill." Sam came into the kitchen, seeming disgruntled. The grill had arrived in the back of Kevin's pick-up but was, evidently, Sam's.

"How are things going out there?" she asked, pushing to her feet. She could surely help with something for dinner. Though husking the corn seemed out of the question with one hand.

"Great." He seemed irritated. He opened the packages of steak and started to season them.

"Are you being sarcastic?"

"No." He sighed. "They're almost done. Mac and Dooley are great at this kind of stuff."

"Good thing you called them then." She stood beside him and decided she could cut and butter the garlic bread. Somehow.

"Yeah, no better way to show off in front of a woman than to have other guys come over and prove that he sucks at something."

She turned to look at him in surprise. "You were trying to show off?"

"At least I didn't want you to know that, of all of us, I'm the least valuable with a set of tools."

She smiled. "They were supposed to fake that they didn't know what they were doing and let you take the credit?"

"Good friends would have."

Danika bumped him with her hip. "I'm guessing there are things that you are better at than they are."

He looked at her. Then stepped behind her, his hands braced on either side of her on the edge of the sink, imprisoning her between the counter and his body. "There are," he said in her ear. He moved his hips forward, pressing a rather firm fly against her butt.

Tingles skipped down her neck, shoulders and arms, across her stomach and in between her legs.

She closed her eyes and rested her head back on his shoulder, forgetting, as she had for most of the day, that she was mad at him for the night before. "You've already got a fan in me."

"Good thing. Because I don't want you to like anyone more than me."

Something about his words made her pause. He was being flirtatious, she knew, but there was an underlying thread of something that made her want to not just tease about it. There was a heart behind the impressive chest pressing against her back. Sam held himself back from people for some reason, but he still liked people, cared about people...and wanted to know they cared about him. So he connected in the only ways he thought were safe—partying with his friends, letting his sisters fuss over him and being a sex god to the women he knew.

"There's more to you than sex, Sam." She should know. She hadn't even had sex with him and she liked him way too much. Sure, he knew his way around the female anatomy, but he was kind and intelligent and fun to be around.

Crap.

She liked him for way more than sex and she wanted him to know it.

Which meant that she'd done something pretty stupid and started to fall for him.

"For instance, you said you were good at grilling. Show me your culinary talents," she said, trying to distract him from the confession she'd almost made and to stop the delicious things he was doing. Like licking the skin along the back of her shirt's neckline.

"I can show you all kinds of talents..."

She pushed back against him, dislodging his hands from the countertop. "Oh, no you don't." She turned quickly, though there were mere inches between them. "You didn't want to show me your stuff last night, so you're not going to start it here, now, in the kitchen with a houseful of people."

It was like she could read his mind. He thought of saying something provocative, but considered what she said.

"You're right." He stepped back. "I shouldn't start something I can't finish."

"Like last night," she said, giving into the temptation she'd been fighting to bring it up.

"I didn't not finish last night," he said with a frown.

"Oh? I don't remember seeing you naked. Seems that's something I would have made note of." She crossed her arms, more to make him back up than anything. He, of course, didn't move a millimeter.

In fact, he leaned in slightly. "I finished my objective last night," he said, looking directly into her eyes. "Very nicely if I do say so myself."

She swallowed, overwhelmed by memories of the night before. Yeah. Nice was a good word. So was spectacular, amazing, and unbelievable.

She was glad she hadn't known she was missing *that* all these years.

"What's your objective for tonight?"

A myriad of emotions played across Sam's face. Surprise, desire, resignation. It was that last one that didn't make any sense. "To prove my manliness...by grilling some kick-ass steaks." He slid to the side and resumed preparation of the meat.

She opened her mouth to reply, but suddenly four other people were in the kitchen with them. Jessica and Sara had arrived and were accompanied by Ben and Mac—or at least the huge pan of some kind of cobbler was accompanied by Ben and Mac.

"We're here!" Sara came into the room and kissed Sam's cheek before enfolding Danika in a huge hug.

Belatedly, Danika returned the squeeze. "Welcome."

The guys gave Sam some trouble about the steak, Mac managed to dip a finger into the corner of the cobbler, and Ben pressed Jessica against the wall next to the fridge for a long, deep kiss. Her cheeks were flushed when he let her up for air but she didn't seem upset. Ben was grinning.

"Good grief." Sara rolled her eyes. "You act like you haven't seen each other in days."

"It's been six hours, forty minutes and twenty seconds," Ben said, his hand cupping the back of Jessica's neck.

Jessica elbowed him in the ribs. "You made that up."

"No, I last saw you when I pulled you into exam one and..."

"Okay!" Jessica slapped her hand over Ben's mouth. She was laughing as she pulled him into the next room.

"Yes, they're always like that," Sara said to Danika. "Can I use your bathroom?"

"Down the hall, you can't miss it."

"I'm hungry." Mac grabbed the plate of steaks and headed out of the kitchen.

"Hey..." But Sam's protest didn't even make Mac glance

back.

"Don't look now, but Mac just watched your sister leave the room," Danika said.

Sam glanced after his friend. "Coincidence," he said.

"Coincidence?"

"That he was looking in that direction when she just happened to leave."

"Uh-huh." Danika rolled her eyes and cut the long loaf of French bread in half lengthwise, holding it down gingerly with her casted hand.

Thankfully, Sam was too distracted by Mac and Sara to notice.

"Mac did not just watch Sara leave the room. Not the way you mean," Sam insisted.

"The way *you* mean, right? You're the one that explained it the other night," she reminded him, sliding a stick of butter from the box on the counter and unwrapping it.

Sam just frowned in response.

"I'll bet he ogled her before she left too," she said with a grin.

"No way."

"I'm sure he's not thinking about her now, either," Danika added, spreading butter over the surface of the bread.

Sam scowled at her, then at the door Mac had gone through. "He's like ten years older than her."

"So?"

"He's known her since she was twelve."

"So?"

"He's more like a big brother than..."

"Than what?" Danika tried to fake a look of innocence.

She didn't think it worked.

"Never mind," Sam muttered.

"I think that there's more there than—"

"No, there isn't."

"It's very possible that Mac wants to—"

"Shut up, Danika."

She turned to stare at him. "Did you just tell me to shut up?"

"Yes. I don't want to talk about my sister being anything

other than a little sister. To *anyone.*"

She couldn't believe he'd told her to shut up. If he could be childish, so could she. She scooped up a square of butter on the end of her knife and flicked it at him, hitting the front of his shirt.

He looked down at the butter, then up at her. "Danika."

She concentrated on the bread in front of her. "Yeah?"

"Did you just throw butter on me?"

"Yep."

"Because I told you to shut up?'

"Yep."

"And if I told you to shut up again?"

"I'd do it again."

"And what if I did this?"

The next thing she knew, the butter was smeared down the side of her face from ear to chin.

She stared up at him, mouth open. "I can't believe you just did that!"

She grabbed the rest of the stick and smashed it against his cheek.

"You're in for it now," he said, quietly. He reached for another stick of butter.

She was in huge trouble. She had nowhere to go. Not that Sam wasn't bigger and faster than her anyway. Still, she found herself fighting the urge to laugh. He hadn't even wiped his face, but stood there looking at her, butter on his cheek, nose and half his mouth.

"You can run, but you can't hide," he growled.

She started to laugh, and backed away faster. "You can't throw butter. It will get all over everything and the make the floor slippery."

He clearly didn't care. He advanced on her, a gleam in his eye.

Danika tried ducking, grabbing a dishtowel and holding it up when Sam continued toward her. She tossed an entire, still-wrapped stick at him, but it bounced of his chest and Sam stepped on it and kept coming with a devious smile on his face.

She backed up until her back was against the wall.

"Now you're in trouble."

"You started it," she protested, around her giggles.

"You buttered me first."

"It was better than throwing the other thing I had close."

"Bread?"

"The knife."

He was one step away from her now and her back was to the wall. She knew she couldn't escape.

"There's only one way out of this," he told her, holding the butter up.

"I'm not scared of butter, Sam." She tried to look nonchalant.

"No, but you're scared of letting me win."

"You sure about that?"

"Oh, I'm sure that you like to be in control, which means having the last word and never saying quit."

She tipped her head and thought about that. How did he know that? "How can you be so sure?"

"A woman who learns all the things you've learned so she doesn't have to ask for help is a woman who fights to the death."

"It's butter," she pointed out. "Harmless."

"But when I drop this butter down the back of your shirt, it means I win."

"Your face is covered!" she exclaimed, unable to contain her smile. "How will we be able to tell who won?"

He moved in until the toes of his shoes touched hers. "You and I will know. That's all that matters. I had the upper hand. You had to surrender."

She struggled to breathe deep as he watched. She didn't know how he knew that it would bug her to give up even a little power, but he was right. "I'll never surrender."

"Oh, you will," he vowed, lifting a hand to cup her cheek.

It was clear to her that he was no longer talking about the butter fight.

"In fact," he said huskily, running his thumb along her jaw, "you'll beg in the end."

She lifted a hand to his face, smoothing his hair back. "I'll be the one begging, huh?"

"Oh, honey, I'm not above begging," he said. "But I'll insist on your submission."

She saw Kevin come into the kitchen behind Sam. Sam,

however, was so intent on her that he didn't notice his friend's arrival. Kevin gave her a wink and she concentrated on not smiling as he pointed to the final unused stick of butter that remained on the counter next to the bread.

"Submission?"

"Complete. Absolute. Unwavering," Sam said, close enough that she could smell the butter on his skin.

Then her mouth slowly curled into a cunning smile. "Talk about the wrong word choice," she murmured.

"Wh…"

A moment later he clearly felt the greasy, mushy sensation of something being dropped down the back of his shirt and sliding along his back.

"Submit to that, my friend." Kevin patted him on the back, smashing the butter and spreading it out under his shirt.

"Kevin. Of all the people I thought I could trust…" Sam started.

"What is going on in here?"

Jessica stood in the doorway to the kitchen staring at her brother and her hostess both with butter on their faces.

"Isn't that just like Sam?" Ben asked from behind her. "Bring other people in to do the floor, someone else to do the cooking, while he gets slippery with a hot girl."

"Hot?" Jessica asked, looking up at him.

"You know what I mean," he said, smiling at her, unconcerned.

"Yeah, you mean, 'she's cute but nothing like you, babe'." Jessica slipped her arm around his waist and pulled him close, giving Danika a wink when their eyes met.

"I was just— What happened in here?" Sara came up short in the doorway. "Is that *butter*?" She'd noticed the smashed stick on the floor.

"Sam," Jessica said simply.

Sara found her brother and nodded with a smile. "Oh."

Danika frowned. Oh? What did that mean? As if it was a given that Sam would be making a mess, or goofing off, or whatever it was they thought he was doing.

Sam turned and grabbed a paper towel from her roll and wiped his face, but said nothing to his sisters.

She stepped around him to face Jessica, Sara and Ben.

Yes, they were Sam's family, but she didn't like that they were assuming Sam was messing around instead of working when clearly the guys had come in and taken over. And she didn't like that Sam was accepting their unfair criticism. "What was that supposed to mean?" Danika asked.

Kevin carefully stepped around Sam and behind Danika, obviously wanting to be out of the line of fire.

Jessica frowned. "What?"

"*I* started the fight, not Sam," Danika told her.

Jessica looked from her to Sam, then back and shrugged. "I just assumed..."

"Exactly." Danika could feel that her cheeks were pink, flushed from the play and now from irritation.

"Danika, don't," Sam said through gritted teeth. He tried grabbing her wrist, but she shook him off.

"Why did you assume it was Sam?"

Sam took a huge step, putting him in front of Danika, facing her. "Don't."

"No." She scowled at him. She pushed around him and faced Jessica again. "You don't give him enough credit. You expect the worst, so you see the worst."

"Sam's a great guy," Jessica said, drawing herself up tall. "I love him very much."

Sam put his hands around Danika's upper arms and pulled her closer to him, her back against his chest. "Don't do this. I'm okay," he said against her hair.

"I know that," she said. "This is for *them.*"

"*No,*" he said firmly. "It's fine..."

"He *is* a great guy who cares so much about you that he doesn't want to let you down," she said to Jessica. "So he never *lets* you see him take things seriously."

Jessica folded her arms. "I—"

"Never mind."

Sam cut Jessica off. He turned Danika abruptly, lifted her and covered her mouth with his. He wrapped one arm around her waist, pinning her against him, the other held her head where he wanted it. He kissed her for several long seconds. In front of everyone. Long and deep.

When he lifted his head, he pinned her with a serious gaze. "Don't say anything else."

"But, I—"

He kissed her again. When he pulled back, he frowned at her. "Not another word."

She opened her mouth. Then shut it, pressed her lips together and nodded.

He started walking forward, with her still against him, her feet swinging a few inches from the floor. "See you all later."

When they'd gone halfway across the living room—the only room currently unoccupied—Danika whispered, "Can I talk now?"

"Are you going to challenge either of my sisters to a duel?"

She rested her forehead against his shoulder, loving the feel of him carrying her even while she acknowledged that it wasn't very liberated of her. "No."

"Are you going to defend my honor to anyone else?"

She chuckled. "No."

"Then yes, you can talk." He let her slide down his body until her feet touched the carpet.

Wow, she wouldn't mind doing that again.

"Okay. What are you doing?"

"Taking you someplace where I can kiss you the way I *really* want to."

"I thought you were doing that to keep me from upsetting your sister." She wiggled against him just because it felt good.

He groaned softly and that made her feel even better.

Chapter Nine

Sam knew that he should let her think that the kiss had only been to occupy her mouth so she would quit talking. He should let them all think that. But he was still reeling from hearing Danika defend him. To Jessica, no less. It made him want to kiss her even more.

He looked down at her. "I don't remember the last time someone stuck up for me."

She frowned. "Why not? You're a good guy. You have lots of friends."

"I do," he agreed. "But I'm also good at not letting things bug me, so they never feel the need to defend me."

"It didn't bug you that they thought you messed up the kitchen?"

"No," he said honestly.

"But it should."

He looked at her, trying to figure out what was behind those three words. "Why?"

"You're okay with them assuming the worst of you because it's easier. But that's crap, Sam. You're worth more than that."

He had no idea what to say to her. Again. That had happened a lot in the few days he'd known her. Among his many talents was the ability to talk to any woman. Yes, a lot of it was B.S. but he was never at a loss for words.

Just then he felt a chunk of butter slide down his back to the waistband of his jeans. He shuddered involuntarily and must have grimaced.

"What?" she asked.

"I, um...need to de-butter myself." It also beautifully

changed the subject.

She looked up at him and a slow, sexy smile stretched her lips. "I'll help."

He didn't know what she had planned exactly, but he would do anything for that smile.

She put her good hand on the bottom of his T-shirt and swiftly pulled it up, baring his stomach. He lifted his arms, helping to slide it the rest of the way off even as he said, "We can't do this right here."

"Why not?"

"Someone might come out here."

"Yeah, they might."

He groaned as she tossed his shirt to one side and ran her hands over his chest. "We'll need water to get the butter off." Though he was imagining all kinds of wonderful reasons that skin, butter, he and Danika could go together.

"There's water in the bathroom. And a lock on the door," she suggested.

The look in her eyes made him groan again. She wanted this as much as he did. The realization was enough to make his already aching erection pulse in anticipation.

He should either kick everyone out or take her to his apartment. He'd imagined her in his bed often enough. But something in him rebelled at the idea. And he knew what it was.

He'd taken a lot of women to his apartment and his bed. Danika was different. He wanted sex with her to be different. Untainted. Special.

Lord, he had it bad.

She took his hand and headed for the bathroom. They had to pass Dooley, who was finishing up the trim work around the new piece of linoleum. He looked up.

"If no one knocks on that door for the next thirty minutes, at least, I'll buy you cheeseburgers every Friday for a month." Sam pointed at the bathroom door as he spoke.

"Fries too?"

"Absolutely."

"You got it." Dooley bent his head back over his work, as if the request was so routine it barely registered.

"Throw in milkshakes too. It will be worth it," Danika

whispered as they slipped the rest of the way down the hall undetected.

She smiled up at him and he didn't care about who else was in the duplex, the melted butter on his back, or that he was going to miss out on the steaks. He wanted her. Now. Against the wall.

The minute the door swung open and Danika hit the light, he nudged her forward, stepped in behind her, kicked the door shut and peeled off her shirt all in one fluid motion.

She gasped as he spun her around and crushed her satin-covered breasts to his chest, catching her mouth in a hot, wet kiss.

The bathroom wasn't very big and it was definitely girly. It was decorated in a soft lavender color with a framed inspirational quote on one wall, lavender-scented liquid soap in the dispenser by the sink next to the bottle of lavender scented hand lotion, with a fluffy lavender rug under their feet.

Not his color. Or his scent.

Which didn't matter at all.

It was a private space where he could get Danika naked and the countertop was wide enough and sturdy enough for her to sit on.

He lifted her up and stepped between her knees. Her hands went around him and her bare palm began rubbing up and down in the slippery streaks of butter on his back.

It felt like massage oil now.

"I want to help you get this off," Danika gasped against his mouth when he finally came up for air.

"I don't mind it suddenly," he told her gruffly. He wasn't going to be able to walk away this time.

Yes, he was going to make love to Dani more than once. And that seemed like the best idea he'd ever had.

She smiled. "Let me do this." She pushed to turn him and he obeyed, but made use of the time by undoing the first button of his jeans.

Danika rubbed her hand up and down along his back, slipping through the butter.

Sam couldn't help but let his head drop forward and moan in pleasure. "Nice."

"Hmm."

Then he felt her tongue against his right shoulder blade.

"God, Dani." He tried to turn, but she squeezed her knees against his hips, preventing the motion.

He could have turned anyway, but chose to let her have her way. It wasn't like he wasn't enjoying himself.

Her tongue ran up and down along the bumps of his spine and his nerve endings burned from there out to his fingertips and toes.

"You taste great," she told him.

He smiled. "Like movie theater popcorn."

"Like sex."

He groaned anew. "I want to taste you too."

"Okay." He felt her shift behind him, then saw her bra hit the floor at his feet.

He tried to turn again, but she squeezed in with her thighs. "Wait."

The next thing he felt were her breasts against his back. The feel of her hard nipples pressing into his skin made him groan. Then she rubbed, sliding her breasts across his back from shoulder blade to shoulder blade.

She eased the pressure of her knees and he turned.

As soon as he faced her, Danika touched herself. Sam felt all the blood drain from his head to his groin. She rubbed the butter over her breast, then drew on her nipple with her greasy fingers.

"See what you think," she urged, spreading her arms.

Her breasts glistened with the butter and Sam felt his knees go weak. He bent his head and took a long bold swipe with his tongue over the curve of her right breast, avoiding the tip.

She groaned and tangled one hand in his hair. He didn't care if his head smelled like butter for a month.

He licked again, then under the lower curve on the left. Then finally came back to the nipple. He licked first, then urged by the pressure of her fingers against his scalp, took it fully in his mouth, sucking butter and the taste of Danika in.

"Love that," she murmured to him, arching closer.

He slid his hands under her butt and lifted her up and forward, against the erection straining against his fly, pressing her breasts to his chest, loving the glide of their oily skin on one another. His mouth captured hers and they shared a slippery kiss that seemed to go on and on, satisfying him one second and then building his hunger the next.

"I want you, Dani. So much," he groaned against her throat as her head feel back. His lips trailed a buttery stripe from her chin to her collarbone.

"Me too, Sam. Please."

"Here." It wasn't exactly a question, but he did need to give her the chance to say no.

She pulled back to look at him. "Really?"

"Of course."

"Everything?"

"Definitely." He tried to capture her lips again, but she dodged him.

"All the way this time? Not just me?"

"What are you talking about? I'm about to explode here, honey." He plucked a slippery nipple and absorbed her groan with his mouth.

When he let her lips go, she said, "What's different suddenly?"

"Suddenly? I've wanted you since I first met you."

She frowned up at him instead of melting like the butter on her skin. "Last night."

"Last night?" As far as he could recall, and granted a lot of blood had routed from his brain, he'd nearly proposed last night.

"You didn't stay in bed, or come back."

Nearly a hundred possible responses ran through his mind, but in her eyes he could see that this was important. "Dani." He gripped her butt and pulled her against him again. "I didn't come back to your bed because I was afraid I'd never leave."

She looked like she wanted to believe him. Then her eyes narrowed suspiciously. "But you fell asleep on the couch, no problem."

"No, I did not," he said firmly. He'd tossed and turned, thinking about how she'd looked when he left her, thinking about the sounds she made, her scent, her taste.

"I came into the living room. You were just lying there. I was still all wound up, and you were practically snoring."

He tipped her chin up, frowning down at her. "Are you

seriously doubting how much I wanted you. How much I want you now?"

"I don't think you had a bad time but..." Her eyes dropped to his collarbone. "You must not like vanilla cupcakes."

Sam remembered every detail of Abi's dessert theory. "I like vanilla cupcakes just fine," he said. He leaned in and put his lips against the skin behind her ear, sucking lightly, then flicking the spot with his tongue. "But you, honey, are strawberry shortcake. My all-time favorite dessert. The one thing that can make me forget everything else."

She met his eyes again, but still seemed not quite convinced. "But I wanted to make you crazy, hot, at my mercy...unable to walk away."

"You did. I was. I'm still here, aren't I?"

"But you did walk away. You were unaffected enough to—"

"Dani," he growled. "I had to jerk off in the shower, thinking about you, to get to sleep. And it still took me hours."

"You...did?"

Her eyes went wide, then flickered to the shower stall behind him. She looked back at him—with interest, if he wasn't mistaken.

He groaned again. "You're thinking about that aren't you?"

"Trying to decide," she confessed.

He shouldn't ask. "Decide what?"

"If I would have rather watched...or helped."

Her grin shouldn't have been provocative. It was more of an I-know-exactly-what-I'm-doing-to-you smile. But it was the sexiest thing he'd ever seen.

"You're going to help. Right now. Right here."

"Great." She reached down and unzipped her jeans and began wiggling her hips trying to lower them one-handed.

Her wiggling against him made Sam almost howl. "Easy, honey."

She looked at him. "You've got to be kidding."

"Kidding about what?"

"I don't want it easy. I want it with you. Hot and hard and fast. Now. Here. *Now*."

In spite of the nearly painful pressure in his jeans, he chuckled. "Dani, it's going to be now. Here. *Now*. But we have to take it easy or it's going to last about three seconds."

"I don't care." She pushed him back, slid to her feet and stripped her jeans and panties off.

He stopped breathing, or forgot about it, or something. All he cared about or could focus on was that Danika was gloriously naked in front of him and was insisting that he make love to her.

And the lighting in the bathroom was exceptional.

Danika kicked her feet free of her jeans and panties, stepped forward and pressed her naked body to Sam's. He bumped against her as he also tried to free his pants from his ankles. With a muttered curse, he kicked his shoes off first, then pulled his legs free. His hands were all over her, stroking her back, her butt, her waist, then up to cup her breasts, rubbing his thumbs across her nipples.

Danika reached around to his back, ran her hand over the butter on his skin and then around to his abdomen and down, taking him in hand, spreading buttery oil over his shaft. "This would taste good butter-flavored too."

Sam swore. The pleasure was nearly painful. "Dani." He sounded like he was begging but couldn't stop. Just as he could not stop his hips from thrusting forward even as he grit his teeth against the sensation and the loss of control he felt on the verge of.

His hand glided down over her stomach to the sweet warm spot between her legs. Without coaching, Danika lifted one foot and propped it on the second shelf of the floor cabinet that supported a glass bowl of potpourri and a candle.

His fingers sank into her and her breath hissed out between her teeth. "*Yes.*"

"No stopping this time," he murmured, stroking deep.

"God, no," she panted. "Please don't stop. Ever." Her hand encircled him and stroked up and down.

"You got it," he replied hoarsely. "Countertop. Now." He pulled back and reached for the condom in the pocket of his jeans. Obviously, he'd known this—or something like it—was inevitable.

Danika slid her bare bottom back up onto the counter and spread her knees.

Sam paused with the condom packet ripped only half open. "You're going to kill me."

She smiled. "I hope not. I'm not near done with you yet."

He ripped the rest of the condom open, slid it on and stepped forward. "I've never been like this—"

She pulled his head forward, kissing him and cutting off what he'd been about to say.

He slipped his hands under her butt again, but this time when he lifted her, he slid in deep.

They both gasped, breaking the kiss.

Danika just froze. Every single muscle fiber in her body seemed to be pulsating and she felt as if she moved even the tiniest bit, she would explode.

She squeezed her legs around Sam, preventing him from moving as well.

"You okay, honey?"

His deep voice against her ear, the fact that he asked, the fact that he was here with her like this, the way she'd wanted for so long, all came together to make the pulsations through her body even stronger.

She took a shaky breath. "I'm..." She had to clear her throat. "I'm overwhelmed."

Sam pulled back to look at her, but she gripped his shoulders.

"Don't move," she gasped.

He stopped, but she felt him smile against her temple. "I have to, Dani."

She shook her head. "No. If you do..."

"Trust me," he whispered.

Rather than move himself though, he lifted with his hands, moving her against him.

She felt the ripples start immediately, like a Fourth of July sparkler had touched along her nerve endings. Her head fell back and her fingers dug into his shoulders, her feet slid up the back of his thighs to link her ankles at his low back.

Then her body overrode her brain. Her back arched, her pelvis pressed closer and her inner muscles tightened.

"That's it," he muttered, looking like he was gritting his teeth. "Just like that."

Then he moved inside of her. It wasn't more than a tiny flex of a muscle, a tightening of his glute muscles, but it sent her over the edge.

She orgasmed. Spectacularly. Gasping his name. Her body pulling him in closer and deeper.

Sam groaned. "You're amazing."

He thrust forward and her body, still tingling, welcomed him. He drew back and thrust again, his hands pressing her hips closer. Her buttocks slipped forward on the countertop until she was no longer supported by anything but Sam's arms. Her legs tightened around him and he brought his hips forward, stroking into her body deeper than anyone had ever been, touching parts of her that yearned for him, wanted him, needed him.

She felt the ripples building again, deeper and bigger than before, rolling waves replacing the electrical sparks, pulling at the very core of her being, making her want to be closer and closer to Sam.

He lifted her away from him, her hips cradled in his big palms, then brought her against him again. Then again. And then her body started pulling at him as well, bringing him closer to the heart of her, deeper and further. Finally, the waves crested and rolled out and over her, touching every cell of her body. She knew she cried out his name, loud enough that someone out in the kitchen would hear, but she didn't care, especially when Sam's groan of completion covered the sound of her own climax.

It was several long moments before he stepped forward and set her back on the countertop. The cold, hard surface replacing his big warm hands made her sit up straight. He pulled free of her body and discarded the condom, then wrapped her in his arms.

With her cheek against his chest, she listened to his heart beating under her ear and his big breaths filling and rushing from his lungs for several seconds.

He tangled his hand in her hair and she felt him kiss the top of her head. "I think I now fully understand the term 'buttery goodness'."

She chuckled. "The pop quizzes helped? I passed the test, Professor?"

His fingers tightened against her scalp. "You got every single thing right," he said in a husky, clearly aroused again—or still—voice.

She pulled back to look up at him and her breath caught at the heat in his eyes. "My teacher should take a lot of the credit."

"Oh, I do, honey. I do."

She laughed. "Of course you do."

"But," he said, loosening his hold on her and moving back. "That was just the level one test. We'll have to see how level two goes."

Her heart tripped. Level two. That insinuated they were going to do it again.

"Level two?" she asked, trying to keep her voice from squeaking.

"*Peanut* butter."

She giggled. And her imagination instantly made up a dozen ways to use the peanut butter with and on Sam.

"I definitely have peanut butter." She nudged him back and slid to the floor.

"Wait. Smooth or chunky?"

She looked up at him from bending to retrieve her jeans. "Chunky might be uncomfortable for some of the stuff I have in mind."

He grinned and Danika paused. Oh, boy. He was cute. And nice. And pretty damned good at the whole orgasm thing.

Crap.

She liked him. A lot.

She didn't *need* him, of course. So she'd never had an orgasm with any other guy. So what? She'd never let herself. That was all. It wasn't anything special about Sam.

And there were a whole lot of other things besides sex that she *didn't* need him for.

She pulled her jeans up, fastening them as she tried to think of a way to keep from throwing herself back into his arms and begging him to do it all over again.

Completely distracted, she pulled her T-shirt on without replacing her bra and then reached back to put her hair into a ponytail. Then she realized that Sam was staring at her.

"What?"

Sam was in trouble. Huge trouble. Never-been-this-bad-before trouble.

He was watching Danika get dressed after sex, something he'd done with more than one woman in his life, but this time he was thinking that he could happily do this every day for the *rest* of his life and never get tired of it.

She was so beautiful. Especially rumpled up from sex with him. And funny. And damned good at the whole sex thing.

Crap.

He liked her. A lot.

But she didn't *need* him. He was the only guy to give her an orgasm, but now that she'd let go and realized how great it was, she would let it happen with another guy.

And the urge to put his fist through a wall at the thought would surely fade over time.

"You just...you look gorgeous."

She smiled. "Thanks."

Even the way she said thanks made him want her.

Yeah, he had it bad.

He reached out and took her elbow tugging her close, wanting to smell her hair, feel the silkiness of her skin, feel her warm breath on him. "Dani, I just..."

"Oh, come on." She gave him a frown. "We have several hours until our one night is over. And I intend to use every minute."

Satisfaction coursed over him. He wasn't entirely sure what he'd been about to say when he pulled her close, but apparently she'd thought he was going to give her some reminder about his one-night rule.

Before he could speak she put her hand against his cheek. "I remember what you said. One night. Don't worry. I'm okay with that. But I do want the whole night."

He was more than happy to give her the whole night. He fully intended to, in fact. But she was *okay* with it? What did that mean? If she was crazy about him, and addicted to him like he was fearing he was becoming to her, she wouldn't be *okay* with it. She'd be resisting it, trying to talk him into more, or distract him, or entice him. Like other women had done. Like *most* other women had done.

He told himself he should appreciate her respect of what he'd said in the beginning. He should be enjoying the fact that he'd done what he'd wanted to do from the first minute he saw her. He should get busy doing more of it before they ran out of time.

Instead he said, "I don't think I fully explained the rules, though."

"There are rules to the rule?"

He shrugged. "More like a definition, I guess."

She let her hand drop from his cheek to his chest and wiggled closer. "Why do I get the impression that this definition might lead to more time without our clothes on?"

"Because you're very intuitive," he said, his hands settling on her hips—and never wanting to move.

"Right. I would have to be incredibly insightful to know that you like it when my clothes are off."

He chuckled. He did like her.

Naked or not.

Which was what he should be most worried about.

"The one night is technically twenty-four hours. We have until this time tomorrow."

She looked at him, unblinking, for several beats. Then she slowly smiled. It was a smile full of I'm-so-on-to-you. "This time tomorrow, huh?" She pressed closer with her hips. "We might be able to get through *half* the things I want to do with you."

He wanted her again. Right now. He leaned in close, fully anticipating the kiss. Her breath was hot against his lips. The kiss was full of heat and promise.

"Let's go," he rasped, pulling back. He needed a shower, he needed Danika again, but... "We have an house full of people to get rid of."

She chuckled. "We can't kick them out."

"Maybe *we* can't, but I sure as hell can." It wasn't like any of them would be surprised.

Besides, this time they needed a soft, horizontal surface.

Unwilling to let her go, Sam kept her hand in his as they headed for the kitchen.

The place was completely quiet.

The kitchen was spotless and devoid of food and coolers.

"They left?" Danika asked.

"Apparently."

"You have good friends," she said, turning and wrapping her arms around his waist.

"Yes. Yes, I do." Good friends to whom he was going to have to explain a lot of stuff about Danika that he didn't understand.

He breathed in the smell of her hair and decided that it was worth it.

She tipped her head back and rose on tiptoe to kiss him, her hands ran over his back down to his butt, pulling him close.

He wanted her, but... He sighed and pulled back. He wanted more than sex. It was official. He was in too deep and was probably going to regret a whole bunch of stuff very soon. But for right now, he was going to enjoy. He wasn't sure exactly what to do, what to say, how to tell her, but he was going to do something he hadn't done since high school.

He was going to *date* a woman.

Not just any woman. Danika Steffen.

"Honey," he said, breaking the kiss. "Don't you want a shower?"

"I'm planning on getting dirty again. Soon. It would be a waste of water."

His erection came fully to life. He tried to think of another excuse not to take her again right here and now. "You're going to be sore if we don't slow down."

"I don't mind." She kissed his chin, then his throat.

Sam groaned, but still put his hands on her shoulders. "We have time," he said, looking directly in her eyes so she understood. "We have plenty of time. Let's just slow down so we can enjoy everything."

He stopped short of repeating and emphasizing *everything.*

"Slow down?" Danika looked like he'd just told her they were going sledding. In July. "Why?"

"Because I'm...starving." So he wasn't entirely ready to tell her what he was feeling. There was time for that too. Once he got used to it himself.

She laughed. "Okay." She disentangled her arms from his waist. "I could eat."

Thirty minutes after having the best sex of either of their lives, they were sitting on the floor next to Danika's coffee table eating pizza. His good friends had taken all the food with them when they'd exited. Including the steaks Sam had paid for.

They talked as they ate. It was as if the physical release

had released everything. They talked about their parents and the heartaches. Sam told her about the night his dad had died and Danika talked about watching her mom become more and more dependent and her father becoming more and more burdened with everything.

But they also talked about the good times. Family game nights, vacations, birthday parties, her dad's practical jokes and his dad being able to eat more onion rings than three teenage boys put together. And they talked about their friends and their sisters. The sisters who were the biggest joy and the biggest headache in their lives.

As it turned out, and much to both of their surprise since the events of the afternoon had been a first for Danika, she got very hungry after sex that included an orgasm.

"This is the best pizza ever," she declared. "I used to think this pizza place was terrible."

He laughed. It was pizza. It was not quite horrible, but far from amazing. "It's the endorphins, I'm sure."

She wiggled her eyebrows. "Maybe this would be a good time for me to try eggplant, because I *hate* eggplant."

He wrinkled his nose. "For eggplant we're going to have to go back into the bedroom for a while."

"I'm ready when you are."

He was definitely ready. He had a feeling he would always be ready for Danika. But he smiled and shook his head. "You're going to need more calories for what I have in mind."

She smiled and reached for another piece.

Oh, yeah, he could definitely do this for—well—a really long time.

He watched her for several minutes, responding to her chatter with well placed "uh-huhs" to keep her thinking he was listening. But she was jumping from one topic to another, laughing at her own comments, and chewing her fourth piece of pizza. It was like she'd drunk three cans of Mountain Dew.

He'd done that to her. He'd made her that happy. A fact he was enjoying immensely.

"If you're not going to make me like eggplant, what do you want to do?" she asked.

"What would you be doing right now if I wasn't here, or if your wrist wasn't in a cast?" He wanted to know about her.

What she did, what she liked, her past, her friends, why she was a social worker, what her twenty-first birthday had been like, who had taken her to prom.

She rolled her eyes. "You don't want to know." She licked pizza sauce from her middle finger.

Sam had to shift to be comfortable in his jeans at that. "I do. What would you be doing?"

"You'll think I'm weird."

Now he was very interested. "Does it involve whips and leather or something?"

She giggled. "No."

"Are you a superhero?"

"I wish."

"You don't have a room wallpapered in photos of Ashton Kutcher where you burn incense on an altar and kiss a life-sized cardboard cutout of him, do you?"

She outright laughed at that. "Nope."

"Okay, I give."

"This week I had plans to clean out my attic."

"Your attic?"

"Well, my half of the attic."

He looked at her suspiciously. "I suppose the boxes are all heavy."

She shook her head. "No. Not all of them. Just the ones I need to look through."

He threw a pillow from the couch at her and she giggled again. "Fine. I'll be the big manly man and go get the boxes of bricks you need to look through." He pushed himself to standing. "But I expect to be rewarded for my hard work."

"Of course." She looked adorable as she tried to get up as well, but her good hand was holding her glass of iced tea.

He reached down and pulled her to her feet, then kissed the top of her head. "Which boxes?"

"You don't have to. It can wait. There are just some pictures my sister wants for her new house. It's not an emergency."

"But this was what you planned to do before you got hurt?" he asked. When she nodded he said, "That's why I'm here. To be sure that things get done even though you have a cast on your wrist."

"The door to the attic is in the outer hallway. I'll have to get you the key." Danika started picking up the wadded napkins and tossing them into the nearly empty pizza box. "My stuff is on the south end of the attic. I wish I could tell you that each box is carefully labeled with what's inside, but the best I did was put my name on them. There are a few with clothes in them and a huge trunk that doesn't need to come down. But there are four or five others I should look through, since I'm not sure where the pictures are."

He had all the boxes clustered in the middle of her living room fifteen minutes later. There were six total and there were sixteen steep, narrow steps up to the attic. Sam was embarrassed to have worked up a sweat by the time he was done.

Danika's face, however, was worth it when she started opening the tops. It was like watching a kid at a birthday party. It had apparently been some time since she'd looked through the boxes.

She pulled out some yearbooks, which Sam picked up and started looking through. She also stacked some photo albums to one side along with several books. She finally withdrew framed photos from box three.

"Here's the one she wants for her mantel." Danika passed him an eight by ten black and white photo of three little girls, standing with their arms around one another in front of a lemonade stand.

"How old are you here?"

"Seven. Carmen is nine and Abi is six."

"You look happy."

She was looking at the photo in his hand instead of at him. "We were. That's one thing I do remember, how happy we all were before..."

Her mother's illness. Sam was still surprised how the knowledge about Danika's childhood with her mom in a wheelchair socked him in the gut.

"I'm sorry that happened," he said sincerely. There wasn't a thing he could do to make that better for her and he hated that.

She looked up at him. "Thanks." She sounded like she meant it. "It's not like we weren't *ever* happy again. It just changed. Everything had to be thought out and planned. If we went to the zoo, would mom get too tired? Would it be impossibly difficult to get her wheelchair into that restaurant? Things like that. And my sisters didn't help."

Sam looked at the grinning little girls in the picture and thought of the women he knew. Carmen was an ER nurse. She was caring and dedicated even while she was being tough and no-nonsense. "What do you mean?"

"Carmen is a take-charge person. She took over all the things she could *do*. She was even in charge of taking mom to her doctor's appointments, which is how she got interested in nursing. But she can't sit still. She was the one who made every outing or family gathering or event into a production. She'd call ahead and make sure everything was set up just right, or she'd call the family and give them instructions about how things would go when they came over for holidays. Things like that. Drove us all nuts.

"Abi, on the other hand, needed two weeks' notice to be a part of anything. She worked two jobs, volunteered, and was in every extracurricular activity she could possibly find so that she could avoid everything at home. She loved our mom, of course, but she was very uncomfortable with the wheelchair and the doctors and the medications. That's why, I think, she went into sales...nothing to do with caregiving. Not her thing."

Sam chuckled and shook his head. "I can relate to a lot of that."

"You can?"

She looked genuinely interested and he figured that if he was going to find out everything he could about her, he'd probably better share a few things himself. "Jessica is exactly like Carmen. She takes charge of things and orders people around. After my dad died she took over. Everything..." He trailed off, swallowing hard.

"I'm sorry about your dad, Sam."

He looked at her, deciding if he should go on. He wanted to. Which never happened. Then he decided that if anyone would understand the pain it would be this woman. "He was shot."

"Oh!" Her eyes were wide. "That's horrible."

"It was," Sam agreed. "Jessica was living in a rough neighborhood. He went over there every day to check on her. One day he got there in time to interrupt a burglary. They shot him and left him lying on her doorstep. He was still alive when Jess got home, but he never regained consciousness."

Danika was staring at him with her hand over her mouth. "How old were you?" she whispered.

"Fifteen."

"Oh, Sam."

"Yeah, it sucked."

"What about your mom?"

"She left when I was five."

"Left?"

"Walked out. Never came back. I remember her, but not well."

"She *left*?" Danika sounded outraged and was now sitting tall. "How? Why?"

Sam felt he corner of his mouth kick up at her obvious indignation. "She wasn't cut out to be a mom."

"But she *was* a mom. That's not something you just undo."

He shrugged. He knew that his mother's abandonment had helped form him as a person, but it bothered him more to talk about his dad than his mom. "You have to understand my dad, I think. He was intense. He had beliefs and he stood by them, put his whole self into them."

"Like the youth center?"

"Right."

"I would think she would have been impressed by that," Danika said.

"It wasn't that easy. Dad was a lawyer and made good money in spite of taking lots of pro bono cases. But he insisted on keeping only what we needed. We had nothing in excess. No TV, no video games, only one car, no vacations, things like that. He knew that there were a lot of people out there who were struggling and he didn't feel right living extravagantly."

"You didn't even have a TV?" Danika asked. "Seriously?"

Sam chuckled. "Seriously. I watched TV at friends' houses, of course, but I didn't have one until Jessica got custody of me and Sara."

"That is true commitment to a cause," she said, with a frown.

"He gave all his extra money away," Sam said feeling the familiar mix of pride and frustration when he thought of his father's lifestyle choices.

"And your mom wanted more?" Danika guessed.

Sam shrugged. "It was more complicated than that. She was a project of his as well."

"A project?"

"She was a runaway when he met her. She was eight years younger than him and he took her under his wing, tried to help her straighten out her life. She saw him as her savior for a long time, but he did everything he could to mold her into the lifestyle he'd always envisioned—kids, stay-home wife, who would work alongside him on his charities. She was unsatisfied. So he talked her into having Jessica. That was okay for a while, but she got restless again. So I came along. Then Sara. It just got to be too much, and none of it was what she chose."

"Your dad told you all of this?" Danika was frowning again.

"No. Our aunt. Dad's sister. But not until after he'd died. Anyway." Sam shifted. "I guess I can relate to having a less-than-perfect childhood."

Danika met his eyes. "I guess so."

"I've never told anyone any of that." Sam wasn't sure why he said that out loud. But it was true. Ben was the only one of his friends who knew the story and that was because Jessica shared it with him. Sam had certainly never told a woman. Of course, he rarely spent time with women that lent itself to talking, not to mention talking about their childhoods.

"I'm glad you told me," Danika said simply.

She didn't say it especially sympathetically, or like she was reading anything into it. She just seemed to sincerely mean that she was glad to know his story.

She turned her attention back to the box in front of her. "Oh my gosh!" She pulled out an aged VCR tape. "This was my mom's favorite movie. We watched it all the time together."

He glanced at the cover. *Groundhog Day*, with Bill Murray.

He chuckled. "I haven't seen that in years."

She nodded staring down at the tape. "We'd watch it and then talk about days that we'd had that we'd like to live over and over."

"Let's watch it," Sam said, setting the picture of Danika and her sisters on the coffee table.

She looked up excitedly. "You'd watch with me?"

"Yes. And then I'd love to hear about some of the days that you'd like to live over and over." He stretched to his feet, prepared to move to the sofa.

"This one."

Her words stopped him and he turned slowly. He looked at her for a long time as the word *yes* raced through his head like the running digital numbers at the stock market.

"I'm pretty fond of this one too."

He wanted to make love to her again. Just like that, he wanted her. Not that he thought the desire had gone away, but all at once it was different, stronger somehow, and almost *more*. Like it had become a necessity versus just a longing.

She seemed to read something in his face, because she rose and laid the tape on the coffee table next to the photo.

"Maybe we'll watch it later."

She pulled her shirt off and reached for his.

"I'll do mine. Keep going," he said, pointing at her jeans as he stripped his shirt off and unzipped his pants.

Within seconds they were naked. She sat on the couch, then lay back while he shoved the coffee table out of the way and knelt beside her, bracing one hand beside her hip.

Sam stroked his hand from her ankle to her knee and down again. "Definitely this one."

He looked at her, proudly displayed before him, confident in her body and his response to her, confident that he wanted her.

All at once, she sat up, leaned over, took his erection in her hand and stroked up and down. Sam thought he was going to die, letting go with a deep, long groan.

His hand went to hers and stopped the motion before his head blew off.

"Am I doing something wrong?" she asked, blinking up innocently.

He didn't buy that for a second. "Um, no." He cleared his throat. "I just wasn't expecting it to...feel...like that."

"No one's ever done this before?"

"It's never been this good." He didn't even have to try to make it sound heartfelt.

"Really?"

His hold on her hand didn't lessen, so instead of stroking, she squeezed gently.

A long breath hissed out between his teeth. "Yeah."

"That's interesting," she said with another squeeze. "How could it be that different?"

Sam's hand dropped limply away from hers and his head dropped forward.

She stroked base to tip and back. "I mean, it's just a hand. How could it—"

"Danika," he interrupted.

"Hmm?" she looked up.

"I can think of something better for your mouth to be doing than arguing with me about this being the best hand job I've ever had."

She grinned, obviously feeling a little surge of feminine power. If she only knew the things he was willing to give her if she kept going.

"You want me to sing?" she asked.

He looked down at her, smiling up impishly at him even as she kept her hand firmly around him.

"*No*, I don't want you to sing."

"Knock-knock jokes?"

"No."

"Whistling?"

Before he could answer she shifted forward and took the tip of him in her mouth.

"*Dani.*"

His hand cupped the back of her head, urging her forward. Not that she needed urging.

She sucked slightly, then took him more fully into her mouth. She lifted her head, swirled her tongue around the tip, and then sucked again.

Nope. He wasn't going to make it. "Okay." He pulled her up and swung her leg over his thighs as he turned so she sat straddling him. His mouth was on her breasts, her nipples, her neck, her shoulders, and back to her breasts. "Dani, Dani," he chanted softly, over and over.

She reached for his jeans that were on the floor in front of the couch and found the condoms in his pocket. There were four left.

She quickly opened one and rolled it into place, then lifted her hips and sank back down, taking him deep.

They both groaned.

He paused, absorbing the feel of her. The position allowed a deeper penetration and it seemed that Danika was content to stay right there. But that wasn't going to happen. His hands went to her hips and started moving her on him. Not that she seemed inclined to quarrel about it. He guided her in a rhythm that quickly, surprisingly, built the heat and the longing. They were moving toward something that stayed just out of reach, building momentum, until at the end they were rushing forward, their breaths and sighs and movements perfectly aligned.

And then they were there at the sweet moment when every sense was engaged and every synapse was firing. Sensations and impressions poured into his mind and heat and fulfillment spread throughout his body.

A moment later Danika slumped against him. Sam's hands spread wide on her low back and he rubbed up and down the bumps of her spine.

It seemed apparent to him what he needed to do— absolutely nothing but hold the woman he was very likely already in love with.

Chapter Ten

They watched the movie, dressed, but lying on the couch, spooning.

"I've never done this before," she told him.

"What?"

"Watched a movie with a guy on a couch."

She thought for sure he'd tease her. Instead, he surprised her by saying, "I've never done this either. With a woman...or a man," he added with a chuckle.

She snuggled in closer, thinking that it wasn't fair for this to feel so good and be something she'd never be able to do again.

Sam didn't want to keep doing stuff like this and she knew from here on out she wouldn't be doing much of anything with other men simply because they would never measure up to Sam Bradford.

Pitiful. But true.

She felt the vibration of his cell phone against her left buttock where it was tucked in his left front pocket.

"Damn." He shifted to slide it out. "Yeah?" he answered a second later.

Danika reached to pause the movie and when she rolled too far away for his taste, Sam tightened his arm around her. Gladly, she sank back into the warmth of his embrace.

"No, I'm still at Dani's."

Another pause as he listened.

"Oh, sorry. Yeah."

Pause.

"I'll go right now."

He flipped his phone shut.

"What's up?" she asked, moving so he could sit up.

"That was Kevin. I totally forgot I was going to touch up the paint around the front windows when we were there Thursday. I told Kevin I was going to do it today."

"Is there a problem?"

"Kevin just assumed that I'd gotten...distracted." Sam leaned over and kissed her shoulder. "He offered to go if I can't make it. But I should be the one."

"Absolutely. Let's go." Danika ran her fingers through her hair.

"I feel bad that I blew this off."

She stopped him and put a hand against his cheek. "You were here because of my wrist. You can't be in two places at once and this doesn't mean that you aren't responsible."

He smiled at her. "I forgot because I was having incredible sex with an amazing woman. That's not as innocent as forgetting because I was nursing someone back to health."

"It still doesn't mean you're a bad person, Sam. You're a little late. You still care about her and you'll still take care of her house."

He grabbed her hand and pulled her in close for a kiss. "Okay. Thank you." Then he kissed her again, longer and sweeter. "It won't take long," he said when he lifted his head.

"Give me one minute," she told him, heading for the bedroom for her shoes.

"You're coming?" he sounded surprised.

"I thought so," she called from the other room.

He had no ready answer for that.

She came back into the living room and leaned against the wall to slip her shoes on. "Is it okay?" She wondered if Sam realized how involved all of this had gotten. She'd met his friends, spent time with them in her house today and now he'd had sex with her twice. Was he starting to see that this wasn't as simple as he liked to keep things, and worse, was he regretting it?

"Of course, it's great if you come along." He seemed sincere. "I'm just surprised that you want to."

She hadn't thought about it. It was something Sam was going to do and she naturally wanted to go along. Should she be concerned about the wanting to be with him all the time?

"I want to," she assured him, shoving the questions to the back of her mind for later.

Seventeen minutes later, they pulled up in front of Natalia's house.

"Her garage is open and the car's here," Sam commented almost to himself as he stopped the car along the curb.

"Maybe she's still home," Danika suggested. "Should we wait?"

"No, we have to check it out." Sam was frowning at the garage as if the building had insulted him. "If she's gone, the garage door should be down. This isn't safe."

"Do you want me to go up to the front door and see if she's home?" Danika asked. "She doesn't know me. I can pretend I'm taking a survey or something."

Sam shook his head. "Even if she is home, the garage door should be down."

"We can mention that if we talk to her." Danika rolled her eyes. "Should I see if she's home?"

Sam shrugged. "It doesn't matter. She doesn't know me either."

"She doesn't even know you?"

"Nope."

"How exactly did you get started doing this?"

"We picked one of the other ladies, Katherine, up in the ambulance one night with chest pains. The other three were there with her. Every minute. I overheard them talking and realized what good friends they were and that Katherine, at least, lived alone and wouldn't be able to take care of things on her own for a while. They were debating how much help they would be able to be. The idea formed." He shrugged. "We started by showing up at Katherine's place with a new alarm system that we told her she had qualified for through a program for older women living alone."

"You made this program for older women up?" Danika asked.

He nodded. "We thought about telling her she'd won it in a contest, but we wanted to do the same thing for the other women who were alone and convincing them that they had all won a contest seemed like a stretch. Instead we asked

Katherine for the names of three friends who could also benefit from a system and she, of course, gave us Barb, Dorothy and Natalia's names."

"You guys are very clever."

"We find a way of doing what needs done. We installed the system for her safety but made a point of choosing the code for it so we could get in any time to take care of the house. We took care of just her at first, but..." He frowned and paused. "I guess I don't know how we found out about the card game every Thursday."

"So Natalia's never met you?" Danika asked, amazed by the story.

"They all met us in the ambulance, but they were pretty upset and didn't register our faces or even ask our names. Then she met me briefly when we came to install the alarm system. But no, she doesn't know who I am or that I come to her house."

"I think that's too bad," Danika said. "She should know how sweet and generous you are."

He shook his head. "No. It's better this way. Easier. I get to feel good about helping her, but I don't have to feel bad about not visiting or forgetting her birthday or anything."

Danika huffed out a frustrated breath. It didn't even occur to Sam that maybe he would like to visit or that Natalia's birthday would...a thought came to mind and she asked him, "When is Natalia's birthday, Sam?"

"August first," he answered. Then he glanced at her.

She was looking at him with raised eyebrows.

"I suppose you think that it's significant that I know when her birthday is?"

"Oh, not at all," she replied. "I also don't think it's significant that she gets a bouquet of flowers from a secret admirer on her birthday. And I don't think it's significant that there's a 'free' extravagant dessert for her at whatever restaurant she and the girls choose for the celebration."

Sam didn't argue, or deny. He just glared at her. "Come on, let's see what's going on."

Danika laughed as she got out and followed him up Natalia's driveway. She'd gotten pretty darned close with those guesses. She knew him. He was a good guy who was sweet and generous and caring.

"Maybe she forgot something inside and is coming back out," Sam said as he approached. "If she sees us, we'll pretend to be appreciating her landscaping."

"Got it," Danika said dutifully, knowing that Sam had likely done the landscaping. She wondered if Natalia thought she'd qualified for free landscaping, too, or if the beautiful bushes, flowers and stones just naturally appeared around her house one weekend. Danika guessed the older woman was brighter than that.

"I'll...um...go...take a look in the back kitchen window," Sam said.

Danika smirked. Sam had no idea what he was doing. But it was sweet that he was here and hadn't just left when he'd seen that Natalia's car was still here.

"I don't think she's here," he said a moment later.

"How can you tell?"

"I can see her answering machine on the counter. She has three messages. She would have listened to them if she was here, right?" He sounded like he had no idea one way or the other.

"Should we go in?"

"I guess."

They had just started toward the door into the house through the garage when a car pulled into the driveway. Danika glanced at Sam and found him looking panicked. But there was no escape now. The people in the car had to have seen them and running would certainly look suspicious.

Two older women got out of the car and started toward the house.

"Oh, hell," Sam muttered.

Another glace at his face showed him looking at the two women, easily in the their mid-seventies, as if they were terrorists come to torture government secrets out of them.

"Hello," the one who had been driving greeted them. "Can I help you?"

"We're um..." Sam started.

Danika took control. "We were admiring the landscaping here and wanted to ask the owner who had done it."

Sam half choked, half coughed behind her.

She ignored him and continued. "We saw the car was here,

but no one answered the front door and we were concerned."

The other woman, who had been in the passenger seat of the car, smiled, but her eyes filled with tears. "That's sweet. But no, no one is home."

"Oh, then we'll just be going," Sam said, grabbing Danika's elbow and dragging her toward the driveway.

Danika dug her heels in and turned back toward the women. "I hope everything is okay." The woman was crying, and there had to be a reason.

"No." The woman sniffed and dabbed her eyes with a tissue that looked to have been used for the same thing repeatedly already. "Everything is not okay."

The driver patted her friend's arm. "We're here to get some of our friend's things. She's in the hospital."

Danika felt Sam tense beside her, but she didn't look at him. His grip on her elbow tightened, but he made no move to walk away now.

"Oh. I'm so sorry. Is it something serious?" These woman had to be two of the four that Sam helped take care of. They obviously didn't know who he was, but he had recognized them. She wanted to find out as much information about Natalia for him as she could without tipping them off. While she thought he should tell them who he was, he had chosen not to and she couldn't ruin that for him.

"A stroke," the driver, the more composed of the two said. "I'm afraid it's quite serious."

"They don't know if she'll wake up," the passenger said.

The woman started truly crying versus just letting tears run over her cheeks and Danika had to hold herself back from reaching out to her. Instead, she turned her attention to another person who needed comforting. She slipped her arm from Sam's grip and instead took his hand in hers, squeezing.

"It doesn't look good," the other woman said, putting her arm around her friend's shoulders. "But we're praying and hoping."

"We will be too," Danika said softly. Then she turned to Sam. "We should go," she whispered.

He was watching the two women let themselves into Natalia's house. She could feel him holding himself back from following them. He wanted to do something. She could sense that.

"Come on, Sam."

They walked back to the car silently. Sam pulled his car keys from his pocket but didn't protest when Danika took them from him and got in the driver's seat.

She didn't pull the car away from the curb right away. She turned to face him. "You okay?"

"No."

"What do you want to do?"

"Go home, I guess." He stared out the front windshield.

"I know what you're going to say, but I think you should go to the hospital."

"Why?"

"To see Natalia."

"What difference would it make?"

Danika frowned at him, even though he wasn't looking at her. "What do you mean?"

"Even if she wakes up, which doesn't sound likely, she won't know me." He sounded and looked defeated and Danika wanted to hug him.

"Then tell her who you are," Danika said. "Now's a good time."

"No." He frowned at the pavement in front of the car. "It won't matter."

Danika sat and let her thoughts turn. Then she said, "You should tell the other women."

"No."

"Sam, come on. They'd love to know that you've been there for her. They'd love to know who you are."

"Danika, I'm *not* doing that. What's the point?"

"They love her. They're hurting. It would make them feel good that someone else cares about her."

"The point was to avoid getting involved and caring..." he mumbled.

She sighed. "Sam, you don't have to talk to someone every day or even know their middle name to *care* about them. Sometimes that just happens. I'm guessing you got to know Natalia pretty well being in her house once a week."

He didn't reply.

"Tell me three things you know about her that most people who spend time with her probably don't know. Maybe something her friends don't even know."

He shook his head.

"Tell me, Sam."

He sighed. "She likes tater tots. She buys like five bags at a time."

Danika smiled. "What else?"

"Her great granddaughter's middle name is Natalia, after her."

"How do you know that?" She assumed he knew about the tater tots because he'd checked to be sure her fridge and freezer were working.

"She had the birth announcement hanging on her fridge for a long time. Then she framed it and hung it in her bedroom."

Danika liked that he'd been paying attention. He didn't want Natalia to know she had a guardian angel, but he was doing a great job of it.

"One more thing," she prompted.

"She's allergic to poppy seeds."

Danika chuckled. "How do you know *that?*"

He smiled. "She had antihistamines on the countertop for the first time in all the months that I'd been going to her house. Then beside her chair in the living room she had several pages printed off the Internet about allergies and she had highlighted and circled poppy seeds on every page that mentioned it."

"You could be a detective," Danika said. "Wow."

He shrugged. "I was in her house once a week for over a year. You're right, you get to know someone that way."

Danika let those words linger in the air for several moments. Then said, "You should go to the hospital."

"I have to tell the guys." He reached for his phone and hit a number on his speed dial.

Danika put the car into drive and pulled away as he called, not wanting Natalia's friends to find them still sitting there without a good reason. Or at least, without a reason that Sam would share with them.

"Kevin, it's me," Sam said a moment later. "Natalia's in the hospital."

"I know. I just got here."

"Where?"

"The hospital," Kevin answered. "Are you coming?"

"Why are you at the hospital?" Sam asked.

"To see Natalia. And Katherine and Dorothy and Barb."

"What do you mean "to see" them? And Katherine and Barb are over here at Natalia's getting her stuff."

"Did you talk to them?" Kevin acted genuinely surprised.

"Well, yeah."

"Did you tell them who you are?"

"Of course not."

"Oh." Now his friend sounded disappointed. "Why not?"

"Why would I? What would that help?"

"I just thought...forget it," Kevin said. "Are you coming over?"

"I don't think so."

"Mac and Dooley are here."

"How'd they know about it?"

Kevin took a deep breath and Sam braced himself. For what, he wasn't sure, but he definitely got the impression that Kevin was hesitant to tell him whatever it was and that probably meant that Sam wasn't going to like it.

"Katherine called Dooley and he called Mac, who called Dorothy to be see if she was okay, but she was already down here so he came down to be with her."

Sam processed that one long sentence slowly. "Katherine called Dooley?" he finally repeated, picking *something* to start with when he wanted an explanation on the whole blessed thing.

"Right."

"How...why... How did she know to call him... How did she have his number?" Sam demanded.

Kevin sighed. "There's something you should know and I suppose this is the best time for it to come out."

Oh, crap. "I don't want to hear this, do I?" he asked his friend.

"Probably not," Kevin admitted. "The thing is...the ladies have known about us for about six months now."

"What?" Sam demanded. "Why?"

"Barb caught me at her house one day. I told her what I was doing, but I only gave myself up. Then Dooley and Mac wanted Dorothy and Katherine to know, too, so they confessed. We've still been going to their houses to check on them, but we don't necessarily go just when they're gone."

"What about Nat-Natalia?" Sam asked, tripping over her name.

"She knows that one of us comes over to her house, too, but we didn't tell her, or the other ladies, about you. We knew it was important to you to keep that secret."

Sam didn't know what to think, or feel, about the revelation. "I've got to go."

"You coming down here?" Kevin asked.

"No." Sam disconnected before Kevin could ask him more, or make him feel guilty. Guilti*er*.

Sam scrubbed his hand over his face feeling agitated and exhausted at the same time.

Would she be okay? If so, could he go back to how things were, him just showing up once a week when she wasn't home? He had a nearly overwhelming urge to storm into the hospital and demand to know what was going on. He also wanted to hug Natalia. And tell her that he cared and wanted her to be okay.

If she wasn't okay...

He shut down that train of thought before it could go any further.

Danika, bless her, didn't try to talk to him any more. She probably knew that he was replaying all of her words about going to the hospital even without her repeating it out loud.

She was right. He'd gotten to know Natalia quite well now that he was thinking about it. The allergic to poppy seeds thing hadn't registered until Dani asked him about it, for instance. Sam leaned his head back against the headrest and let his mind wander over Natalia's house, over her life, or at least the snapshot of it he'd been given.

She drank coffee out of the same cup every day. He'd been there on almost every day of the week at some point and that cup was always the one sitting next to the sink with the millimeter of coffee left in the bottom. There were others in the cupboard of course, but that was the one she used. He assumed there was some significance to that, and now he was curious about the story behind that cup.

Other things started coming to mind quickly, as if he'd let the plug out of the dam he'd put on the realizations and...okay, *emotions*, he had about Natalia.

She watched CBS most often. When he turned on the TV to check it, no matter what day or time he was there, it was always on CBS. From her refrigerator and the cards and letters on her kitchen counter he knew that she had fifteen grandchildren and three great grandchildren. Her oldest son lived in Tennessee. She saved pennies in an old-fashioned milk bottle on her dresser, collected thimbles that were displayed in a shadow box in her living room and she'd read the entire series *The Chronicles of Narnia* in the past year. That was an easier one though. She'd had the books on the table next to her chair each week.

Sam felt his throat thicken. He supposed in many ways the look into Natalia's life that he'd been given was more accurately who she was than most, or any, other people in her life saw. After all, when was anyone more themselves than when they were alone at home? Even when a person had guests over they cleaned and tidied. She wouldn't have left her favorite coffee cup or books lying around if she'd known he was coming over.

"You okay?"

Dani's soft question opened his eyes. They were parked in front of her building.

Was he okay?

He was confused. Worried too. And sad. Even if Natalia survived the stroke, there was a chance there would be long-term impairments. She might not be able to go home and live alone anymore. If someone moved in with her, she wouldn't need him checking on things. If she lived somewhere else, it would likely be an assisted living apartment, or even a nursing facility. Again, she wouldn't need him anymore.

"No," he said hoarsely. "I'm not okay."

"What can I do?"

He rolled his head to look at her. Danika. He was glad she was there.

That didn't make sense either.

Except in the context of what he already feared—he was falling for her.

"Let me come upstairs."

She nodded. She didn't seem surprised or confused about his request. It seemed to be what she'd expected.

"Let me stay all night." He'd never asked that. He'd never wanted to. But now he wanted nothing more. "In your bed."

"Of course," she said simply.

They didn't say a word as they climbed the steps and Danika opened the door. As soon as it closed behind them, she turned. She tossed the keys on the table and leaned around him to lock the door. Then she wrapped her arms around his neck and pulled him close for the kiss he needed desperately.

He held her against him with his palms wide on her hips, devouring her lips, drinking her in, loving the feel of her in his arms. Living, breathing, wanting him with her, in her home.

Both her hands were on his head, and the fingers of her unrestricted hand curled into his hair, while he considered taking her up against the wall in her foyer, or on top of the new flooring his friends had helped lay. Instead, he dipped his knees and swung her up into his arms. She didn't stop kissing him for even a second.

They made it to the bedroom, to an actual mattress, finally. He let her feet touch the floor and she immediately moved to lie back on the bed. He followed her down. They didn't need words, there was no rushing, it was like they each knew just what the other wanted and needed. Their lips met, their hands roamed, discarding clothing until there was only skin and they came together slowly and sweetly.

It lasted longer than the other times and when he climaxed, Sam knew that in spite of all the experience and the reputation, he had only just now made love to a woman.

"We need chicken."

Danika opened one eye and saw that it was eight-seventeen in the morning. She'd slept like a log. In between bouts of making love with Sam. It seemed that every two to three hours he'd need her again. He'd reach for her and she always went. It was like it was a need for him rather that just physical desire. There was something Sam was looking for and he seemed to think that she could give it.

There had been no real talking. There had been some sexy comments that fired her blood, some sweet murmurings that made her heart beat even faster and some moans and sighs that made her feel a surge of power that was growing addictive.

But he hadn't opened up about how he was feeling about Natalia or her hospitalization, or anything besides how much he wanted her.

"Fried chicken. Lots of it."

She rolled to her back and squinted at him. "You're kidding, right?"

He grinned at her from the foot of the bed. He was fully clothed. "Nope. Fried chicken. Right now."

"You want me to make you fried chicken at eight o'clock in the morning?" She wasn't even sure she knew how to make fried chicken.

"No, no." He reached for the sheet covering her and started pulling it down her body. "We'll buy it."

She grabbed for the sheet, but he was too quick. He swept it off of her and the bed, his eyes lingering with appreciation on her now uncovered, naked body. She blushed, but didn't try to hide.

"Buy it where?" she asked, swinging her legs over the side of the bed to sit up.

"Buy what?"

She looked over her shoulder to find his eyes studying the profile of her breast.

"The chicken."

"What chicken?"

She laughed and grabbed the T-shirt lying on the floor, holding it against her chest. He blinked and looked up at her. "The chicken you claim we need to have," she said.

He made a production of blinking and searching his mind for the recent memory. Then he grinned. "We'll get it at George's."

"George?" she asked.

"You're too talkative in the morning." He pushed her, literally, in the direction of the bathroom. "I just called George. By the time you've showered, he'll have it ready. We'll get the chicken and go up."

"Up where?" she asked, just before the door slammed behind her, enclosing her in the bathroom.

"To the hospital," he said through the door. "They've been there all night and Mac and Dooley love fried chicken."

She opened her mouth to tell him that fried chicken before

ten a.m. was impossible, but she couldn't make the words to discourage him. It was sweet that he wanted to feed his friends and it was wonderful that he wanted to go up to the hospital.

George turned out to be the owner of the appropriately named *George's Chicken*, a small, open-late restaurant that Sam and his ambulance crew frequented after their late shifts. Apparently George didn't do much beyond chicken and some potato salad and baked beans, but he didn't need to. He was famous for the battered, deep-fried chicken he served for cheap prices. In fact, to hear Sam tell it, Danika was the only hospital employee who *didn't* know about George and his chicken.

George met them at the door with a huge cardboard box filled with Styrofoam containers of chicken, potatoes and beans. He'd even put several cold cans of soda in. He'd gone down and cooked just for Sam and his friends and Danika liked him simply because of that.

A few minutes later they stepped off the elevator on the fourth floor where Natalia had been admitted. The waiting room was full of big guys and little ladies. Dooley was slumped in the corner of a sofa, his head back, still snoring softly. Mac was sitting in a deep chair, feet on the coffee table, watching the *Today Show*. Kevin was reading in another chair in the corner. The ladies, Katherine, Dorothy and Barb, were seated around one of the small round tables, sipping coffee. The room was filled with only the sound of Matt Lauer and Meredith Vieira bantering with a chef who was showing them something spectacular—according to Meredith anyway—to do with tomatoes. No one was talking. In fact, they all looked exhausted. And worried.

"Hey, keep it down up here," Sam said.

Everyone turned to look at once. They all looked slightly stunned. Whether it was the lack of sleep, the fried chicken as breakfast food, or that Sam was there, Danika couldn't tell.

Mac got to his feet first. "Hey, Sam. Dani."

She didn't mind that Mac called her Dani for some reason. Maybe because it was meant affectionately, because she was a part of the group, because she was with Sam.

"George got up early just for you all," Sam said, setting the box in the middle of the table.

The guys descended on the box, but there was plenty for everyone and Danika was surprised to see even the women

215

partaking of chicken. They declared it delicious and confessed that they hadn't eaten for hours.

It was several long minutes before it happened.

Katherine looked up to thank Sam, and frowned. "Aren't you the man who was at Natalia's house yesterday when we stopped for her things?"

Sam struggled to swallow his bite of food, while his friends all turned to look at him. None of them said a word, however. In fact, they continued chewing, clearly not trying to think of a way to help Sam out.

Danika hated the look on Sam's face. He looked panicked.

A guy like Sam never panicked. He knew what he was doing all the time. He was a born charmer with women, a paramedic who didn't even blink when he saw a human body with it's vital organs exposed, a guy who went out of his way to help an older, widowed woman keep her house going.

"Yes, he is," she said for him. "His friends had mentioned her house to us and as we said, we wanted to look at her landscaping."

His friends simply switched their attention from Sam to Danika to Sam. Katherine looked puzzled. "Why didn't you mention that you knew these boys?"

"We didn't know that you knew them," Danika said.

"Oh. I suppose I just assumed they would have mentioned all of us if they spoke about Natalia," Katherine said.

That earned Danika a frown from Dooley, Katherine's self-appointed guardian angel.

Finally Sam sighed. "We weren't there for the landscaping."

Danika slumped back in relief. He wasn't going to let Katherine have her feelings hurt by the thought that Dooley hadn't mentioned her.

"I'm the one who's been taking care of Natalia's house," he confessed. "Like Dooley's been looking out for you."

Katherine was obviously surprised. "You did this too?"

"It was actually his idea," Kevin finally spoke up. "He wanted it to be anonymous though, so we never told you his name."

"But..." Katherine looked around the table.

The other women were just as befuddled, it seemed. "Why..." Dorothy said, without finishing the thought.

"You should have told her," Barb said.

Sam shook his head. "I didn't need for her to know my name. I just liked helping her out."

"But she...she knew someone came in and helped out, and she wanted to know who it was. I told her how Doug and I would sit and have coffee together when he came over and she was so envious," Katherine said.

"I told her that Mac likes my homemade cinnamon rolls," Dorothy added. "She asked me if it was Mac that came to her house and if so what she could bake for him. Since I didn't know who it was, I couldn't tell her. That bothered her."

"She makes fantastic banana bread," Katherine said and all the women nodded.

"And when I told her that I'd given Kevin one of my late husband's favorite novels, she wanted so much to give something special to whoever came to her house too," Barb said.

Danika wanted to hug someone. She wasn't sure if it was one of the ladies, or all of them, or one of these men who had become such important people to these sweet women and allowed them to dote on them. She suspected that the things the women did for them were better for the women than they even were for the guys. But she was pretty sure that the person she wanted to hug most was Sam.

"I just..."

She held her breath, praying that he wouldn't say something like *I didn't tell her who I was because I didn't want to have coffee with her or get gifts from her.*

But he said simply, "I just wanted to help her."

Katherine nodded and covered her plate with her napkin. "I know, honey. And you did." She sounded sad though.

"It's just that, when you live alone in a house that used to have people and noise and conversation, it's so quiet sometimes," Barb commented.

"And when you used to cook for a family and now you don't have that chance, it's nice to do that once in awhile," Dorothy added.

Sam looked miserable.

Kevin rubbed a hand over Barb's shoulder and Dooley smiled at Katherine affectionately.

"Have you ever seen her map collection?" Barb asked Sam. He shook his head and she smiled. "It's...impressive."

"She has nearly one hundred maps," Dorothy said. "She's collected them from all of the places she's ever been."

"Wow." Danika said, interested. "She traveled that much?"

Dorothy smiled. "Some of the maps are of things like zoos or museums. But yes, she's been a number of places and always kept the maps."

"Wow."

"She's been to Disney World five times," Barb said.

"That's the one in California or Florida?" Katherine asked.

"California."

"Florida."

Barb and Dorothy looked at each other and laughed.

"Florida," Sam confirmed.

Danika looked at him, trying to gauge his mood.

"She loves Disney stuff," Barb went on.

Sam looked...constipated. That was the best description. He looked incredibly uncomfortable but unable to make an excuse for leaving.

"But not as much as she loves Nebraska Husker football," Katherine said.

Sam's head came up. "She likes football?"

Katherine shook her head with a smile. "Not football in general. Only college football and only Big Twelve. She's a die-hard Husker fan. Has been her whole life."

Now there was a very strange tension radiating from Sam. Danika wanted to touch his arm, but he seemed so wound up she was afraid he'd jump out of his chair.

"I, um. I..." He shoved back from the table, making the Styrofoam coffee cups wobble dangerously. "I'm going to go for a walk."

Everyone stared at him as he stalked toward the hallway. At the edge of the waiting room, he stopped. He turned back, looking right at Danika. "Are you coming?"

She scrambled—rather ungracefully—to her feet, once again threatening the contents of the coffee cups. "Of course."

Once she was at his side, he took her hand, and they started down the hall. They'd gone about a hundred feet when she said, "Where are we going?"

"Away from the waiting room."

"Mission accomplished," she muttered.

He stopped and turned to face her, dropping her hand and shoving his fingers through his hair. "Why doesn't she have any Disney stuff in her house?"

Danika stared at him. "What?"

"Natalia supposedly loves Disney. She's been there five times. I've never seen a single mouse ear in her house."

Danika had the impression she needed to tread softly. "I don't know. Maybe she had it in a box in the attic or something."

"No," he said firmly. "If someone likes something so much, they have evidence of it around."

He had a point. It was also, apparently, an important one.

"And I love Husker football."

"That's required for being a citizen of the state of Nebraska isn't it?" she joked.

"No, I mean I *love* it."

"That's—"

"I didn't see any Husker memorabilia in her house either."

Finally Danika held a hand up to stop him. "I can see you're agitated about this. But I don't understand why you care so much how Natalia decorated her house."

"I just..." He scratched the back of his head. "I thought I knew her."

She had no idea what to say to that.

"I've been in her house once a week, or more, for the past year. I know her favorite TV show, what she reads, her favorite snack foods."

"Of course you do," Danika said. "You know a lot about her."

"No," he denied. "I know some things. But not a lot."

She got it. Sam cared about Natalia. Danika had known it, of course. Sam was a good-hearted guy. Of course he would come to care about the woman he had taken care of for so long. But he *cared* about Natalia and though he hadn't sat in that waiting room all night long, he was scared he was going to lose her.

"I think you should go in and see her."

He shook his head immediately. "No."

"Why not?"

"What good would that do? She's unconscious. And she doesn't know me. She doesn't know my voice."

"That doesn't matter," Danika said. "Having someone hold your hand and tell you they care about you is a good thing no matter what."

"What would I say?"

She crossed her arms. "You're really not going in there?"

"I came up here today for the guys. And girls. They needed to eat."

"The food is great. Very considerate. But it's possible they need more than chicken."

"I don't suppose you mean I should go get dessert?"

"No."

He sighed. "I didn't think so."

"They need to talk about Natalia. And frankly I think you should hear it."

He rolled his neck and she heard the cracking from where she stood. "I don't know."

"Sam, you can't have it both ways!" she finally exclaimed. "You can't want to know all about her and not want to go into her room at the hospital or talk to her best friends about her."

He frowned at her. "Talking with them makes me feel bad."

She frowned back. "They are three very sweet women who care about their friend who is lying in a hospital bed. How can they make you feel bad?"

"I feel guilty!" he shot back. "I've been changing her damned light bulbs for over a year, but when she got sick I wasn't there. The *paramedic* made sure that her toilet flushed, but wasn't there when she had a medical emergency."

"You can't blame yourself for this," she said, disbelieving what she was hearing. "How could you have possibly known that she needed help? No one expects you to be there all the time, at exactly the perfect moment."

"Exactly! I don't want anyone expecting anything, because of stuff like this!" He grit his teeth and pulled a deep breath through his nose. "No one is blaming me, no one is expecting a thing from me."

"But you want them to," she said quietly. "You want to be a part of this."

"I can't help that I care about her, Danika," he exclaimed. "I didn't want to. I *don't* want to. But here I am."

He was driving her crazy. "Oh, shut up already!"

That made him stop and blink at her. "What?"

"Shut up. Quit feeling sorry for yourself. Quit making this about you."

She didn't blame him for staring now. That was harsh. But still, something had to snap him out of this pity party.

"Are you yelling at me?" he asked, stunned. "While Natalia's here, in the hospital, unconscious and I'm feeling horrible...you're yelling at me?"

Danika frowned and rocked back on her heels, crossing her arms. "Yeah, I guess I am."

"Wow," he muttered. "That isn't very supportive."

Danika snorted. "I'm supposed to be supportive of you falling apart when Natalia needs you?"

"I'm not falling apart."

"You were."

He scowled at her. "Like I said, not supportive. At all."

"You need someone to support you?" she asked.

"Maybe."

"And you want it to be me?"

"Maybe."

"Fine. I'll support you."

He looked suspicious. "And?"

"I'll support you while you go in and talk to Natalia."

He said nothing for several seconds. Then, "You're going with me."

He felt like he was five years old and approaching the door to his kindergarten room on the first day of school. He had held on tight to someone's hand that day too.

"It's going to be fine," Danika whispered, squeezing his hand.

It was stupid, but he did feel better when she did that.

"What do I say?"

She shrugged. "Talk to her about the 1997 National Championship."

He looked at her, a smile, surprisingly, stretching his mouth. "You know about Nebraska's '97 National Championship?"

"And the '94 and '95 Championships," she said smugly. "But Eric Crouch is my favorite quarterback."

"You like football?"

"Of course. I was born and raised in Husker Nation." She grinned.

They both sobered a moment later as they stepped into room four twenty-two. Natalia's room was bright and sunny, but the woman lying in the bed was pale and hooked up to monitors and machines. Her eyes were closed, her breathing shallow, and it made them forget everything else.

She'd been unconscious since long before the paramedics arrived at her house. She was breathing on her own, but she hadn't awakened.

Sam swallowed. It was worse than he'd expected.

He'd seen Natalia in person only the one time he'd gone to install her security system. Otherwise he, of course, avoided running into her. But he'd seen numerous photos. Natalia was an obviously naturally happy person. She had a great smile. And she wore purple a lot.

She was wearing a pale blue hospital gown now. She'd probably hate the color.

Danika nudged him. He stepped forward. He was never intimidated by hospitals, or medical equipment, the things that were a natural part of his daily work life. Now, though, his heart was pounding and he had to remind himself to breathe.

"I'll bet Natalia thinks Eric Crouch is the best-looking Nebraska quarterback too," Danika said. She stood on the opposite side of the bed so that Natalia lay between them and Sam missed the contact of having her hand in his.

He swallowed and concentrated on what she'd said. "Natalia appreciates Nebraska football for the superior offensive strategy and the kick-ass defensive line," he said.

Danika smiled. "Speaking of the defense, they had some hunks too."

Sam rolled his eyes and felt himself smile, something he didn't think possible inside Natalia's hospital room. "Never mind their record number of All Americans. It's all about the looks, right?"

"All Americans are impressive," Danika conceded. "Not to mention the fact that they have the fourth-most all-time victories of any NCAA division I-A team."

For the next thirty minutes they sat by Natalia's bed and talked football—past players, statistics, coaches, if firing the athletic director in 2007 had been the right thing to do. They agreed that it had been. They included Natalia with questions like, "don't you agree?" and statements such as, "I know Natalia remembers the Matt Davison catch against Missouri in 1997."

Finally, a nurse came in to check Natalia's vital signs and Sam let himself stand and walk away. "I need to get some stuff done," he said.

Danika looked worried. "Are you going to come back?"

"Definitely."

He felt agitated. He needed to do something for Natalia, get something for her. *Something.* Though he had no idea what. Flowers weren't good enough, a teddy bear wasn't right, balloons didn't send the message he wanted. He didn't know exactly what it was, but he thought that once he was in her house he'd find just the right thing to bring, to comfort her and make her smile when she finally woke up.

He'd start by going to her house and making sure her fridge was cleaned out and her plants were watered and her mail and newspaper were brought in. Then maybe he would bring some of her favorite things. She needed the throw blanket she always used in her chair in the living room and a few photos. At least. Her friends had brought personal items like her toothbrush and some clothing items, but she needed some personal effects. Something to make the sterile room more...like home. Like Natalia.

This wasn't right. The first time he spent time with her and she was unconscious and they were here, in this cold room. He couldn't ask her about her special coffee cup, or confess that he liked *ER* reruns too—of which she owned the DVDs for seasons one through six—or talk about her trips and ask about her maps.

He leaned over the bed and placed a kiss against her forehead. "Get better," he whispered.

Danika simply slipped her hand back into his as he came around the end of the bed. It was good that he could do something sappy like kiss Natalia when Danika was there. It was good that she'd made him come in here. It was just good being with her.

"I'll see you later?" he said when they stopped by the elevator.

She seemed startled. "Sure."

"You don't mind do you? I know Mac will give you a ride home. I just have some stuff I need to do."

He couldn't explain it. He liked having Danika with him through this. Loved it in fact. She had made it bearable.

So he had to get some distance. It would be easy to lean on her, to continue to let her lead him through what he should be doing. But he had to know—would he still be a good guy, making the right decisions, if she wasn't by his side?

Because, if not, he was in huge trouble.

He'd have to keep her by his side forever. And that didn't seem likely.

Chapter Eleven

Natalia passed away the next morning. She'd awakened briefly, smiled at her three best friends, looked at the photograph that Sam had brought of all of her children, grandchildren and great grandchildren gathered around her at her last birthday. Then she'd closed her eyes and drifted peacefully back into unconsciousness. Her heart stopped less than a minute later.

Sam wasn't there.

Everyone was glad that it had gone relatively quickly and painlessly for her.

Which Sam thought was stupid.

Natalia was gone. Forever. And they were glad? Of course he knew they didn't mean that they were glad she was gone. But how could any of them be *glad* about anything?

He ignored all nine calls from Danika and got drunk that night. He didn't even go to her duplex. Because he knew that she'd make him feel better and frankly he wanted to feel horrible for a while.

The funeral was on Friday and her family chose to have a wake the evening before the service. It felt very strange to Sam to be walking through the front door versus the garage door, a door that opened to him without the need for the security code that he'd made up for her.

Sam also felt strange going to the wake without Danika. Which was crazy considering that he'd spent twenty-some odd years going lots of places without her and being just fine with it.

Then there was the suit jacket. Sam never dressed up and he'd had to go buy a dark jacket, though he couldn't bring himself to buy or wear a tie.

He was very uncomfortable inside a house that he'd come to be very, well, comfortable in over time. He had been in every corner. He'd cleaned it, fixed it, and checked it. Now he was a guest. Even though the woman they were honoring didn't really know him, and her family certainly didn't.

It was more like he was crashing the wake.

"Hey, Sam."

"Thank God," he muttered as Mac greeted him from the dining room. He smiled at the granddaughter who had handed him the program with Natalia's photo on the front. Inside was her obituary and the address for everyone to send contributions to a local literacy program in lieu of flowers or plants.

He was torn between crumpling it up and framing the front photo.

"Want something to eat?" Kevin asked him as Sam discovered his other friends already there and standing around the buffet, looking as uncomfortable in their suits as he felt. They were all wearing ties, though, which added to the strangeness of the whole thing.

"Sure."

They took a plate of food each and headed to find chairs. They made small talk, which was ridiculous, because they'd never made small talk, ever. Of course, none of them had ever been to a wake. Additionally, none of them really knew the woman the wake was for.

Well, Sam knew her. But no one knew that he knew her.

Finally, his sisters and Ben showed up, which made the small talk a little less small.

"Kevin?" Another granddaughter smiled at his friend.

"Hi, Amanda."

"I just wanted to let you know that Mr. Stearn would like you guys at the church at nine-thirty. Is that okay?"

Kevin glanced at Mac and Dooley, who nodded. "We'll be there," Kevin said.

"Thank you." Amanda smiled and headed back across the room.

"What's up?" Sara asked Mac.

Sam could have kissed her for asking the question he wanted to ask but didn't know how.

Mac glanced at Sam. "We've been asked to be pallbearers

for the funeral tomorrow."

Now everyone glanced at him.

"Oh," Sara said, obviously surprised. "That's...nice. You agreed?"

"It is nice," Mac said. "And yes, we agreed."

Sam wasn't sure how to label the emotion he was feeling. Hurt was probably closest. Even though Dorothy, Barb and Katherine had learned the truth about him taking care of Natalia, they still hadn't asked him to be a part of her service.

Which was fine. He hadn't wanted her to know who he was because he didn't want recognition for what he'd done. He'd taken care of her without needing or wanting anything in return. So, this was fine.

"The ladies had each written out their wishes for their funerals," Kevin said, clearly addressing Sam. "Natalia had asked that we be three of her pallbearers. I think she'd assumed that it was one of us taking care of her house even though none of us would confess."

"Did you spend time with her?" Sam asked.

"Some," Kevin said. "A few times when she was at one of the other houses and we were there. She was very sweet. We all liked her very much."

Sam nodded. "Good. I'm glad you agreed to do it." And he was. These three men were some of the best men he knew. They would be properly honored to be a part of Natalia's service and they would appropriately honor her with their presence at her funeral.

"We know you should be a part of it too," Mac said. "The girls have been talking about it. But no one wanted to do anything besides what Natalia had in her letter."

Sam shook his head. "No. That's the right thing, to follow what she wanted." He rubbed his hand over the left side of his chest. This was what he wanted—to feel bad. And he did.

The service at the wake was nice. Several of her grandchildren spoke about Natalia, her three friends sang one of her favorite songs and they showed a slide show of many photos Natalia herself had taken. Apparently, she had boxes and boxes of photos in her attic.

Sam had seen the boxes, but he'd never opened them.

Just like Natalia's life. He'd seen it, but he'd never gotten into it.

He felt like shit.

After the service, no one in their group seemed in a hurry to leave. Kevin, Dooley, and Mac had offered to help clean the house up after everyone left and there were still some malingerers. It was fine with Sam. He fully intended to stay and help clean up. That's what he'd been doing in this house for more than a year. It was fitting that he be there to clean up after the service honoring Natalia's life.

He was also very aware that this was the last time he would be in Natalia's house. That, on the other hand, didn't seem right at all. The last time he'd been in here had been with Danika when she'd hurt her wrist.

That night had changed a lot of things for him.

"Where's Dani?" Mac asked as if reading his mind.

Sam was sure that everyone had been dying to ask all day, but had fought the urge. Until now. Now the ties were off, the buffet mostly empty and they were all sitting around Natalia's dining room, their chairs in a circle. Ben had been called into work and Sara and Jessica had taken off when he'd left. Sam hadn't missed Sara's hand on Mac's shoulder just before she'd gone, but he was ignoring it because he didn't want to deal with it meaning anything more than one friend comforting another.

Now it was just the guys and, as usual, there were no boundaries.

Mac flipped his wrist sending a playing card from the deck he held sailing toward the target. The big plastic bowl had held potato chips earlier, but was now empty and sat on the floor between the chairs Mac, Dooley and Kevin occupied. Whoever got the most cards into the bowl won.

"I thought she'd be with you," Mac added.

"I didn't think she'd find this particularly entertaining," Sam said.

Dooley raised an eyebrow. "I don't think this is intended to be entertaining."

"She didn't know Natalia."

"She could have been here for you."

"For what?"

"To make you feel better."

"I have you guys for that," Sam said sarcastically.

"I am *not* going to make you feel better the same way Danika can," Mac said.

"Thank God." Dooley landed two of his cards in the bowl. "I don't want to see *you* naked, Mac. No offense, but Danika has way better breasts than you do."

"Agreed," Mac said, tipping back his glass of punch.

Sam looked around at his friends. Unbelievable. They were talking about Danika being naked at Natalia's wake. "How about some respect, guys?"

Mac hit his shot too. "I think distracting you from your depression is better than respect."

"I can't believe I'm going to agree even remotely about the lack of respect," Kevin commented, his card landing next to the bowl. "But your depression definitely needs distracting."

"And talking about Danika naked is the best you could do?" Sam asked, wishing that he could ignore his friends.

"Danika naked doesn't distract you?" Dooley asked. "Because the thought of it definitely distracts me."

Sam scowled at him. "You are *not* thinking about Danika naked."

"I can't help it. We're talking about it. How can I not think about it?"

"He's got a point," Mac said.

"Shut up," Sam growled.

"You shouldn't be talking about your friend's girlfriend like that," Kevin said.

Sam said nothing, knowing that his silence would be deafening, but unable to bring himself to deny, or confirm, what Danika was to him.

"Girlfriend?" Dooley said on cue, flipping three cards into the bowl one right after the other.

Mac didn't wait for Sam to comment. "He's sleeping with her, but you don't bring a bed bunny to the hospital to see a sick friend." Mac mimicked Dooley's trick, landing four cards in the bowl.

"Bed bunny?" Dooley asked.

"It's not a bad term," Kevin said.

"It's a perfect term," Mac said. "She's sweet and cute. Wildcat doesn't fit Danika, for instance. Or tiger."

It did. But Sam wasn't about to say so. His friends were

looking for a reaction from him.

"She's way too hot to be a bunny," Dooley scoffed. "Bunnies are cuddly and soft."

"Maybe she's the snuggling type," Kevin offered. He flipped five cards in before missing.

She was that, too, but Sam kept his mouth shut.

"Snuggling after wearing a guy out," Dooley quipped.

"She might wear a guy like Kevin out," Mac said. "But I don't know about Bradford. It would take some skill and endurance."

Sam grit his teeth. He wanted to wallow in his misery over not taking the chance to get to know the woman whose vents and gutters he'd cleaned for nineteen months, a woman who, according to everything he was learning, he would have liked very much. Not to mention wallowing in his guilt about not letting her fuss over him as she apparently wanted to do and the way the other ladies had obviously enjoyed doing with his friends.

Instead, he was thinking about Danika, naked, quite effectively wearing him out and not only making him snuggle, but making him like it.

"Sam's an altruistic kind of guy." Dooley expertly flipped the rest of his cards into the bowl in rapid succession. "I'm sure he didn't mind her giving it her best shot."

"If he did mind, there will be plenty of other volunteers for her to try on," Mac said.

That was more than Sam could resist reacting to.

"Dammit!" Sam shoved back in his chair. "You guys are bastards," he muttered, pulling his car keys from his pocket.

"Where do you think you're going?"

"To Danika's." He should have said *Out for coffee* or *To get my jacket* or anything else, but they would know the truth anyway.

"To distract you?" Dooley asked.

Sam rebelled against that idea. He wasn't going to use Danika to take his mind off of Natalia and this long day, or the long day that would be tomorrow. He just wanted to be with her.

"I want to see her."

"Do you?" Dooley asked, looking completely serious.

"Of course."

"Why didn't you ask her to come with you today?" Mac asked.

Sam didn't want to admit that he was starting to need to have her around. "I couldn't get her naked here," he said flippantly.

"That's all you want her for?" Dooley asked.

"Maybe."

"You sure about that?"

Sam shifted his weight to his other foot. "Maybe."

"Get sure." Kevin stretched to his feet slowly.

"What?" Sam sighed. He didn't want to fight with Kevin about this. Of all his friends, Kevin was the hardest to rile up, but when he felt strongly about something he would stand up to anyone. He was also an ex-college football player. A defensive lineman. Which made him taller, wider and even more solid than Sam. Or anyone else they spent time with.

"Get sure before you go over there," Kevin said.

"What do you mean?"

"Get sure about what you want." This time it was Mac that spoke. "Don't mess with her, Sam."

"Danika knows how it is. She *likes* being naked with me," Sam said defensively, in spite of his attempt to avoid sounding defensive.

Dooley joined in the conversation. "That's your claim to fame, right?"

"What's that supposed to mean?"

"You're giving her your best, right Sam?" Dooley asked.

Sam didn't like this at all. "Nothing less."

"You sure about *that*?" Kevin asked.

"What the hell are you guys talking about?" Sam finally demanded.

Kevin tucked his hands in his front pants pockets. But Sam wasn't fooled into thinking he was nonchalant. "Danika deserves more and if you won't give it, then you'd better back off and let someone else try."

Several things occurred to Sam all at one time. One, his friends didn't just like Danika. They were feeling protective of her. Two, he wished that he *could* give her more. Three, there wasn't even one guy that Sam could think of that was good enough for Danika. Other than him, anyway. Four, that was a big problem.

He hated the idea of Danika with another guy, but if he wasn't willing to be everything for her, then he had to let her find someone who was. He'd kept Natalia from having a psuedo-son to dote on like Katherine and Dorothy and Barb had in his friends. They'd had regular visits and someone to bake for and someone new to tell their old stories to. Natalia hadn't had that, because of him.

Sara had pointed out that Sam had stopped being there for her, as well. He hadn't helped her with her cheerleading tryouts. There were lots of other things he hadn't helped her with either. And she'd deserved to have a brother who was there for her.

He couldn't keep Danika from having what she needed just because he wasn't willing to give it. He couldn't change things with Natalia, or Sara, but he could with Danika.

"Uh, huh," Kevin said, when Sam failed to respond. "Sit your ass down in that chair until you change your mind."

Sam sat.

"Then you guys shut the hell up about Danika being naked. You're driving me nuts."

"Good to know," Dooley said, sharing a look with Mac.

Sam chose not to interpret the look.

"I could date her," Dooley volunteered. "I'm not completely opposed to commitment."

Sam scowled at him. "Excuse me?"

"I'm just saying...if you think she should date someone else, then maybe it should be someone you know and can trust to be good to her."

"Your idea of a romantic dinner is buying her two hot dogs at the baseball game instead of one," Sam said.

"And the last time you bought a woman something to wear it was a tattoo," Mac added.

"Didn't you once tell me that your biggest turn-on is a woman who can drink straight Jack Daniels without shuddering?" Kevin asked.

"I'm not good enough for her?" Dooley asked, feigning offense, but grinning as he said it.

"You're not exactly her type," Sam said, feeling secure that

Dooley was kidding about asking Danika out.

"I could ask her out though," Kevin said. "I know about romance."

Sam turned to look at his friend who sounded dead serious. "You?"

"I'm a nice guy," Kevin said matter-of-factly. "I'm intelligent, good-looking, interesting and she wouldn't have to worry that I was only in it for the sex."

No. That was very true. Kevin was celibate. He hadn't always been, but since finding Jesus three years ago, he'd pledged to wait until marriage.

"I don't..." Sam coughed and started again. "I don't think you're quite right for Danika either."

Kevin looked interested when he asked, "Why is that?"

"She, um." Sam didn't know how to say what he wanted to say. "She's a very...passionate woman."

"She needs sex." Dooley slapped Kevin on the back. "Sorry, dude."

"It is possible for people to have relationships without sex. It's worth waiting for," Kevin said.

"Asking Danika to wait for sex would be like asking a dolphin to wait to swim," Sam said without thinking.

Kevin grinned at him. "I could make her not mind waiting. And there are other ways to be...intimate...than intercourse."

Sam was about to put his fist into the face of the nicest guy he knew. The images that came to mind with Kevin's comment were enough to make him want to pummel his God-fearing friend.

"Nah, I'll take care of it," Mac said.

"What do you mean?" Sam asked, his jaw tight.

"I don't have any problem sleeping with her without marrying her," Mac said. "And I can definitely be romantic."

"Are whips and handcuffs romantic?" Dooley asked.

"You are *not* dating, Danika. Or anything else," Sam said adamantly.

"I'm a nice guy." Mac didn't seem insulted by Sam's statement.

"You are a nice guy," Sam agreed. "But Danika isn't in your league, Mac."

Mac liked things kinky. Sometimes with more than one girl

at a time. It was absolutely amazing to Sam the things Mac could talk a woman into doing. None of it was dangerous and there was never anything against anyone's wishes. But he had a talent for picking women who had a lot of the same wishes he did.

"You think I'm too much for her?"

"Definitely."

"Maybe she needs her horizons expanded."

"No."

"Maybe she needs—"

"*No.* Whatever it is."

"Then what does she need?" Kevin asked.

Sam turned to face his other friend. He started to answer, then stopped.

Shit.

He knew exactly what Danika needed.

She needed a guy who could keep up with her, who could make her laugh, who could keep her safe and who would take care of her in spite of her insistence that she didn't need it. She needed a guy who wouldn't be intimidated by her independence and who would let her express it as often as possible. She also needed a guy who would appreciate her, who would realize what a lucky S.O.B. he was that she was with him, and who would take her to sex toy shops, but who would also take her out for ice cream. She needed someone who could make her moan in bed but who would also love being with her...anywhere.

She needed *him.*

Or a guy exactly like him. With the exception of his not wanting to be involved in a relationship.

"I'll take care of it," he said, somewhat begrudgingly.

"What does that mean?" Kevin asked, looking concerned.

"I know what, or should I say who, Danika needs."

"Why am I feeling that our plan to make you realize how you feel about her might have backfired?" Kevin asked, looking even more concerned.

"Oh no. It worked like a charm," Sam assured them. "I know exactly how I feel about her."

Even though he couldn't do anything about it other than walk away before one, or both, of them got hurt.

She hadn't been invited. But she wasn't sure that people were actually invited to funerals.

Danika was a smart woman, however, and she didn't like lying to herself. She was here for two reasons. One, Natalia had been important to Sam and that made Danika like her and want to honor her in some way. Two, Sam would be here and she wanted to see him.

She hadn't seen or heard from him since he'd left her by the hospital elevators. She'd left him a hundred messages but he hadn't returned any calls.

Still she was here.

She was chasing him. But she was worried about him. And she wanted to see him, even if it was across a church.

There was an empty seat near the back off the aisle that she slipped into as the family was being escorted into the sanctuary. From so far back and behind, dressed in various dark shades, she figured it would be difficult to tell which man in the first few pews was Sam. But it only took her a minute to find the back of his head. She stared at him, wishing she could go to him, wishing she knew what was going through his head right then, wishing she could make it better.

Thirty minutes later, the three men to his right rose and joined the other three pallbearers to escort Natalia's casket down the aisle to the waiting hearse. Sam turned to watch Mac, Dooley and Kevin carry Natalia past her family and friends. He was in the fourth row and rose, holding Sara's hand, followed by Jessica and Ben, and joined the procession of mourners.

He wasn't a pallbearer. That had to be hard.

His face looked strained and she wanted to cry. She wanted to hug him. She wanted to...make him cocoa. She'd always found that comforting. She had no idea if Sam even liked cocoa, but she had a crazy urge to comfort him and no idea how to do it or if Sam even wanted to be comforted by her.

As he and his sister approached, Sam's eyes flickered past her face, then came back to rest on hers. There was an instant of surprise, then what almost looked like relief. As he passed her he reached out and snagged her hand, tugging her forward and into the procession with him.

Once they were outside, Sam dropped Sara's hand and she moved to stand by her sister, but he kept a hold of Danika.

They watched solemnly as the casket was lifted into the back of the car, then shut the door.

"Sara, Danika is..."

"I'm riding with Ben and Jess," Sara said.

"We're driving separate," Jessica added. "From you," she clarified.

Sam didn't argue or even seem to take time to think about it. "That'll work."

He turned her in the direction of the parking lot across the street from the church. They walked in silence and he opened the car door for her, letting go of her hand only because he had to shut the door and get in on the driver's side.

It was four blocks into the drive before he said, "Natalia picked her pallbearers. I wasn't one of them."

"That was your own fault." With anyone else she would not have chosen those as her first words to him in days. But she knew that he was expecting it and there was no sense in sugarcoating what he already knew.

"Yeah."

"I'm sorry, though. I know you wish you could have been part of it."

"I'm sorry too."

It was as if the last few days hadn't existed without contact or conversation between them. She felt very comfortable saying, "I guess you've realized that caring about people isn't necessarily a choice we make. You tried to keep your distance, and you still ended up loving her." It wasn't rubbing it in. It was voicing what he needed to acknowledge and what she suspected he already had, to himself.

"Yeah."

They said nothing for a few seconds.

Sam broke the silence. "Just when I realized that I wanted to know her, and spend time with her and let her know me, she's gone."

"You were important to her, though. She didn't have to know your name or face for you to matter to her. Even though you held yourself back, you were still important in her life."

"I do want to be important to people. I also want a guarantee that I won't mess it up."

"Why should you get a guarantee?" She frowned at the road

in front of the car. "The rest of us don't. We all screw up sometimes. Life and relationships are messy. Broken wrists and strokes and worse happen. What matters is that we keep hoping and trying and loving anyway."

"I'm learning that. And that taking care of people isn't only about fixing leaky faucets or ceiling fans."

"That's...good." It was a sadly inadequate word, but she was too surprised to come up with a better one. In fact, his words resonated. Being taken care of wasn't just about things like that either. She'd wanted to be independent, to physically take care of herself, and she could fix almost anything that broke in her house. But that didn't mean she didn't need someone else around.

Just as Sam had loved and been important to Natalia even without meaning to, Danika couldn't help that taking care of her own needs didn't feel like enough anymore.

"I want you to know that I've been thinking about you."

"You have?" She wanted to add, *Then why haven't I seen you?* but held back.

He turned to look at her and though he could only take his eyes off the road for a moment, his gaze seemed to burn into hers. "Every minute."

They arrived at the cemetery before she could think of something appropriate to say.

He didn't let go of her hand through the entire graveside service. He took once last look at Natalia's casket and headstone, then turned away and followed the other mourners back to their cars.

"Will you take a walk with me?" He'd pulled the passenger side door open.

"Here?"

"Yeah."

She looked around. The cemetery was peaceful. It was a beautiful sunny day. Maybe a little strange, but if this was what Sam needed, then it was fine with her. "Okay."

He shut the door and took her hand, heading in the opposite direction from Natalia's grave.

"I was wondering," he said as they walked. "If you ever thought that maybe your dad didn't mind."

Danika replayed his words but realized that no, she didn't

know what he was talking about.

"What?"

He stopped in front of a huge stone angel statue and faced her, dropping her hand to put his hands into his pants pockets. "I think you need to consider that your dad didn't mind taking care of your mom." He was watching her face and must have seen something that made him want to go on. "I know you think that your mom felt like a burden and I think that you've spent all these years believing that too. But it's very possible that your dad considered it an honor to take care of the woman that he loved. He was able to give her things she needed. When you love someone, that's a good feeling. I think he might have felt good about that."

Danika wasn't sure if her mind was blank or if there were too many things in it all at once to make any sense. Either way, she had no idea what to say.

Sam didn't seem to care. He went on. "And I think you also have to consider that your mom still did things for him. She couldn't do laundry or take a walk with him, but she was still there for him to talk to, to be his companion, to hold his hand, to listen to him rant about a bad day at work, or tell him that she was proud of him when something great happened."

Danika's mind started replaying snapshots of her parents, as if someone had started a slide show in her head. Her mom sitting next to her dad on the couch watching a movie, her running her fingers through his hair as he rested his head against the back of the chair, her smearing cake frosting across his lips from his birthday cake and then kissing it off.

She nodded. "I'll consider it."

He stepped closer, but kept his hands in his pockets. "And I know you think you don't ever want to be close to someone, you don't ever want to need anyone, but Dani, you can't help it. You need someone who can look at old photos with you and hear your stories so you can keep your mom alive. You need someone who can appreciate your use of power tools and buy you the latest, greatest thing each Christmas because you won't buy it for yourself."

He paused for breath. Her heart had started to pound with his first sentence and she knew she was staring at him. But, wow, did all of that sound good.

"You need someone who can...rub your neck at night when

it's tight after a long day. Or someone who can..." he paused to think again, "...eat all the food that you love to make but won't make for just you."

She had yet to blink but she said, "Maybe I do." She sounded like she'd swallowed down the wrong pipe.

"You do," he said resolutely.

"I think you're right." She wanted to throw her arms around him, kiss him, dance with him, spin around like little kids until they were so dizzy they fell back onto the grass.

"Good." He looked relieved.

She almost laughed. Had he thought she'd say no? She wanted Sam in her life. For all of the reasons he'd said and just because he was Sam. She felt good with him and wrong without him. It was that simple.

"Good," he said again, as she reached for him. "Then I think you should call Matt. Tonight."

She froze with her arm extended toward him. "Matt?"

"Matt Dawson."

Her arm dropped. "What are you talking about?"

"Matt is the perfect guy for you."

The pounding of her heart in her ears turned to a strange rushing sound. "You think I should ask Matt Dawson out?"

"Yes. Unless you want him to ask you. I know he's interested. I'll tell him—"

"No!" She was almost certain that she was going to vomit.

"He'd be an imbecile to not be interested, Dani. I'll subtly hint that—"

"*God,* no," she said firmly.

She was such an idiot. She'd thought Sam was talking about himself. One more second and she would have said something completely humiliating. "I'll, um... I'll take care of it."

Of course, humiliation would likely be an improvement over the sick to her stomach, tight in the chest, stinging behind the eyes she was feeling now. There was *no way* she was calling Matt—or any other guy. Ever probably. But she wasn't going to tell Sam he'd ruined her for other men. He was quite clearly done with whatever it was they'd been doing.

She wanted to bang her head against the side of his car, but thought that would be an obvious sign that she wasn't okay. Instead, she calmly walked back and got into the car. On the way back to the church, Danika finally processed and admitted into her conscious mind the fact that Sam really was asking her to date another man.

"Do you want his home number?" Sam asked as he pulled up next to her car.

She looked at him quickly. He sounded a little sick himself. "No. I'll be seeing him."

"You will?"

Was that a frown she saw on her new matchmaker's face? She hoped so.

"Yeah." She held up her right wrist.

"Oh, right." He did frown this time. "You're going to ask him out during a checkup?"

"No."

"Good."

"I'll wait until after the checkup."

Another frown. "Next Thursday, right?"

"Right." The frown increased. "Oh."

Was that too soon? Or waiting too long in Sam's opinion? She couldn't care less.

She wrenched open her car door and got out, slamming it behind her, but unable to get rid of enough adrenaline.

"Dani are you...okay?"

She whipped around to find him standing beside the car, watching her worriedly.

He was an idiot, she decided. He was an idiot if he thought she could be okay with this. He was an idiot to think that Matt Dawson could replace him for her. He was an idiot if he didn't want to be with her himself.

"You bet," she said with forced cheeriness. "I'm fantastic."

Something softened in his face. "I know."

And she wanted to smack him.

He knew she was fantastic? Sure. Right. Of course. Because he was pawning her off on another man before she could get needier with him.

She was just fucking fantastic.

She tipped her chin up and met his eyes. "Goodbye, Sam."

Then she turned and walked away. From Sam Bradford. Something she would never have guessed she'd ever want to do. But in that moment, he was the last person she wanted to be with. It probably wouldn't last, but she was going to enjoy a few seconds of not wanting to cry, curl into a ball, or smash something.

It was Danika's date night with Matt. Sam hadn't forgotten. Even if he'd tried, everyone in the damned hospital had been talking about the two of them being seen together over the past two weeks and four days. He'd heard exactly how many cups of coffee they'd had and how long each one of them took to drink.

The fact that they'd finally taken their relationship out of the hospital was a relief. Or should have been. While they were in the hospital he'd had a play-by-play account of their get-togethers. Now he had to *wonder* what they were doing which, given his imagination and experience, was downright scary.

His so-called best friends were not helping.

"I can't believe he was a slow starter," Mac said. He curled his middle finger against his thumb, then flicked it out, shooting the wadded gum wrapper across the table, aiming for the goal—the Styrofoam cup lying on its side in front of Dooley. He missed. "Dawson seems like the kind of guy to take a woman out, come on strong, lots of romance, something right out of the gate."

"Something that involves alcohol," Dooley agreed. "And skimpy clothes."

"At least not work clothes and cafeteria coffee," Mac said.

"The cafeteria coffee isn't so bad," Kevin said. "It's better than the stuff at the Quick Mart."

"He's not going to take a woman to Quick Mart," Mac said, rolling his eyes.

"I'm just saying," Kevin muttered.

"He bought her lunch twice here too. I hope he takes her out for real food this time." Dooley shot his gum wrapper straight into the cup in front of Kevin.

Mac hit his next shot too. "I think he should skip dinner and go for chocolate-dipped strawberries and champagne."

"That's pretty romantic for you," Kevin commented, his wrapper shooting off the end of the table. It joined at least twenty others. Apparently gum-wrapper-table-hockey didn't include a clean-up crew.

"They'd be eating them in bed, of course." Mac wiggled his eyebrows. "Or just the chocolate sauce and forget the strawberries."

Sam gripped his pencil tighter and kept his eyes on his Sudoku puzzle, but the image of Danika in nothing but chocolate wouldn't leave him.

The crew needed a call. Something to do. Something to interrupt conversation. Something where everyone lived, but that took some brainpower and time on the part of his crew. And did not involve insane amounts of chewing gum.

"Did it occur to you two that Matt might *like* her and doesn't want to sleep with her right away?" Kevin asked.

Sam hadn't filled a number in on the puzzle in at least five minutes. He kept writing a six in the third box from the top, erasing it, then writing it again.

Six was the time Matt was supposed to pick Danika up, according to hospital gossip.

Hospital gossip was frighteningly accurate.

"Oh, he likes her," Mac said. "What's not to like?"

Kevin nodded. "Women like Danika are worth drinking a few bad cups of coffee."

"Thought you said the cafeteria coffee wasn't that bad," Dooley said.

Kevin gave him an irritated frown.

Sam almost broke his pencil.

He knew his friends were messing with him. He could not rise to their bait. They wanted him to react to show that he cared about Danika, that he didn't want her out with someone else, that he did *not* want her out with frickin' Matt Dawson. Even though it was his dumbass idea.

As if her dating someone else, someone who seemed good for her, would magically make him not want her himself.

Yeah, great dumbass idea.

"Is he the type to get her into bed tonight?" Dooley asked, shooting three wrappers into the cup one right after the other.

"I can't think of why not," Mac said, mimicking Dooley's trick, but missing on two.

Sam couldn't think of a reason why not either.

"Maybe *she's* not the type to jump into bed with someone on the first date," Kevin pointed out. He flipped five wrappers in before missing.

Maybe, Sam thought. But she was the type to go to an adult toy shop with a virtual stranger.

He'd like to think that it was because it had been him, but he wasn't quite in the frame of mind to let his ego talk him into that. Matt Dawson was the only guy Sam knew who could rival his reputation.

The reputation that had led to him being set up with her in the first place. When she needed him sexually. She wasn't supposed to need a man in any other way. She only wanted sex. And orgasms.

But it sounded like she and Dawson were getting to know each other.

Which was tying Sam up in knots.

That was the stupid part. The idea of another man so much as holding Danika's hand made his blood pressure go up. In fact, he'd been purposely ignoring the idea that there might be anything more than handholding between Danika and Matt.

Now, though, the idea of Matt enjoying the simplest things—singing along to the radio with her, or sharing her toothpaste, or learning if she liked red or black licorice better, or helping her fold towels—made Sam almost crazier with jealousy than the idea that Matt might sleep with her.

Which proved that he was insane.

He didn't even know which licorice she liked best. Or if she even liked licorice.

And—God help him—he really did want to know how Dani felt about licorice.

Which made that the moment when Sam realized that he was in love with Danika Steffen.

The sex was the best he'd ever had.

Being the one that got to share every aspect of her life was more than he'd ever even imagined having.

"Maybe Matt will change her mind about sex on the first date," Mac said.

Sam did break the pencil then. "You guys suck." Sam stalked to the next desk and jerked open the drawer, could find only an ink pen—which was more commitment than he liked to give even a puzzle—and slammed it shut again, more ticked off than he'd started.

He managed to fill in two boxes in the second row of his puzzle, with his mind mostly not on Danika, and his friends managed to talk about something else for ten minutes.

"Good thing we changed her garbage disposal, though," Dooley said. "Wouldn't want the surgeon getting his hands dirty."

Mac snorted. "Like Dawson would know the first thing about impellers."

Sam frowned, but none of them noticed as they were pretending he was not in the room as they talked about his personal life. It was subtle and indirect, but they were making their point loud and clear. They thought he was a dumbass for telling Danika to date Matt Dawson.

They could join the club.

"What about her garbage disposal?"

Dooley didn't look at him when he answered, "We replaced it last week."

"It was this week," Kevin corrected.

"It was Saturday," Dooley said. "That was technically still last week. Sunday starts the new week."

"Yes. But it wasn't Saturday. It was Sunday night," Kevin said.

"It was not. That movie was on. That one with Bruce Willis."

"It was Kevin Costner and it was on Sunday night."

"You sure?"

"That's why they called it the Sunday Night Movie."

"*Anyway,*" Sam interrupted, trying to remember why he liked these guys. "You replaced Danika's garbage disposal?"

"It broke," Dooley said with a shrug.

Sam gritted his teeth. "I assumed."

"And she couldn't do it with her wrist," Mac said.

"She still has the brace on?" He'd been wondering how her wrist was doing.

"No, but Matt wants her to take it easy with it until she has some physical therapy on it," Mac explained.

"So she asked you to do the garbage disposal?" Sam asked, ignoring the mention of Matt.

"Yeah. She figured we knew how," Mac said.

"Which we did," Dooley said.

Sam frowned. He wouldn't have known how to fix her garbage disposal.

None of them were trying to date her, she'd needed help and Sam had made it clear he didn't want to be involved, so she'd called his buddies. No big deal. It was good she felt she could ask them for help and Sam was grateful they were good guys and went over. It was great, even.

"No more fixing stuff at Danika's," he said firmly.

Three pairs of eyes focused on him. One looked surprised, one looked thoughtful and one was frowning.

"What are you talking about?" Dooley asked.

"I'm talking about you guys not going over to Danika's to fix stuff anymore."

"Why, exactly?" Mac asked.

"Because..." He was an idiot. He'd acted like an ass. And he obviously wasn't done yet.

He was in love with her and he had to do something about it. Having his friends over there helping her out, taking care of her, wasn't going to work. Danika was his and so were her problems, needs and desires.

He was going to need to learn how to fix a fricking garbage disposal. Among other things.

Many other things.

"Because I said so."

"You've got to be shitting me—"

Four pagers went off all at the same time.

Thankfully, they had a call.

They arrived at the scene fourteen minutes later. It was a huge old white house on the corner, with a wraparound porch and five steps leading to the front walk, which stretched for almost fifty feet to the street. It was the middle of that strip of pavement where a white-haired little lady sat, surrounded by neighbors.

Sam pushed through the small crowd, followed by Dooley and Mac with a stretcher.

"Evenin' ma'am," Sam said, squatting next to the woman. "I understand you had a little spill."

The woman gave him a wobbly smile. "My hip hurts."

"Yes, ma'am." It was very likely a hip fracture. "What's your name?"

"Donna."

"Do you know what day it is Donna?"

"Thursday."

"Do you know where you are?"

"On my front sidewalk."

Sam smiled. "Can you give me your address?"

"But you're already here."

His smile grew and he squeezed her hand. "I need to see that you know your address so I know you don't have a head injury, Donna."

"Oh." She rattled off her address.

"Thanks," Sam said when she got it right. "Did you hit your head?" He started feeling through the fluffy white curls for bumps or abrasions.

"I think I did," she admitted.

"Did anyone see the fall?" he asked. No one had. "Does your head or neck hurt?" he asked Donna.

"Yes," she nodded. "The back of my head."

Mac and Dooley moved in and one applied a neck collar as a precaution. She lived alone and her estimate about what time she'd come out to get her mail was fuzzy, leading Sam to wonder if she might have blacked out. Still, she was oriented and making sense and was able to move her fingers and toes and feel Dooley touching the lower leg on the side she'd hurt. All good signs.

Mac and Sam moved her carefully onto the gurney as Dooley held it steady. They lifted the gurney to its full height once she was secure and they started to roll it toward the ambulance.

"Do you think I broke it?" Donna asked Sam, who was steering the head end of the rolling table.

He looked down at her, wondering if he should be completely honest. She looked scared. Finally he said, "There's a chance."

"What do they do then?"

"The doctor will have to talk with you about that. I'm just your charioteer." He gave her a wink that did get a smile.

"Sometimes they operate on hips," she said. "My friend Elizabeth had that happen."

"Sometimes they do," Sam agreed. "Have you had a surgery

on any of your joints before?"

"No. Thank goodness," Donna added.

Sam chuckled and had to agree. Then he tried to remember who was on call that night for orthopedics. Whoever was on call would take care of Donna. Unless she specifically requested another member of the orthopedic surgical team. Then that surgeon would be paged for the consult and resultant operation.

He leaned in closer to her ear. "Matt Dawson is an excellent orthopedic surgeon. If you end up needing one tonight."

"Oh?" Donna asked. "Thank you."

"You bet." Sam was very comfortable with suggesting Donna request one of the finest surgeons in the city.

Danika would understand if her date got interrupted for a medical emergency.

Donna deserved the best, after all.

Chapter Twelve

Danika was whistling "Roll Out the Barrel" as she headed down the hallway after spending fifteen minutes convincing Tommie that he needed to go to the shelter for the night. He had initially asked for "Brad", but Sam wasn't working days and when informed of that, Tommie had asked for someone else for the first time ever.

"Stephanie" had shown up with orange Jell-O—in three individual cups—and Pepsi.

She was feeling pretty good.

At least Tommie wanted her.

So what if he was a homeless, eccentric, in-need-of-a-shower man twenty years her senior?

She rounded the corner and her whistle abruptly died right in the midst of havin' the blues on the run. She was in front of Jessica Bradford Torres' office. And the door was open. Which meant Danika probably had to go in.

Dang.

She'd avoided this up until now. It was unusual for Jessica to be available. She was the Chief Nursing Officer for the ER and was generally in the trenches with her troops versus sitting behind her desk. But it was a semi-quiet day in the ER—something no one said out loud lest it jinx the situation—and it looked like Jessica was in her office catching up on paperwork.

Danika couldn't just walk by.

A deep breath and silent pep talk later, Danika knocked on the door.

Jessica's head came up. "Hi, Danika." She didn't seem particularly surprised to see her brother's...whatever...in her office.

"Hi, Jessica. Can I talk to you for a minute?"

"Of course." Jessica laid her pen down and folded her arms on top of her desk. "I'll take any chance to get away from paperwork."

Danika stepped across the threshold but wasn't prepared to sit. She wasn't quite that comfortable with Sam's older sister. God only knew what Jessica thought of the whole situation.

"I just felt that I needed to apologize," Danika said. "I shouldn't have yelled at you the other day at my house."

Jessica's eyes widened. "Really?"

Danika paused. "Really what?"

"I hardly ever get anyone apologizing for anything. Wow, I don't know what to say."

Danika smiled. "Well, yes, that's what I'm doing."

"Wouldn't you know it?" Jessica asked.

"Know what?"

"Someone finally comes to apologize and it's someone who doesn't have anything to be sorry for. Just my luck." She was smiling as she said it.

"I yelled at you. Sa—he's your brother. I shouldn't have butted in."

"Why not?" Jessica asked. "You were right. We don't give Sam a lot of credit, and he does deserve it. He's a great guy. But it's easier for me to just let him be the way he is."

Danika felt a stupid lump form in her throat. She could only nod.

"I don't know if anyone has ever stuck up for Sam," Jessica said thoughtfully. "He's always fun-loving and laid back and the good-time guy. I don't think anyone has ever believed he needed sticking up for."

She leaned back in her chair. "The thing is, Sam is easy to get along with. He drives me nuts sometimes because he's *so* laid back, but in reality, Sam's attitude made my life easier in a lot of ways." She crossed her arms and focused her eyes on the clock on the corner of her desk rather than on Danika.

"After our dad died, I was barely able to take care of Sara, run the house and handle school. Sam not only never asked me for anything, he also never made me worry about him. At least, not *real* worry. I worried that he was staying out too late, blowing his money on stupid stuff, not studying enough. Those were things I knew how to fix, mostly. But I never had to wonder if he was happy or sad or depressed. He was just...Sam. He was even-keel. I couldn't give him a lot of responsibility but I also didn't have to sit up with him at night when he had a nightmare, with no clue what to say or do, like I did with Sara. He was easier for me. And I let it stay that way because it was...easier."

Danika wasn't sure how much to say. She'd come in to apologize but now found herself wanting to say more in Sam's defense.

Well, Jessica thought she'd been right before...

"I think he *acted* even-keel, Jessica. Because he knew it was easier for you to think of him that way."

Jessica nodded. "Now I can see that...because now I can handle that fact. Back then, having two kids needing me to be their emotional support when I was hardly holding my own emotions together would have sent me over the edge."

He'd been taking care of Jessica even back then. Not only by staying away and not letting her learn to depend on him, but by keeping his needs and emotions out of her way.

"Have you ever seen him sad or upset or angry?" Danika asked.

Jessica shook her head. "The other night at the center when he thought you hurt your knee was the first time I've seen him rattled in...maybe ever. Then at Natalia's funeral. I hadn't seen him sad like that since my dad's funeral. He avoids getting into situations where he might get sad, or rattled, or anything. Usually, anyway."

Something about hearing that she had been a cause of emotions Sam usually kept suppressed gave Danika a thrill. Not because she wanted Sam to be upset, but it was nice to know that he cared enough to react without being able to carefully check his emotions.

"Because he doesn't want people to worry about him."

Jessica nodded her agreement. "He doesn't want to be the cause of any turmoil in anyone's life. He doesn't want to burden anyone with his emotions or problems, just like he doesn't want anyone to depend on him and then be let down."

Danika hated that. She hated that he wasn't letting other people close. She hated that he was scared. He was confident and strong and compassionate and did the right thing. He deserved...everything.

"Sam needs someone to make him see that it's okay for him to be more than fun-loving and even-keel and the good-time guy," Danika said. "He's been playing that role for so long, I think he honestly thinks that's who he is and when that doesn't work, he doesn't know what to do." Danika took a deep breath. "When that doesn't work, he gets someone else to take his place."

Jessica sat forward again. "I think you're right."

"Talk to him." Danika said it with more force than she'd intended, but Jessica didn't act the least bit offended. "Tell him that you don't expect him to always be happy and upbeat. Tell him that if he wants to take care of people, then it has to be a two-way street. He needs to get involved. And let them get involved with him."

Jessica was looking at her intently now. "I'll definitely talk to him, Danika. I have some apologizing to do myself." She leaned forward onto her elbows. "But I hope you're the type of woman to take her own advice."

For some reason Danika's heart rate sped up. "What do you mean?" She didn't have anything to apologize to Sam for. *He* had been the idiot.

"I think that you might have a better chance of convincing him he wants to be involved."

"Why would I have a better chance?"

"Because he's in love with you and it isn't going to be long before he can't stay away from you. And instead of calling you and taking you on a date, or showing up at your door with roses, he's going to take care of you. From afar. If you let him."

Danika felt a huge rush of air inflate her lungs. Holy crap. Sam loved her. Part of her mind thought maybe she should protest Jessica's statement, but she felt it. She felt that it was true. As was the part about Sam taking care of her.

"I have to make it all or nothing with him, don't I?" Danika asked.

Jessica nodded. "You have to be firm. He can be very charming, and clever, about getting his way."

"But he hasn't come up against someone who cares as much as I do how this turns out." Danika realized how true that was as she said it. She was going to tell him it was all or nothing...but she wouldn't let him quit until it was *all*. For both of them.

"He'd rather move a heavy couch or do a bunch of yard work than sit and keep someone company or give advice," Jessica said.

"Because he doesn't think he's good at that stuff."

"Right."

"That's not going to fly anymore," Danika said decisively. "I don't let people rearrange my furniture and I don't have a yard."

"Also, if he ever shows up with a set of tools, I would strongly recommend you keep him away from your dishwasher. And your toilet. Oh, and your stereo system."

"Oh?" Danika asked, fighting a smile. "Why is that?"

Jessica grimaced. "Just trust me."

The games began the next day.

In truth, they might have started two days prior once she thought about it, but she couldn't prove it. Her carpet just seemed cleaner than it had the day before.

On Monday, she put burned-out light bulbs in two lamps and the front hallway fixture.

That evening they had all been changed.

On Tuesday, she broke the latch on the cabinet in the bathroom. On purpose.

That evening the entire cabinet was new. As was the bottle of mouthwash inside.

Danika had to simply shake her head and laugh. She was completely in love with him. No question about it. He didn't know how to fix the latch...he still made sure that she had a working cabinet in her bathroom. Replacing the whole thing was over-the-top, but it meant that he didn't mind her noticing the things he was doing for her. That had to be a good sign.

On Wednesday, she took a deep, brave breath and "accidentally" left her freezer door open. It wouldn't defrost completely before the end of the workday, but it would leak, and she'd lose some ice cream. But Sam was worth it.

When she got home, there wasn't a drop on the floor and there were two full cartons of ice cream where there had been only one that morning.

She smiled at the fact that he cared so much, and at how

obvious he was being, and smiled thinking that he must know she was doing these things on purpose as well.

Then she frowned. How much longer would this go on? Why hadn't he called, or come over when she was home, or found her at the hospital? If he was in love with her, how was he standing this time and distance apart?

She wanted to go after him. Badly. But she wanted him to be the one to decide to be fully present in her life.

On Thursday she started to loosen the leg on her coffee table. But just as it started to tip toward that corner, she stopped. They'd eaten pizza together at that coffee table. His friends had set cans of beer and soda on it when they'd come over to finish her floor. Sam had needed to shove it out of the way to make love to her on the couch.

She suddenly missed him so much it literally hurt. She was tired of this. Three days was long enough. She wanted to see him, talk to him, eat a grilled cheese sandwich with him.

She didn't leave anything for him to do. Everything was in working order and in its place when she left for work. It was time for him to know, and accept, that he needed to be in her life whether or not her wrist—or coffee table—was broken.

She stopped by the gym on her way home, then the grocery store. Not because she loved the elliptical machine—that was so not the case—or because she needed the yogurt and bread she picked up, but because she didn't want to go home. For the past few days, ever since she first suspected that he would show up to check on her, she'd looked forward to going home and seeing what he'd done. She'd liked knowing that he'd been there. Each time, deep down, she'd also hoped for a note, or even for him to still be there when she walked in the door.

Of course, he wouldn't have known that she hadn't broken anything for him today. Maybe with nothing to do he would finally realize that he'd rather see her than her appliances. Maybe he would see that he wanted to be around even when there was nothing he could do for her besides just be with her. Maybe he'd stay.

She took her steps instead of the elevator. After all, she was already sweating.

But he wasn't there.

In fact, as far as she could tell, he hadn't been there at all.

Which kind of pissed her off.

Now he wasn't even going to secretly take care of her? What was that all about? What about being madly in love with her? What if another light bulb had burned out?

Good job being in love there, Sam.

She stomped into her bathroom, practically ripping the shower curtain from the rod when she yanked it open. She turned on the faucet in the tub, then pulled the curtain shut again, and lifted the lever that started the spray before turning to undress as it warmed up.

A second later the shower turned into a Yellowstone National Park geyser.

Water shot straight up from the connection between the showerhead and the wall pipe. In seconds, every surface in her bathroom was dripping. Including her.

She struggled for nearly a minute before she managed to get the water turned off with her bum hand. By then the water was running into her eyes

Saying things that would make her mother blush, Danika got up onto the side of the tub to look at the showerhead. It wasn't that old. There hadn't been so much as a tiny prior leak. What the hell had happened...

It took her less than a minute to realize that someone had sabotaged her showerhead.

She didn't need even a millisecond to figure out who.

Danika stood on the edge of her bathtub, staring at a white plastic showerhead, processing that the man she loved had done the exact *opposite* of fixing and taking care of everything without fanfare or attention...the opposite of every instinct he seemed to have.

He'd made a damned mess for her. A *huge* damned mess. An *obvious* huge, damned mess. He had to know that she would take one look and know that it was intentional.

This wasn't helpful, it wasn't considerate, it wasn't Sam. And doing it had probably driven him crazy. Thinking about the mess, thinking about her struggling with it with her hand, pondering how mad she was going to be and how apparent it would be that Sam had done it had to be making him nuts.

It could mean only one thing.

Well, two.

It could mean he had tried to fix it—for some reason—and

had botched it. Or it could mean that he wanted her to come to him.

But why this? Something she could either fix herself or go out and quite easily buy a replacement? Why had he done this? She figured it out almost immediately. He was surrendering. He was showing her that not only was he not going to fix everything, he was also going to sometimes make messes that she would have to fix. And he was okay with that.

It certainly wasn't subtle, she thought as she watched water drip from the lavender towel hanging on the rod straight across from the shower. It was also in the bathroom. The room where they'd finally made love. Was that symbolic?

She was going to make a complete ass of herself if he hadn't done this, or hadn't intended it to mean anything.

Because, whatever he'd intended, what he was going to get was a soaking wet kind-of girlfriend showing up in the middle of his work shift and making a public spectacle of this whole thing.

"Stop trying to fix my stuff!"

Sam smiled as the familiar voice and exasperated tone came from behind him. She sounded irritated. But she was here.

He stopped and turned in the middle of the busiest hallway intersection in the hospital. The hallway to his left led off to the cafeteria, the parking garage behind him, the lab to his right and the ER in front of him, where Danika had clearly just come from.

The charming quip never made it off of his tongue.

Danika was dripping wet. Her hair hung in a limp, wet ponytail against her shoulder, she was devoid of makeup and was still wearing a tiny pink baby-doll T-shirt with gray cotton workout pants. Both of which were soaked...and clingy.

In spite of the fact that she looked like a street urchin, he had to clear his throat before he spoke. She was a sexy street urchin.

"It's about time you got down here. I've been coming to your house, slaving away for you, for seven days."

"Slaving..." she started to snort, then stopped. "Seven?"

He watched her mentally trying to figure out what he'd been doing in her place for seven days. It had only been four days ago that he'd started noticing things were truly broken around her place. It had been two days ago that he'd realized she was doing it on purpose. Which had thrilled him. She wanted him there.

"How was I supposed to know that you wanted me to come to you? Normal people call people they want to see. Or show up to see *them*. Or send an e-mail or text."

He fought his smile, but thoroughly enjoyed—without hiding it—her ranting and raving. She was here. She was so beautiful, and smart, and passionate and...his.

He crossed the distance between them in three strides, stopping right in front of her, but she was so far into her tirade that she simply tipped her head back and looked up at him as she went on.

"And besides, you spent *months* not wanting Natalia to find out who you were and would have freaked out if she would have showed up down here. So how should I know—"

There were some things he really wanted to say to her. There was only one thing to do.

He pulled her up against him, tangled one hand in her hair, settled the other on her butt and covered her moving lips with his.

She gave a soft sigh and her eyes opened very slowly when he lifted his head several minutes later. They were in the midst of the most un-private spot in the hospital, but he didn't care and he didn't think Danika noticed.

He could listen to that sigh for the rest of his life. In fact, he fully intended to.

And the best way to start that was with a few important words. He knew she loved him—whether he deserved it or not—but he had a little groveling to do.

"Danika, I love you. I was a jackass. I get that I need to let people need me and I want the first one to be you. Please promise me that you will fix everything that breaks in my life, that you'll forgive me for the messes I make."

She just stood blinking up at him. Without a word.

"And that you will never, *ever*, even smile at Matt Dawson again."

Still no response.

"And I promise that I will be there for you. I want to be involved in everything you do, take care of everything I can, know everything about you..." She wasn't saying anything and it was beginning to bother him. "You okay?"

She finally spoke. "Did you say you were a jackass?"

He raised an eyebrow. "Yes."

"Have you ever admitted, to a woman, that you were a jackass before?"

"Did you hear the part about me loving you?"

"Yeah. I know you do. Answer the question."

He grinned. "No, I've never told a woman I was a jackass before."

"But you have been one?"

"Without a doubt. Though I don't think quite to this extent before."

She seemed to consider that for a moment. "Hmm. I like it."

"I have a feeling we should both get used to it."

"You being a jackass, or you admitting it?"

Sam sighed. "Probably both."

"Can I smile at other men?"

"Just not Dawson."

"Okay."

Okay. That was Danika. Sweet, to the point.

"What were you saying before?" he asked.

"I was asking how I should know that you wanted me to come down here when all this time you've been avoiding being involved," she said, picking up exactly where she'd left off.

He grinned and held her face in his hands. "Because you know me, honey."

She sighed again. If he was the kind of guy to use the word *dreamily* he would have used it to describe her sigh. "Yeah, I knew. After a couple of days."

"Exam room six has a door and blinds on the windows..."

"No." But she smiled and put her hand on his chest. "I want more than that, Sam. From you. With you."

"For the record, whenever I refer to sex, that includes toys, oral, flavored body oil...all of that. Whatever you want."

She rolled her eyes but her smile grew. "I mean more than any of that. I want to just be together, talk—"

"About sex?"

257

"No. Politics, movies, the weather."

He moved his hips, pressing against her. "You can talk about anything you want as long as I'm deep inside you while you do it."

Her breath hitched, but she kept going. "No. In fact, I'm thinking maybe we shouldn't have sex for a while."

He knew she was kidding, but his stomach still knotted. "Don't *ever* say that again."

"But I love you."

Wanting to hear those three words over and over until he was at least one hundred and forty years old, he said, "I love you too."

"You do." She said it matter-of-factly. "More than anyone in the world."

"Yes. And that means that we should have *lots* of sex. All the time."

"Not until you believe that you have more to offer than that. And fixing things around the house."

"Um, I have a secret," he said. "I can't actually fix anything."

"Yes, I'm aware," she said dryly. "Hence the fact that I'm here looking...bedraggled."

He chuckled. It was a good word. Her hair was beginning to dry and curl at the temples. He flicked one of the curls. "You're bedraggled because I happen to be good at messing stuff up."

"Sam, you're not. You're so much more—"

"I know," he interrupted. "I was kidding." He didn't mean it when he said he was good at messing up. Anymore. He wasn't a screwup. As Sara had pointed out, if he messed up on purpose it didn't count.

Besides, he was turning over a new leaf. His sisters had come to him four days ago and they'd had a nice, long talk about the past and how they felt and what they were each doing about it. They'd agreed to focus on the future and making it everything they wished their past could have been. He was ready to be there, one hundred percent, for everyone he loved, and, though it scared him to death, he was ready to make—and keep—some promises.

Danika's eyes softened with tenderness. "There is something I need you for—only you."

"Does it involve lace or need batteries?" he asked hopefully.
She shook her head. "This." She held up a map.
He took it from her fingers. "South Dakota?"
"Take me there."
"To South Dakota."
"Yes. The Black Hills. Mount Rushmore."
"You know that whole City of Gold in *National Treasure 2* isn't real, right?"
"I need someone to go with me who I can stand being cooped up in a car with for ten hours. I need someone who will stop at every tourist attraction and interesting site along the way, including the Corn Palace. I need someone who will just stand and gaze at Mount Rushmore and feel the majesty and not laugh when I get choked up. And I need someone who will listen to me go on and on about why Thomas Jefferson is my favorite President."
She took a deep breath and looked into his eyes. "And you will, right, Sam? Because you love me and want to share my life and be that person I need for the things *I* need."
He was going to make some smart-ass comment about the Corn Palace, but he looked down into the face of the woman he was going to love for the rest of his life and simply nodded. "It will be my pleasure."
Which was, amazingly, completely true. He would probably never know how to fix a garbage disposal or rewire a ceiling fan, but that wasn't what Danika needed. Thank God. He would, however, love watching her face while she looked at Mount Rushmore and he would love to hold her hand while they talked about dead presidents, and absolutely anything else in the world. No one else could do that like he could, because no one else would ever love her like he did.
"You know, everything's going to be a lot easier if you just marry me," he said.
Her eyebrows rose slightly. "Easier?"
"You're going to be running over to my apartment to fix things all the time. It'd be easier on you if we just lived together and you only had one place to take care of."
"We have to get married to do that?"
"Of course. You can't live together without being married."
"And we're not going to sleep together until the wedding

night, right?"

"Let's not get crazy." He looped his arm around her waist and started for the parking lot outside of the ER.

They were almost to his car when she stopped and drew him up short. "Guess we're taking my car."

She was looking at the two front tires of his car. The very flat front tires of his car.

"Guess so." He grinned down at her.

She looked at his grin and suddenly realization dawned on her face. "Sam, did you flatten your car tires?"

"Why would I do that?"

"So you could call me and get me down here to change them for you."

"Hmm, that would have been a pretty good idea."

"I can't change a car tire with a bad wrist." She wiggled that bad wrist as she said it.

"But you would have come down here to help me anyway, right?"

She sighed, shook her head, then smiled up at him with resignation. "Yes. Of course I would have."

"And you can change a car tire by yourself?" he asked. "When your wrist is working?"

"Of course."

He rolled his eyes. Of course. He looked down at her. "I'm not going to kiss you right now."

"Why not?"

"Because I won't be able to stop. Let's go somewhere that we can do that for a long, long time. Naked."

Danika grinned up at him. "We are so going to get along fine. Forever."

He grabbed her hand and started for her car. "We can call the tow truck while we drive."

They had just pulled away when she said, "Do *you* know how to change a tire, Sam?"

He cleared his throat and got busy watching the stop light.

"Sam?" She repeated.

He didn't look at her, but he heard the amusement in her tone.

"It's been awhile," he muttered.

There was a long pause, then a loud snort of laughter. He

felt his lips curl up in response. "Don't worry," she said, giggling. "I'll teach you."

"I have some things I can teach you, too, you know," he growled.

"Oh, I'm counting on it."

She cuddled up next to him, and as he slipped his arm around her, he knew that he could absolutely be everything Danika needed.

Which was going to be everything he'd ever needed too.

About the Author

Erin Nicholas has been reading and writing romantic fiction since her mother gave her a romance novel in high school and she discovered happily-ever-after suddenly went a little beyond glass slippers and fairy godmothers! She lives in the Midwest with her husband who only wants to read the sex scenes in her books, her kids who will *never* read the sex scenes in her books, and family and friends who say they're shocked by the sex scenes in her books (yeah, right!).

To learn more about Erin Nicholas please visit www.ErinNicholas.com or her blog at http://ninenaughtynovelists.blogspot.com/. Send an email to Erin at Erin@ErinNicholas.com or join her Yahoo! group to join in the fun with other readers as well as Erin: http://groups.yahoo.com/group/ErinNicholas/

To save one good man, she'll have to let her
inner bad girl out to play...

Just Right
© *2010 Erin Nicholas*
The Bradfords, Book 1

ER nurse Jessica Bradford is a good girl. Okay, a reformed bad girl, but she's done her late father proud. Now she's one step away from landing Dr. Perfect, aka handsome, sexy, heroic Ben Torres—the hot fudge *and* cherry on top of her hard work scooping out a respectable life.

Ben learned the art of sacrifice from his missionary parents, but when a drunk driver he saved kills three people, he quits. To be precise, the fist he plants in the man's face gets him suspended. And the first dish he wants on his newly empty plate is Jessica—preferably naked.

Jessica can't believe the Ben she's found drowning his sorrows in a bar is her knight in shining scrubs. And he won't be pried loose until she bets 48 hours of her time in a game of pool. She loses. And the next morning she stands to lose much more.

The Chief of Staff's recommendation for the promotion she's been after rides on her ability to keep Ben out of trouble until things blow over.

Except "trouble" is all Ben wants. And despite herself, Jessica finds that she's more than willing to go down with him...

Warning: Contains hot love in a store dressing room and in the front seat of a car—at the expense of a very nice strawberry patch, unfortunately—oh, and hooker boots. Can't forget the hooker boots.

Available now in ebook and print from Samhain Publishing.

GREAT
CHEAP
FUN

Discover eBooks!

THE FASTEST WAY TO GET THE HOTTEST NAMES

Get your favorite authors on your favorite reader, long before they're out in print! Ebooks from Samhain go wherever you go, and work with whatever you carry—Palm, PDF, Mobi, Kindle, nook, and more.

WWW.SAMHAINPUBLISHING.COM

9 781609 280925